OLD
SCORES

SCOTT MACKAY

OLD SCORES

ST. MARTIN'S MINOTAUR ≈ NEW YORK

OLD SCORES. Copyright © 2003 by Scott Mackay. All rights reserved. Printed in the United States of America. No part of this book may be used or reproduced in any manner whatsoever without written permission except in the case of brief quotations embodied in critical articles or reviews. For information, address St. Martin's Press, 175 Fifth Avenue, New York, N.Y. 10010.

www.minotaurbooks.com

ISBN 0-312-30841-8

First Edition: September 2003

0 9 8 7 6 5 4 3 2 1

TO MY BROTHER, IAN—
THE DIODES RULE.

ACKNOWLEDGMENTS

The author wishes to thank the following
people for help in certain aspects of this novel:
Nidia Vargas-Molnar, Michael Hofmann,
Anton Hofmann of Fenelon Falls,
Anton Hofmann of Germany, Dr. Thomas Kiss,
Claire Mackay, Cindy Walker, Joanie Mackay,
Donald Crowe, Jeanie Doggett, Ian Mackay,
Paul Robinson, John Catto, John Hamilton,
Gordon Hawes, Peter Robinson, Joshua Bilmes,
and Marc Resnick.

OLD SCORES

DETECTIVE BARRY GILBERT STUDIED GLEN Boyd's dead body. Boyd lay on his back in the middle of the queen-size bed, his turquoise satin dressing gown flung open, his blue boxer shorts partially visible, a woolly mat of curly gray hair thick upon his chest. A woman's silk scarf was tied around his neck. Boyd was profoundly cyanotic, his skin the bluish-gray color of a strangulation victim. Gilbert was surprised to see how frail Boyd was, not like the Boyd he once knew.

Gilbert glanced at Constable Virginia Virelli, first officer on the scene. She stood rigidly at the end of the bed, a young woman, nervous, subdued, her hands behind her back, staring straight ahead. Her blond hair was tied tightly in a short ponytail.

"Your first homicide?" he asked.

"Yes," she said.

"You don't have to be nervous," said Gilbert. "He's not going to get up and bite you."

She tried to grin but couldn't. "Thank you, sir," she said.

"And don't call me sir. Call me Barry. How old are you?"

"Twenty-three."

"And where's your partner?" he asked.

"Downstairs taking the credit agent's statement."

"And did you speak to the credit agent yourself?" asked Gilbert.

"Yes, sir, I did."

"And did you catch his name?"

"Ryan Gill, sir," she said.

"And what did he say?"

"He said he came to make a collection call on behalf of Evergreen Property Management. The victim was five months behind in his rent. When he came upstairs he found the door partially open. He knocked but no one answered. So he came inside." She glanced around the big one-room apartment. "He discovered the victim lying on the bed, sir. He called nine-one-one."

Gilbert nodded. "Thank you."

Officer Virelli peered at Gilbert.

"What are you looking at?" he asked.

"You're wearing a tuxedo, sir," she said.

He grinned. "It's my birthday," he said. "My wife and I were at the theater when headquarters called. She was taking me out."

"Oh," she said. A strained smile came to her face. "Many happy returns, sir."

He could see she was still having a hard time acting normal around Boyd.

"Thank you," he said. "It's my fiftieth. I never thought I'd see the day."

"Congratulations, sir," she said. "You don't look fifty."

He gazed at the young officer, realizing he was over twice her age.

"Thanks," he said.

He glanced at the disarray around the apartment: the broken plate on the floor, the clothes scattered everywhere, the chair knocked down beside the table. Had there been a struggle, he wondered?

"Has Detective Lombardo been notified?" he asked.

"Yes, sir," said Constable Virelli. "I spoke to him personally. He should be here any minute."

This time she managed a grin.

"Why are you grinning?" he asked.

Her grin disappeared. "No reason, sir," she said.

Gilbert frowned. "Let me guess," he said. "He asked you out, didn't he?"

Constable Virelli's grin came back. The color climbed to her face. "No, sir," she said. "But he sure can be charming."

Gilbert shook his head. "Oh, he's charming all right." He slid his hand into his pocket where he felt his theater ticket stub. "You might as well help your partner," he said. He knew she wanted to get away from Boyd's body. "I don't think there's anything else you can do here." He noticed Boyd had three toenails painted red with nail polish. "I'll call if I need help."

"Thank you, sir," she said.

She left the apartment, trying to put some confidence in her stride.

Gilbert looked at Glen Boyd. He never thought he would see the man again. Funny how he should be standing here like this. The apartment, open-concept, was a bachelor pad, with the kitchenette built right into the wall, and the rest of the place a bedroom, living room, and dining room combined. Funny how life could play pranks like this. He wasn't upset, just unsettled. Boyd looked so old. He had a crescent-shaped welt on his forehead, as if he'd been hit with something. An unopened packet of cocaine, five or six grams, rested on the bedside table. So did a bunch of weird candles. The smell of urine rose from the bed. Boyd looked as if he'd been flung onto the bed. Was he strangled next to the laundry hamper, or the piano, or the dining room table, then moved to the bed? Did the messy apartment in fact indicate a struggle? Or was Boyd just a messy guy?

Boyd still had long hair after all these years. Most of it was gray. Despite the cyanotic color of his skin, Boyd's nose was red and raw. Habitual cocaine use, thought Gilbert. Life in the fast lane, that was Glen Boyd's credo. An earring was skewered through his left ear, and eyeliner lined his eyes. The right sleeve of his turquoise dressing gown, pushed up, revealed a peppering of track marks.

Gilbert took his hand out of his pocket and rocked on his heels a few times. The open skylight let in mild June air. He loosened his black bow tie. A door to the right led to Boyd's office, a second-floor storefront affair facing Queen Street. Out the open kitchenette window he heard a streetcar rumble by. Framed photographs hung above the battered piano. Gilbert walked over and had a look.

In one photograph, Boyd stood with members of Led Zeppelin outside the old Masonic Temple, where all the old bands used to play. It was all coming back now, Glen Boyd, the concert-promoter legend of the 1970s, the rock-and-roll mogul who had brought so many great acts to Toronto. Another photograph showed Boyd backstage at Maple Leaf Gardens with Stevie Nicks and Christine McVie of Fleetwood Mac. Bands from a bygone era, he thought, before Boyd's name had faded from the entertainment pages. In another photograph, Boyd, with spiky pink hair and a nose ring, posed in the green room at Massey Hall with members of the Toronto supergroup Mother Courage. Gilbert shook his head. Mother Courage. No one ever talked about them anymore. So many photographs of Boyd with famous people who weren't so famous anymore. Why did people in the entertainment industry always have vanity walls like this? Why did they have such big egos? Why couldn't they just be normal?

He looked at the smashed plate. It lay only a few feet away from the piano bench. A hanging wire connected two of the pieces. Looking closer, Gilbert saw that it was actually an ornamental plate, something to be hung on a wall, and in fact, one of the picture hangers on the wall was empty, the spot showing a vague outline of the plate. Put the pieces of the plate together and you had a couple of men on donkeys crossing some mountains. Had the plate been thrown, used as a projectile during a struggle? He looked at the spilled jar of coins at the end of the piano. The jar looked as if it might have been thrown as well.

"Barry?" Lombardo called.

"Up here," he answered. "First door on your right."

Joe appeared in the doorway, impeccably dressed, a handsome young man of thirty-four. He walked over to the bed and had a look at Boyd. Gilbert joined him. The bed was a water bed. Who had water beds these days? A lava lamp stood on the bed-side table amid all the crazy candles.

"A credit agent found him," said Gilbert.

"A credit agent?"

A pigeon landed briefly on the skylight, then flew away.

"He was five months behind in his rent," said Gilbert. "At least that's what Constable Virelli told me."

Lombardo's eyes brightened. "Did you see Constable Virelli?" he asked.

Gilbert frowned wearily. "I saw her."

"She's a knockout," said Joe. "Italian, too." Lombardo's eyes narrowed. "Only I wonder why her folks called her Virginia?" His lips pursed. "Virginia's not an Italian name."

Gilbert's shoulders sank. "Do you know what Virginia means, Joe?" he asked.

Lombardo frowned. "Here we go," he said.

"She's a nice kid, Joe," said Gilbert. "Emphasis on *kid*."

"She looked a little pale."

"It's her first," said Gilbert. He motioned at Boyd. "I'd say it happened sometime in the last couple hours." He lifted Boyd's arm. It was cool to the touch, and skinny. "You've got the blood sinking to the underside here," said Gilbert, showing Lombardo the limb's lividity. To demonstrate another point, he let the arm drop. It fell as limply as a wet noodle. "But there's no rigor mortis yet." Gilbert checked his watch. "Which means the time of death was probably around nine-thirty."

Lombardo was staring at him now. "You're wearing a tuxedo."

Gilbert grinned. "It's my birthday. Regina took me to the theater. I got beeped at intermission."

"Oh, yeah, that's right," said Joe. "Happy birthday. It's the big five-O, isn't it?"

"Yeah."

"And you don't look a day over sixty. Congratulations."

"Thanks," said Gilbert grimly.

"Listen, after we finish up here, let me take you out for a drink. Where's Regina? Is she still at the theater? We could pick her up."

Gilbert hesitated. "I'm not sure where she is," he said. "I lost her."

"You lost her?" said Lombardo. "At the theater?"

"Yes."

"Weren't you sitting with her?"

"I was," he said. "But we got separated at intermission. I got paged. I went to answer the page. I had to find a public telephone because my cell isn't working. When I got back, I couldn't find Regina anywhere."

Lombardo shook his head.

"Usually when you turn fifty you lose your keys or your glasses, but not your wife. I guess senility's going to hit you big-time."

Gilbert frowned. "No, seriously, I looked all over the place. I don't know what happened to her. The little bell dinged, and everybody went back to their seats, and I still couldn't find her. It's got me a little worried, to tell you the truth."

Lombardo rubbed his five-o'clock stubble. "Maybe there was

a long line-up at the ladies' can," he said. From out the open sky-light, Gilbert heard a ship moan on Lake Ontario. "I'm sure she's sitting in her seat wondering where you are." Lombardo smiled sympathetically. "Christ, some birthday."

"When you're on-call," said Gilbert, "you're on-call."

Lombardo glanced at Boyd's office door. "What's out front there?" he asked.

"Boyd's office," said Gilbert.

"He ran a business from here?"

Gilbert nodded. "Glen Boyd International Artists," he said.

"Why's that name sound familiar?" asked Lombardo.

"Boyd was a famous rock concert promoter back in the seventies and eighties," said Gilbert. "He brought a lot of name acts to town."

"Oh, yeah?" said Lombardo. "Like who?"

"Like Led Zeppelin, Judy Pelaez, and Aerosmith, for starters." Gilbert searched his memory. "Plus a lot of Canadian bands like the Guess Who, Lighthouse, and Mother Courage. In fact, I think he managed Mother Courage for a while."

Lombardo smiled nostalgically. "Now *there's* a name from the past," he said.

"I've still got some of their albums," said Gilbert. "Did I ever tell you Regina actually went to high school with one of the band members? Michelle Morrison? The girl who played keyboards?"

Lombardo squinted. "The dishy one?"

Gilbert shook his head and sighed. "All women are dishy to you, Joe."

* * *

While they waited for the Crime Scene Unit and the coroner's van to arrive, Gilbert and Lombardo investigated the premises more thoroughly.

While Lombardo searched the office, Gilbert continued with the apartment.

He looked at the jar and all the spilled coins again. The two-quart Mason jar was so sturdy it hadn't been broken in the fall. He knelt. He looked more closely at the coins. Half of them were from foreign countries—English farthings, French francs, Italian lire, Greek drachmas—all of them old, no euros, a possible indication that Boyd's jet-setting days were long over.

Then he looked at the plate again. Men on donkeys crossing mountains. Two big pieces attached by a hanging wire, with a few smaller pieces around them. He stood up. Boyd's international playground had shrunk to this crappy little apartment on Queen Street, he decided. Served the bastard right.

He spied a few sickly marijuana plants growing on the windowsill. Plus a lot of pill bottles. He struggled to remain dispassionate about Boyd, but it was hard, especially after what Boyd had done to Regina. He looked at the piano, tinkled the keys. It was out of tune. He looked at all the old photographs again. Should he be working this case? He wasn't sure.

He looked at the photographs once more. Time had stopped for Glen Boyd around 1985, judging from these photographs. He saw photographs of Boyd with Culture Club, Platinum Blond, and Deborah Harry. Here was an earlier one—Boyd with legendary folk singer Judy Pelaez. Hadn't they been married for a while? The big famous HOLLYWOOD sign in Los Angeles stood on a hill behind them. He studied Judy Pelaez, a beautiful wisp of a woman wearing a clingy sweater and a black beret. Another name from the past. He frowned. The seventies. Gone. But not forgotten.

He went back to Boyd's bedside. Did he hate the man, or was hate too good for Boyd? *How many hearts have you broken*, Gilbert wondered? *And how many lives have you ruined?* He remembered Boyd's face well. While still broad and forceful, its lines and wrinkles told a tale of drug and alcohol abuse. He reached up and touched his own face. By comparison, his own face was smooth. Boyd was so terribly thin. Maybe he had AIDS. With all those track marks on his arm, Gilbert wouldn't have been surprised.

In fact, Boyd was the one black mark in his life. Even now, twenty-three years later, he felt the echoes of those intense nine months—when Regina, through Michelle Morrison, had come under this man's thrall. He shook himself. He was over it. Of course he was. This was just another case. And he could work this case. It was all a matter of police procedure. As long as he remembered that, focused on that, this case would be a breeze.

He leaned closer. What was that? A blond hair on the duvet beside Boyd's shoulder. He pulled out a latex glove, slipped it on, lifted the hair, and examined it in the light. Regina had blond hair. He chuckled because he actually caught himself feeling nervous about the blond hair. How ridiculous, that events from twenty-three years ago could still do this to him. He shook his head and took out a plastic evidence bag. He slipped the hair into the bag and zip-locked it shut.

He caught a whiff of something. He sniffed the air. Over and above the acid scent of Boyd's urine, he smelled perfume. The perfume was coming from the scarf. Perhaps the scarf belonged to one of Boyd's lady friends. Boyd was certainly known for his lady friends.

He walked to the office door and looked inside.

Two desks occupied much of the cramped space. One of the telephones looked as if it had been thrown to the floor. Lombardo sat at the far desk flipping through a book of cryptic crosswords. Five Rubik's Cubes sat on the desk amid a scattering of disorganized papers. The computer screen-saver displayed one of M. C. Escher's optically confusing etchings.

"The guy was a puzzle freak," said Lombardo.

"That's what I remember about him," said Gilbert.

"You know the guy?" said Lombardo.

"From way back when." Gilbert reined himself in, deciding to downplay it for Lombardo. "Just in passing. Through Michelle Morrison, my wife's old high school chum. You know. The dishy one."

Lombardo gestured at Boyd's computer. "I was hoping it would take me right in. But he's buggered it up with passwords."

"That sounds like Boyd."

"It won't even let me into the operating system," said Lombardo.

"I wouldn't be surprised if he's rigged it with passwords on every single application," commented Gilbert. "He was like that. Regina said he liked crosswords and acrostics, and had a real head for puzzles. Look at his screen saver. That's a puzzle in itself."

Gilbert decided he might be useful on this case after all. At least he knew something about the man.

Lombardo shook his head. "I guess we're going to have to get Computer Support to crack it for us."

Gilbert raised his eyebrows. "Everybody's dumping on them before summer vacation," he said. "We may have to get in line. Those guys are busy right now."

When Gilbert and Lombardo finished with the crime scene, they left Boyd's office-slash-apartment and walked south on John Street to King Street. The CN Tower rose before them, dwarfing the impressive towers of the financial district, a giant concrete needle with a donut-shaped viewing complex two-thirds up. The night was hot and humid. People out for a good time crowded the sidewalks. Gilbert and Lombardo turned left on King Street and walked to the Royal Alex. Theatergoers were just coming out.

Lombardo inspected the theater's glittering marquee.

"*Mamma Mia*," he said. "I hear that's good."

"Regina's a big ABBA fan from way back," he said. "She knows all the songs."

ABBA. Another band from the 1970s. The evening definitely had a theme.

They crossed the street and scouted the crowd.

Theater patrons made their way through the usual souvenir hawkers, ranks of taxis, and tour buses to the neighboring streets. Partiers and revelers jammed King Street. The Skydome arched to the south like a giant white bubble. A panhandler held a sign—HOMELESS, PLEASE HELP. I WILL PRAY FOR YOU—and jiggled a paper cup for coins. The air smelled of too much ground-clinging ozone and car exhaust.

They kept looking for Regina over the next fifteen minutes but they couldn't find her.

"See what I mean?" said Gilbert. "I lost her."

"The next time you go to the theater, tie your wrists together with yarn. I hear that works well with the day-care set. It might work for old people, too."

Gilbert shook his head. "Maybe she went back to the car."

"Where'd you park?" asked Lombardo.

"On Peter Street," said Gilbert.

They backtracked to Peter Street and headed north. Trendy bars and fashionable nightclubs lined the street. So many young people. This was young-people heaven. If you had the ten- or twenty-dollar cover charge, knew the right dance moves, and were under twenty-five, you could have a real good time here.

They got to Gilbert's Windstar five minutes later. A sensible family vehicle. Far different from the flashy Maserati he remembered Boyd driving.

Regina wasn't there.

"I wonder where she is?" said Gilbert, his concern mounting.

"So you lost her at intermission?" said Lombardo. "Didn't you go out together at intermission?"

"No," said Gilbert. "She went out before intermission. Come to think of it, she went out a good deal before intermission. She's been having this problem. I won't go into it. Maybe she went to the washroom, like you said. I wish my cell phone wasn't broken."

Joe took out his own cell phone. "Here," he said. "Use mine. Call her at home. Maybe she's there."

Gilbert took the phone and dialed.

Jennifer, his elder daughter, now home from nursing college for the summer, picked up after the third ring.

"Jennifer, it's Dad. Is Mom there?"

There was an odd pause. "She's out with Nina right now," said Jennifer. "She's taking Nina for a walk."

That seemed strange.

"For a walk?" he said.

"Nina got some bad news today," said Jennifer.

Gilbert glanced at Lombardo. "What kind of bad news?" he asked.

"A friend of hers got tested for AIDS," said Jennifer. "The test came back HIV-positive. Nina's all upset about it."

Now that Jennifer mentioned it, Gilbert remembered talk recently around the breakfast table about Nina's friend.

"Oh. That's too bad."

"You know how Nina starts to hyperventilate when she gets upset," said Jennifer.

"That bad?" said Gilbert.

"Mom thought she'd better take her for a walk," said Jennifer. "Mom says you disappeared on her."

"We lost track of each other at intermission. I got called to a murder."

"That's what we thought," she said.

Gilbert gazed across the parking lot at the sign that said EVENT PARKING, $18.00.

"Tell her I'm coming home," he said. "I should be there in twenty minutes."

"Okay," said Jennifer.

Gilbert hung up.

"What happened?" asked Lombardo.

"Nina learned one of her friends is HIV-positive. It's made

her all upset. Regina went home to console her. You know how Nina gets."

Lombardo eyes grew somber. "Jeez," he said. "That's too bad."

Gilbert took a deep breath and sighed. "I better go," he said. "Nina probably thinks it's the end of the world. We'll have to have that drink some other time, Joe."

"Sure," said Lombardo. "And listen . . . I can handle the autopsy tomorrow. It's Saturday. Just lay low. You didn't have much of a birthday tonight. Take the day off and enjoy yourself."

Gilbert smiled. "Thanks, Joe," he said. "I might just do that."

AT HOME, GILBERT FOUND REGINA sitting at the kitchen table with Nina, his younger daughter. Nina had her chair drawn right next her mother's, and her cheek rested against Regina's shoulder. Jennifer sat in the chair opposite watching her little sister with an expression Gilbert couldn't readily decipher. The clock in the hall chimed midnight.

"So," he said. "I'm sorry about your friend." He got no reaction. "Do we know her?" he asked. "Is she a good friend of yours?"

"Not really," said Nina, in a voice so soft, so unlike Nina's usual voice, Gilbert knew he had to be missing something.

"Do we know her parents?" he asked.

"Her's a him," corrected Jennifer.

"Oh," said Gilbert.

Gilbert waited for some explanation. The mood in the kitchen was an odd one.

"Mike Topalovich," Regina finally said. "He's a grade-twelve student. A year ahead of Nina."

"Oh."

"Barry, could I talk to you?" said Regina.

He looked at his wife. Something was definitely up.

"Sure," he said.

They went out into the hall.

"What's going on?" he asked.

"Mike Topalovich fools around," she said. "He fools around a lot."

He shook his head. "He should have been more careful. He should have worn a condom. Better yet, he should have abstained."

"Barry . . ." Out the open window he heard the Galloway teens splashing around in their pool, having a late-night pool party. "Barry . . . Mike . . . he fooled around with Nina. Jennifer had instructions not to tell you on the phone. I wanted to wait until you got home."

He grew still, his breath seeping out his lungs as if through a slow leak, the pit of his stomach turning icy with mounting anxiety.

Regina started to cry—a stifled sob, a quick sniff. She snatched a Kleenex from the box on the telephone table.

"Christ," said Gilbert.

"She thinks she's infected . . . and she . . ." Regina struggled against her tears. "How do we know she's not? I mean . . . how can we . . . there's no practical way . . . unless we—"

"We'll have to get her tested," said Gilbert abruptly, loudly, as he shifted into damage-control mode.

Regina dabbed her tears with the Kleenex. Gilbert felt as if the tentacles of ice in his stomach were now spreading outward to the rest of his body.

"Dr. MacPherson's open on Saturdays, isn't he?" said Regina.

"From nine till one," he said. "And I think the lab's open till noon."

"Because the sooner we get her tested—"

"I'll take her first thing tomorrow," he said.

Regina looked at the floor, letting her hair fall past her cheeks. Gilbert took her in his arms. The waterworks came faster.

"Oh . . . Barry . . ."

"I've given her the lecture," he said. "It's not as if I haven't talked to her about it."

"And I've spoken to her, too," said Regina.

"Why would she . . . I mean, what happened? How could she have been so stupid? She's a bright girl. She's consistently in the top of her class. And why with Mike Topalovich? Was she going out with him? I don't remember seeing him around. The last one I remember is Jeff what's-his-name. And that had to be two years ago."

"I know," she said.

"Has she explained it to you?" he asked.

Peals of laughter came from the swimming pool in the Galloway's backyard. Funny how those kids could be having a good time when over here Nina was face-to-face—at the tragically young age of seventeen—with her own mortality.

"She said it was casual," said Regina.

Gilbert felt his face warming. "Casual?" he said.

"Keep your voice down."

"Nina's having casual sex?"

"They were at a party. There was some wine. They went up to the bedroom. I guess they didn't mean to . . . but they did."

The ice tentacles continued to claw their way through his body. "And how long ago was this?" he asked.

"Back in February. During Reading Week."

"I don't believe this. And the guy's just finding out now? Who knows how long he's had it for? Who knows how many other girls he's infected? What a supreme jerk. What the hell was he thinking? And what was Nina thinking?"

"Don't give her a big lecture," cautioned Regina, finally getting her tears under control. "It'll only make matters worse. You can see why I had to leave the theater in such a hurry. When I phoned home out in the lobby to check on them, and Nina gave me the news . . . to tell you the truth, I didn't even look for you when I couldn't find you right away. I took a taxi straight home."

He sighed. "I was called to a murder," he said.

"I thought as much."

That it was Glen Boyd's murder now seemed immaterial.

"And I'm not going to give her a lecture," he said. "She looks terrified."

Regina glanced at him somberly. "Wouldn't you be?"

"Has she had sex with anybody else?" he asked. "Because if she has, we have to . . . you know . . . contact the families."

"She says not," answered Regina. "Mike's . . . well . . . her first. And her only . . . so far."

They went back into the kitchen. Nina glanced at him with

trepidation—as if in fact she expected a lecture. But he didn't give her one. Regina sat down next to her. Gilbert put on his best fatherly smile.

"It's all right, Nina," he said. "Mom told me. Don't worry. We'll go see Dr. MacPherson tomorrow."

Her shoulders eased. Gilbert hated to see her pretty face so streaked with tears. He didn't think he'd ever seen her eyes so puffy before. He didn't know what to say. He felt as if some load-bearing piece of his soul was about to break. His little Nina, that bit of sunshine that made the whole household happy, now with the fear of death in her eyes.

"I'm sorry, Daddy," she said, her voice breaking through her distress. *Daddy*. He couldn't remember the last time she'd called him that. It was always *Dad* these days, now that she was getting older. She clutched her mother's arm and pressed her cheek against Regina's shoulder again. "I guess I'm going to die," she said, and a whole new flood of tears sprang to her eyes.

He had to do something to put her mind at ease.

"Let's not jump to conclusions," he said. "Just because Mike Topalovich is HIV-positive doesn't mean you are. You had your little thing with him when, back in February?"

"Yes."

"It's now June," he said. "We'll have to hope he became infected sometime after February." He reached over and stroked her face, not mad at all, just wanting to comfort her. "In the meantime, we'll see Dr. MacPherson tomorrow. This new murder—Joe said I didn't have to come to the autopsy tomorrow, that he'd look after it. So I've got the day free. We'll go first thing. We'll have the doctor order the test right away. And then we'll wait for the results. We'll ask Dr. MacPherson to put a rush on it. Don't worry, Nina. Everything's going to be fine."

But he wasn't so sure.

On his way up to bed, he spied the day's mail on the hall table. One of the pieces looked like a birthday card. He lifted the mauve envelope and checked the return address. Miami, Florida. From his brother, Howard. He opened the envelope and pulled out the card. It showed a man playing golf. A happy theme on this otherwise unhappy day.

Inside, he found something less than happy, a newspaper clipping from the *Miami Herald* showing Howard, a homicide detective with the Miami-Dade Police Department, arresting a suspect in front of the suspect's mobile home. He read Howard's short note.

Happy Fiftieth, bro'. I finally got this bastard, Ricardo Relós, the guy who raped and murdered his thirteen-year-old niece. I may not be smiling in this picture, but I was smiling inside. Many happy returns. We'll see you in November. It'll be good to hit the fairway with you again. Howard.

Gilbert shook his head. Happy birthday, wrapped in the bad karma of a killer. He couldn't seem to escape that particular juxtaposition today. Ricardo Relós. And his niece, Mariana. Now he remembered. A real coup for Howard. But one that just depressed Gilbert right now.

Regina was already in bed with the light out when he got upstairs. He lay quietly beside her, trying not to disturb her, and stared up at the ceiling.

If things had gone according to plan, he and Regina would be making love right now, a birthday present from her to him. Not that it mattered anymore. His stomach had congealed into a ball of worry. He lay there rigidly, thinking not of his birthday but of how his daughter Nina might be HIV-positive. One minute you could be watching *Mamma Mia* and tapping your foot to old ABBA songs, the next, your daughter could be HIV-positive. A summer breeze billowed the bedroom curtains. Fate's pranks were sometimes cruel.

"You asleep?" he asked Regina.

"My mind keeps going round in circles," she said.

"Because I should tell you about this new case," he said. "It's a little different."

"We're not going to need a protection detail like we did with Edgar Lau, are we?"

"No. At least I don't think so."

"Then why's it different?" she asked.

"Because I know the victim."

She paused. "You do?"

"Yes," he said. "You do, too."

"I do?" she said. She propped herself up on her elbow. "Who?" she asked.

"Glen Boyd."

She grew still. The corners of her lips turned downward, something he picked out in the glow of the streetlight coming in through their bedroom window. A knit came to her brow. He didn't know what to make of it. And the look in her eyes, what was that? Pity? Sorrow? Regret? Her chin dipped, her hair shifted, and she looked sad. He felt sorry for her.

"He was strangled," he said. "About the time we lost track of each other at the Royal Alex."

He thought Regina would say something. But she didn't. She finally took a deep breath. A small noise came from her throat. Not sorrow, not pity, not even regret, just a distant ache.

"Thank you," she said.

Why so stiff? Why so formal? She sounded like a queen who'd just been told that her kingdom had been lost. She wouldn't say more. She turned from him. She was hiding. She didn't want him to see her. True to character, she hid her misery from others. He stroked her shoulder, but she stayed turned from him. That load-bearing piece inside his soul sagged another millimeter or two. *Happy birthday,* he thought. He hoped his fifty-first would be better.

Gilbert and Nina sat in Dr. MacPherson's waiting room the next morning.

"We're lucky to have Dr. MacPherson," Gilbert told Nina. "Not many doctors work on Saturdays. He's a dying breed."

Nina didn't say anything, stared at the picture on the wall, an odd print of a nineteenth-century bathing pavilion with nineteenth-century ladies in funny old bathing suits, and nineteenth-century gents in equally quaint swimming apparel. The secretary wasn't in. Not on Saturdays. Her desk was piled with the morning's charts. Nina's was in there among them.

A short en-suite corridor led past the copy and fax room to the doctor's office. Gilbert heard the door open and a Filipino woman say in a thick Tagalog accent, "Thank you, doctor." A moment later, the Filipino woman bustled out with a prescription in her hand.

Then Dr. MacPherson appeared. He walked to his secretary's desk, picked up Nina's file, and flipped through it. He was tall, over six feet, walked in a slouched manner, was about fifty-five, wore Hush Puppies, a white labcoat, and, because it was Saturday, a pair of blue jeans.

He came out past the glass partition into the waiting room, peered at them from over the rims of his glasses, and beckoned them with his finger.

"Nina," he said.

They got up. The doctor walked back to his office, shuffling like an extra from *Night of the Living Dead*. Gilbert and Nina followed.

"Have a seat," said Dr. MacPherson, in a bored and detached manner. They sat. The doctor took his own chair, slouched in it, put his elbows on his desk, and gazed at them as if he had no idea who they were. "What can I do for you?" he asked.

"Well . . . we . . ." Gilbert looked out the window where he saw Toronto Transit bus barns across the street. The morning was sunny and hot, such a contrast from the way he felt inside. "We think Nina might have HIV."

"HIV?" said Dr. MacPherson, whacking the last letter, now waking up. "You think, or you know?"

Gilbert's heart beat faster. For some reason he couldn't look the doctor in the eye, as if Nina getting HIV was his own personal failing. He stared instead at the antique wind-up piggy bank, a teddy bear that snatched a penny from a honey pot and put it in a tree stump, something the doctor entertained kid patients with.

"The evidence is fairly strong," said Gilbert. "The timing might be called into question. But we're worried enough to think Nina should be tested."

The doctor turned to Nina. "And when do you think you were exposed, Nina?" he asked.

The color rose to Nina's face, and she looked so scared Gilbert thought she was going to faint. "February," she said.

"And how were you exposed?"

At first she didn't seem to understand, but then she got it.

"Unprotected sex," she said.

"Do you want your father to be here for this?" asked the doctor. "In these cases, I'm legally obliged to give you the option of privacy."

She nodded. "I want him to be here," she said.

"Okay," he said. "So you had unprotected sex in February. Do you remember roughly the date?"

"The twenty-fifth."

"Exactly the twenty-fifth?"

"There was a party," she said. "I remember the date."

"So essentially three months ago."

In a small fragile voice, she said, "Yes."

"And your partner—I'm assuming he knows he's HIV-positive, and that's how you found out?"

"Yes."

"And is he your only partner?"

"Yes."

"And when did he find out he was HIV-positive?" asked Dr. MacPherson.

"Yesterday."

"And how many tests has he had?" he asked. "Do you know?"

She raised her eyebrows, as if she wondered how this could possibly matter. "I don't know," she said. "I guess only one."

"And he showed up positive the first time?"

"I think so."

Dr. MacPherson flipped through some notes in Nina's chart, but Gilbert could tell he wasn't reading them. He was thinking. Going over the timing maybe?

"Well . . . I guess we should get you tested, then," he said, as if it were no big deal. "But it's unlikely we'll get a useful result three months after exposure."

Gilbert cocked his brow. "What do you mean?"

The doctor leaned back in his chair.

"Well . . . the tests we do for HIV are sensitive to a specific HIV antibody," he explained. "Your immune system starts to make these antibodies three months, give or take, after you've been exposed. If you test *too* soon you'll come back negative, and we'll have to test again." He turned to Nina. "Health Canada recommends waiting three to six months after initial exposure as a way to keep things cost effective. And you've barely broken the three-month mark."

Gilbert frowned. "I don't care about cost effective," he said. "This is my daughter."

Dr. MacPherson raised his hands. "I know . . . I know . . . and we'll get her tested. Cost effective and peace of mind don't seem to have any real-value connection as far as Health Canada is concerned. By all means, we'll get her tested." He opened a drawer and pulled out a test requisition form. "But she may have to be tested again at the four-month mark, and again at the five-month mark . . . and maybe even again at the six-month mark if the early tests come back negative."

Gilbert felt his shoulders sinking. This was going to turn into a bigger waiting game than he thought.

"Can't we do home tests?" asked Nina, now squirming a bit. "I hear they have home testing kits. If I'm going to have to do three or four . . . I find this all so . . . embarrassing."

"I wouldn't go with the home kits, Nina," said Dr. MacPherson. "They're only ninety percent accurate. And they're prone to false positives."

"I just thought of something," said Gilbert, his pulse quickening with dread. "If it takes at least three months for the test to detect the antibodies, and Nina's partner found out he was HIV-positive only yesterday, then that means he was probably infected longer than three months ago, before he and Nina had intercourse."

"That's probably a safe assumption," said the doctor.

"Then that means she's probably infected," said Gilbert.

Dr. MacPherson's face settled. "Unfortunately, that's true."

"Then what chance does she have?" asked Gilbert, his face growing flushed.

"Not a good one, I'm afraid," said Dr. MacPherson. "If her partner came back positive on his first test, and it's a true positive, it's likely he's been infected for a good long while. The antibodies have had a chance to build, and that takes time. Over three months, on average. So you're right, there's a strong possibility Nina is indeed infected."

To hear the doctor say it was nearly more than Gilbert could bear.

"So she has no chance, then?" he said, his dread turning into a mounting wave of panic.

He glanced at Nina. Tears came to her eyes. She, too, had been shocked by the doctor's words.

"I wouldn't say she has *no* chance," said Dr. MacPherson. He lifted the Kleenex box and handed it to Nina. "People produce antibodies at different rates. Average trigger levels for HIV are three to six months. Some people produce trigger levels after only three weeks. Nina's partner might have been exposed after February. It wouldn't be entirely beyond the realm of possibility for him to produce antibodies more quickly than other people. So let's not give up all hope just yet. Let's get her tested. Take this requisition down to the lab this morning. They're open till noon." He turned to Nina. "If it comes back negative—and by the way, it takes six or seven days to get the results back—we'll have you tested again the first week of July."

"We'll be at the cottage the first week of July," said Gilbert.

"Then the second week of July," said the doctor. "If it comes back negative again, we'll test her the first week of August. As far as negatives are concerned, test reliability increases with time. If the test comes back negative six months from the time of suspected exposure, there's nearly a hundred percent chance you're virus-free. At that point I usually say there's no need for further testing. But if you're still concerned, we can retest at nine months. And to hell with cost effectiveness."

IN THE HOMICIDE OFFICE ON Monday morning, Lombardo had the results of the Boyd autopsy.

"A few surprises," he said. "His arm was broken."

"It was?" said Gilbert. His mind was still half on Nina.

"A fracture in his ulna up near the elbow of his left arm."

"I didn't see any swelling or bruising," said Gilbert, forcing himself to get back on track.

"Dr. Blackstein said it was apparent only on X-ray."

"And the fracture was fresh?" asked Gilbert.

"No more than twenty-four hours old."

Gilbert shook his head. "If his arm was broken, why didn't he go to the hospital?"

Lombardo raised his eyebrows. "Remember all those painkillers we found?" he said. "Up on the windowsill and in the medicine cabinet? Maybe he thought it was just a sprain. If he took enough painkillers, he wouldn't feel much pain. Which brings us to the next surprise." Up at the front, Carol Reid, the squad secretary, came in with a flowerpot full of red begonias. "Dr. Blackstein's not prepared to rule manner of death was definitely strangulation."

Gilbert was indeed surprised by this. "Why not?"

"Because the trauma to Boyd's hyoid bone and thyroid cartilage wasn't significant enough to fit the usual pattern of strangulation," said Lombardo. "Nor were the ligature markings on Boyd's throat deep enough."

"Yes, but he was blue," said Gilbert. "He was cyanosed."

"I know," said Lombardo. "And Dr. Blackstein is definitely willing to rule cause of death as respiratory insufficiency. But as for the *manner* of death . . . in this particular case, because of all the drugs we found, and because Dr. Blackstein suspects Boyd took a good deal of those drugs for his broken arm . . . well . . . he says the manner of death could be either strangulation *or* a drug overdose. A drug overdose often causes respiratory arrest. Dr. Blackstein wants a toxicologist to look at the case before he rubber-stamps the manner of death."

"That's going to take a while," said Gilbert.

"Dr. Blackstein thinks we might push it faster if we ask Toxicology to test for only the drugs we found in Boyd's apartment."

Gilbert thought about it. "Even with streamlined testing, it's going to take at least eight weeks."

"That's what we've got to work with," said Lombardo. "He says we should still go ahead and investigate the case as if it were a homicide. He says strangulation is by far the likelier scenario."

Gilbert tapped his paperweight made of bullets. Forgetting Blackstein's preliminary conclusions, he now considered the specific findings of the autopsy report itself. Trauma was slight. That could say something about the strength or size of the killer. He raised the point with Lombardo.

"It seems to me that in the absence of the usual pronounced trauma, we can guess the murderer wasn't particularly strong, and that he was small in stature. We might be looking at an older individual."

Lombardo thought about it. "Or a woman," he suggested.

This stopped Gilbert. He hadn't considered this possibility. He swallowed. He had a sudden thought. A ridiculous, bizarre thought, a thought he shouldn't be thinking at all: Regina. A crazy thought. How was he going to keep objective on this case? He forced himself back on track a second time.

"Did Blackstein find any useable DNA evidence anywhere on the corpse?" he asked.

"Some skin flakes underneath the fingernails of each hand," said Lombardo. "It looks like there was a struggle after all. Boyd grabbed whoever was attacking him and he got trace amounts of their skin lodged under his fingernails. Were you able to reach Boyd's secretary at all?"

"Actually, she phoned me," said Gilbert. "Stacy Todd's her name. She's asking me whether she can get into the office today. She says there'll be a ton of e-mail and voice mail inquiries because of all this. I've made an appointment to see her at noon today. I'm going to pick her up at her apartment, then we'll drive over. I'll find out what she knows."

"Okay," said Joe. "I'm going to Computer Support to see

how they're doing with Boyd's PC. I've twisted some arms. They say they're at least going to start on it." Lombardo glanced at his watch, a sporty little number with Roman numerals. "We'll hook up sometime this afternoon then?"

"Sure," said Gilbert. "I'll bring back coffee."

Gilbert killed time until his Stacy Todd appointment by doing some deskwork on the Glen Boyd case.

He checked for outstanding warrants, prior arrests, and previous convictions on the man, and found three marijuana possession charges, all dating from before 1985. Fraud had a bad-check case on him from 1997. Patrol arrested him for public drunkenness in 1999. More interestingly—and of possible value to his case—Glen Boyd had filed a harassment complaint against former Mother Courage guitarist Phil Thompson just this year. Accompanying the complaint was a restraining order: Phil Thompson wasn't allowed anywhere near Glen Boyd.

So. Friction between Glen Boyd and Phil Thompson. Definitely something worth looking into.

He ran a search for priors on Phil Thompson and found nothing but a current driver's license suspension for driving under the influence. As Gilbert had once been a Mother Courage fan, he now recalled how Thompson had been arrested a couple of times in the United States, once in Denver for lighting his guitar on fire and throwing it into the audience, and once in Houston for stripping naked at one of his concerts. But these ancient antics didn't concern Gilbert. Not the way this restraining order did. Gilbert tapped his fingers a few times against his mouse pad, then scrolled down. Here was an actual on-line copy of the restraining order. He cut and pasted it into the Boyd case file for future reference. There were no useful details in the order, nothing indicating the reasons for it, but that particular information gap might easily be filled by talking to Phil Thompson personally.

First he had to worry about Stacy Todd.

Gilbert went to the car pool, signed out an unmarked Lumina, and drove to Stacy Todd's apartment on Queen Street West—not the trendy part of Queen Street, but the part out near Lansdowne, a stone's-throw away from the sprawling skid row of Parkdale. She lived in a pluralistic little community of musicians, artists, and prostitutes.

Stacy's apartment occupied the third floor of a shopfront building. Looking up, Gilbert saw a dozen pigeons sitting on her window ledge. A streetcar rumbled westbound. He crossed the tracks to the sidewalk and rang Stacy's buzzer. A moment later, Stacy came downstairs—quickly, loudly, an avalanche of legs and feet.

She opened the door. She was a tall, thin, tired-looking woman in her mid-fifties. She wore black stretchy pants tight to her legs, a black sweatshirt, and red running shoes. She wore glasses with oversized lenses and dipping arms, the frames transparent pink. She had blue eyes and blond hair. She gave him a shy but pained grin.

"Hi," she said. "Detective Gilbert?"

He pulled out his badge and identification and showed them to her.

"I'm glad you could take the time to see me," he said.

"No," she said. "I'm glad you're giving me the chance to get into the office." She made way, swept her palm toward the stairs. "Let's go up," she said. "I'll put the kettle on. I've got some seed cakes."

He followed her up the stairs. Seed cakes? What the heck were seed cakes?

The first thing that struck him about Stacy's apartment were all the gift baskets sitting on a long worktable against the wall. She had them filled with designer soaps, bath beads, small cans of expensive salmon, little packages of rye squares, various wines, and boxes of gourmet crackers. She had them decorated with blue, yellow, and pink cellophane. She caught him looking.

"I do gift baskets," she said. "These small ones are eighteen dollars. These ones here are twenty-seven. And the large ones back there are forty-nine. If you're ever stuck for a gift idea, call me. I'll give you my card before you go. I also do catering."

He gazed at the baskets some more. "Boyd doesn't pay you enough?" he asked.

"This is a hobby," she said. "I do it for fun. If I make some money at it, so much the better."

He followed her into the kitchen. He sat down and watched her fix tea. She looked unwell. She looked as if she'd been up all night. Her face was pale, and the rims of her eyes were red. She spooned a green leafy substance into a stainless steel tea ball.

"What's that?" he asked, knowing Boyd had always been a big pot smoker.

"It's mint," she said. "Is that all right?"

Mint tea. And seed cakes. "Sure," he said. "Why not? But do you mind if I use your washroom first? It's hot out. I want to splash my face."

"Sure," she said. "Just down the hall."

He went to the washroom. He wanted a chance to look around. A plain-view search. You never knew what you were going to find. The washroom was spotless. The wastepaper basket was empty except for one small item of interest, a hospital identification bracelet from Mount Joseph Hospital. He splashed his face and returned to the kitchen.

"You were in the hospital recently?" he said.

"Pardon?"

"I saw the hospital identification band in the wastepaper basket."

She nodded. He again noted how unwell she looked. "I'm a diabetic," she said. "I had a bit of an episode on Friday so I thought I'd better have it checked out."

"My brother's a diabetic, too," he said. "Insulin dependent. He has to go in every three months."

"It's not nice," she said. "The doctor was going to keep me in. But then I learned about Glen, and I knew there would be a ton of calls."

"You don't look too hot," he said.

"I'm fine," she said.

Once she'd served tea, he began with his questions.

"So when was the last time you saw Boyd?" he asked.

"Friday afternoon," she said.

"In the office?"

"In the office," she said.

"And how was he?"

"He was . . . preoccupied," said Stacy. "That's nothing unusual. He's always preoccupied."

"So you went home at the usual time on Friday?" he asked.

"Yes."

"And then you had your episode here in the apartment?"

"Yes."

"You're sure you're up to driving to the office?"

"I've got to," she said.

"Okay." He glanced cautiously at his seed cake, wondering if he should eat it. "So on Friday, when you were at work, did Glen mention anything out of the ordinary?"

"Only that he was having dinner with Judy Pelaez that night," said Stacy.

"*The* Judy Pelaez?" asked Gilbert.

Stacy nodded. "She flew up from San Francisco to see Glen."

Gilbert thought of Judy Pelaez, the petite, pretty folksinger who sang such achingly sad love ballads as "River of Tears," "The Bluest Bird in the World," and "So Cool You're Cold," recalled the versatile quality of her voice, one moment husky and low, the next moment sweet and high.

"So in other words, there's a good possibility Judy Pelaez was the last one to see Boyd alive."

"I can't say," she answered. "He was booked to have dinner with her. Whether he showed up is anybody's guess. Glen's notorious for not showing up these days."

Gilbert thought about it. It certainly warranted further inquiry.

"Weren't Boyd and Judy married for a while?" he asked.

"Yes." Stacy gave him a questioning look. "You knew they had kids together, didn't you?" she said.

"I might have read it somewhere," he said.

"A daughter, Morningstar. She's sixteen. And Delta, their son. He's eighteen."

Morningstar and Delta. Mint tea and seed cakes. God. "So she came up to see him?" he said.

"Yes."

"Any idea why?"

"She comes up every so often," said Stacy. "Looking for bookings. And also to see Glen. I wish there was something GBIA could do for her, but there's not. No one wants to book her anymore. She came out with that new album a few years back but it bombed. She's lost her voice. Only die-hard Judy Pelaez fans bought it."

"And were they cordial with each other? Glen and Judy?"

Stacy looked away, picked a burnt sesame seed from her seed cake, and put it on her napkin.

"On their good days, yes," she said. "But I don't know why she bothers." Stacy glanced at the kitchen windowsill where some chives grew in a terra-cotta pot. "Before yesterday, Judy still insisted on thinking they had a future together. It's sad. I guess when you have kids together . . . you know . . . she thought he would finally come back to her. So she comes up every year. To plead with him. It can't be good for her. Or for her kids."

"Did Boyd help her out at all? Like child support, or whatever, for the kids?"

"Sometimes," said Stacy. "But he's made a few bad business decisions over the last few years, and it's hit him hard. He hasn't contributed significant amounts recently. Judy asks him for money whenever she comes up. I think last week she asked for more than usual. They had a big row about it. I heard them fighting. On their bad days they fight. Boy, do they fight. And then I guess he told her he was seeing someone new. He shouldn't have done that. She came raging into my office and asked me who it was. I didn't know. I try to stay out of Glen's personal life as much as I can. Judy was livid. I haven't seen her that angry in a long time."

"So Judy's never gotten over Boyd?" he said.

"That would be putting it mildly," replied Stacy.

"And is Judy still in town?"

Because if Judy were still in town, he would definitely have to talk to her.

"Yes. I spoke to her this morning."

"And do you know where she's staying?" asked Gilbert.

"At the Best Western Primrose, on Carleton and Jarvis."

Gilbert took a sip of his tea. Minty. Not bad. Then he glanced at his seed cake. He thought he'd leave the seed cake alone.

"Tell me," he said, "do you know if she's a natural blond?"

He sure would like to put his mind at ease about the blond hair, get a blond suspect, not Regina, so he could consider the possibility of a DNA comparison test.

"She's gone gray," said Stacy. "But she dyes it back to her original blond."

This was good.

For now, he left it. For now, he moved on.

"Do you know anything about the restraining order Glen Boyd filed against Phil Thompson?" he asked.

Her cup stopped halfway to her lips—he couldn't help noticing the design on the cup, a series of interlocking electric guitars, and in black lettering along the bottom, GUITAR SUMMIT '99.

"You'd have to talk to the company lawyer, Daniel Lynn, about that," she said. "He's advised me not to talk about it."

He grew suddenly curious about the other band members of Mother Courage.

"Tell me, is Michelle Morrison still around?" he asked. "She and my wife were high school friends. They went to North Toronto together in the sixties."

A pigeon landed on the kitchen windowsill and looked in on them, then flew off.

"Michelle opened a flower shop in 'eighty-nine and now has five locations citywide."

"I understand Glen Boyd managed Mother Courage for a while."

"I wouldn't say it was an amicable partnership, but yes, he did."

"I was a big fan," said Gilbert. "I have some of their albums. What happened to Carol White?"

"Oh . . . Carol. I'm afraid Carol died a few years back."

"Really?"

"She died of cancer. I'm not sure what kind. She was a sweet, sweet lady."

"What about Paul?" asked Gilbert.

"Paul moved to London, England. He produces New Age music there."

"And what about Ted Aver?" asked Gilbert, picturing the famous drummer. "He was always my favorite."

Stacy stroked the edge of her mug. "You knew about his motorcycle accident, didn't you?" she asked.

His eyes widened. "No," he said. "What happened?"

"He was sideswiped by a truck while riding his Harley up to Stouffville a few years back," said Stacy. "He's been in a wheelchair ever since. He's a paraplegic."

"Really?"

"He loved his Harley."

"He can't even play drums anymore?" asked Gilbert. "The foot pedals and so forth?"

"Oh, no, he still plays," said Stacy, then glanced at her watch. "I should go to the office soon. The voice mail will be backed up completely."

"But how can he manage the bass drum and the hi-hat?" asked Gilbert, trying to picture it.

"He's got this chin brace that works the bass drum, and an elbow brace that works the hi-hat," she said. "You should see him play. He's amazing to watch."

"But he doesn't play professionally anymore, does he?"

"No. He doesn't have to. He's done extremely well in business investments."

Gilbert nodded, relieved to hear that his favorite Mother Courage band member had made a decent and successful life for himself, post rock-stardom.

"What about Phil?" he asked, because he thought he might as well take one more stab at Phil. "What's he doing these days?"

She sighed, looked away.

"Phil's been trying to resurrect his pop-star status ever since Mother Courage went belly-up in 'eighty-three," she said. "He gigs around in bar bands to keep himself going, and as far as I know, he's trying to get a solo album off the ground, and of course he makes a bit of money from his yearly guitar retreat in Bobcaygean. But I think he never got over the breakup of the band. He's never moved past the band, into new things, the way the others have. He was a big star. A *really* big star. And when you're *that* big, it's hard to be small again."

Gilbert drove Stacy Todd to Glen Boyd International Artists. He asked her for Phil Thompson's telephone number. She went to her Rolodex, jotted Phil Thompson's number down, and gave it to him.

"I'll give you Ted's as well," she said. "Ted was Glen's voice of reason. And here's the company lawyer's number, too, Daniel Lynn, in case you want to talk to him about that restraining order. He's up on Bay. In the Polo Center."

"Thanks," said Gilbert.

She looked around the office.

"You took Glen's computer," she said.

"We had to. I hope you have all the necessary files and applications you need on your own PC."

"My own computer is the office workhorse," she said. "Glen's was just his personal toy. I doubt you'll find anything useful on it."

He gazed at her. She looked positively pale, and her forehead was clammy. But she looked as if she were going to soldier on anyway.

"I'm going to take a look in the other room again," he said. "Call me when you're done. We're going to have to leave together. I can't leave you here alone. Sorry."

While Stacy went about her business, Gilbert went into the apartment.

He walked over to the piano, an instrument he had once played badly in high school. The broken plate and jar of coins still lay on the floor. He could see that Nigel Gower from Auxiliary Services had dusted them for prints. He tried a few bars of "The Bluest Bird in the World." He managed to tinkle his way through most of the chorus, singing in a tuneless voice as he went: "I don't want to hear your endless lies, or your sad good-byes, I just want to fly away, like the bluest bird in the world . . . spread my wings and fly away . . . fly away . . ."

How could anybody write anything so melancholy? He thought of the things Stacy had said about Judy Pelaez, how the folksinger pleaded every year for Boyd to come back to her, remembered how Lombardo said the murderer might have been a woman. He glanced down at the piano bench and saw some papers and music sticking out from underneath the lid. He would speak to Judy Pelaez, and it would be odd because she had a famous face, a face he'd seen in pictures, television, and on the Internet, one that adorned three of his own records at home. He would find out why she was so sad, why she never got over Boyd, and why she had tortured herself by believing Boyd would some-day come back to her.

He opened the piano bench and found a photograph of Regina and Glen resting on top of all the music.

He froze.

His arm went limp and his finger accidentally stroked high C. The damper was broken on that particular key and the note resonated, sterile and lonely, on and on, until it faded like an aging rock star, finally disappearing into the noise of the Queen Street traffic.

He lifted the photograph. His emotional gyroscope went a-kilter, and he had to fight to get himself under control.

The photograph showed a twenty-eight-year-old Regina and a thirty-four-year-old Glen Boyd sitting on a stone balustrade overlooking the French Riviera. Boyd had his arm around Regina. Regina wore a peculiar grin. She looked like she was suppressing a laugh—as if Boyd had just told her a joke. Some bougainvillea cascaded from a garden trellis. Boyd smiled that devil-may-care smile he had. They were *happy*. Regina was *happy*.

That didn't bother him so much.

What bothered him was that the photograph should be here in the first place.

Right on top of all the music.

Within easy reach.

As if in fact Regina still had a cherished place in Boyd's life.

CHAPTER
FOUR

AS GILBERT REACHED BAY STREET, he gazed up at the Polo Center. He wiped his brow with the back of his hand—it was hot, and the weatherman was calling for a heat wave. Except for a few interesting curves and a semicircular courtyard, the Polo Center was a generic skyscraper of glass and steel—bright, reflective, and futuristic. He pushed his way through the revolving doors into the marble lobby, grateful for the air-conditioning. He took the elevator to the third floor.

On the third floor he found his way to suite 308, the offices of Clifton, Simhi, and Lynn, Barristers and Solicitors. He went inside and presented himself to the receptionist, a young man in a white shirt and red tie.

"Can I help you?" asked the man.

"I have a three o'clock appointment with Daniel Lynn." He

showed his badge and ID. "I'm Detective-Sergeant Barry Gilbert of Metro Homicide. He's squeezing me in."

The receptionist glanced at Gilbert's ID, then gestured at the chairs in the waiting area.

"Have a seat," he said. "He'll be with you shortly."

Gilbert sat down in the waiting area.

Daniel Lynn emerged with a client ten minutes later. The client, a middle-aged man with curly dark hair and a mustache, looked grim, as if his meeting with Lynn had gone badly. He didn't shake Daniel Lynn's hand—didn't even say good-bye—just walked right out and disappeared into the corridor.

"I don't think we'll be seeing him again," said Lynn to the receptionist.

The receptionist smiled sweetly at Lynn. It occurred to Gilbert that the young man might be gay.

"This is Detective-Sergeant Barry Gilbert of Metro Homicide," said the receptionist.

Gilbert rose. He didn't particularly like lawyers, but Lynn looked decent enough, a tall man close to sixty, fit-looking, impeccably groomed, conservatively dressed, slim, handsome, with a swimmer's build.

"Detective Gilbert," said Lynn, extending his hand. "A pleasure."

The two men shook hands.

"Thanks for taking the time to see me on such short notice," said Gilbert.

A look of dismay came to Lynn's blue eyes. "Poor old Glen," he said. "Let's go into my office, shall we, and see if we can sort him out?"

Gilbert followed Lynn into his office. Lynn had a puzzling accent. Gilbert couldn't place it. It sounded Glaswegian, or Dutch South African.

"Have a seat," said Lynn.

Gilbert sat down. "I can't place your accent," he said. "Are you South African?"

Lynn grinned like Prince Philip on the Queen's birthday. "I'm Jamaican," he said.

"Jamaican?" said Gilbert.

"Yes," said Lynn. "A *white* Jamaican. There aren't many of us, but we do exist. She was a British colony, after all, for the longest time."

"So you're originally British."

"Actually, my grandfather emigrated from Wales. He came from Cardiff and started a coffee plantation in the Blue Mountains near Mavis Bank. That's just north of Kingston. A lovely spot, really. The high altitude moderates the heat comfortably. I grew up there. So I don't consider myself British. Or Welsh for that matter. I'm second-generation Jamaican. Have you ever tasted Blue Mountain coffee, Detective Gilbert?"

"No," said Gilbert.

Lynn lifted the phone and dialed the outer office. "How do you take it?" he asked.

"With cream and sugar."

"Donald, could you bring in two of the Blue Mountain, both with cream and sugar." He hung up. "My uncle has the place now. Most of his market is in Japan. I don't know why the Japanese love Blue Mountain coffee the way they do, but they're willing to pay outrageous prices for it."

While they waited for Donald to bring in their coffee, Gilbert and Lynn got down to business.

"I understand you have to honor counsel-client confidentiality," said Gilbert, "even when the client has become deceased—"

Lynn quieted him with a wave of his hand.

"Detective Gilbert, you have my full cooperation. This is a murder. I'm not going to confound you with the need for court orders. Glen was not only a client, he was my good friend. I want to catch his murderer as much as you do."

Gilbert warmed to the man. His fervency seemed genuine.

"Then maybe we can start with this restraining order Glen Boyd filed against Phil Thompson," he said. Gilbert took out his notebook. "Do you know anything about it?"

A grin came to Lynn's face. "I knew you were going to ask me about that."

Gilbert shrugged. "Can you blame me?"

Lynn leaned back in his chair, rolling it a few inches from his desk, crossed his legs, and clasped his hands over his knee.

"Let's see," he said. "Where to begin." He leveled his friendly blue eyes at Gilbert. "Phil Thompson has a lot of outstanding concerns with Glen Boyd. And unfortunately most of them have never been resolved. I believe at last count we were defending Glen against seven Thompson-filed lawsuits. Mr. Thompson believes Glen owes him a great deal of money. But legally, Glen's company, GBIA, owes Phil Thompson nothing. In the framework of the restraining order, you can see where this might fit."

On Bay Street, a bus rumbled by.

"Go on," said Gilbert.

Lynn's jacket slid back, revealing a gold pen in his shirt pocket. "Are you familiar with Mother Courage at all?" he asked.

"Who isn't?"

"Right, then," said Lynn. His brow settled, and he sat forward. "Popularity is a fickle bird, Detective Gilbert. That's something Phil Thompson has never understood. Mother Courage was hugely successful in the mid-seventies. But by the end of the decade, Phil, who was the de facto head of the group, should have had the good sense to call it quits. Punk rock and New Wave were all the rage by then, and power bands who played stadium rock were dinosaurs. I think everybody else in the group sensed this. But Phil . . . Phil believed Mother Courage could go on forever."

Lynn shook his head as if at the folly of mankind.

"Phil liked fame," he continued. "They all did. But Phil was addicted to it. Fame was like a drug to him. He liked to go into any restaurant anywhere in the Western world and have people ask him for his autograph. He liked to see album sales soar. He liked to do interviews. And I suppose it shocked him when the interviews tapered off and his record sales dipped, and no one recognized him anymore."

A knock came at the door and Donald entered with two cups of Blue Mountain coffee.

"Here we go," said Lynn. "Jamaica's finest. Thank you, Donald."

Donald placed the coffee on the desk and quietly left the room.

"You're in for a treat," Lynn said. "Try it."

Gilbert lifted his cup and sipped. His eyebrows rose. "That *is* good," he said.

Lynn grinned. "I'll have my uncle send you a pound," he said. "I'll have him mark it: HOMICIDE. He should get a kick out of that."

"You don't have to do that," said Gilbert. "Don't put your uncle to all that trouble."

"He's always looking for Blue Mountain converts," said Lynn. "It will be no trouble at all." He lifted his own cup and took a sip. "Now . . . where were we?" Lynn's eyes narrowed as he looked out the window. "Oh, yes. Phil was always . . . how shall I put this . . . always trying to convince the world that Mother Courage could go the distance, that they were in it for the long haul, like the Rolling Stones or . . . or Aerosmith, for instance. But Mother Courage simply didn't have the staying power of those other bands. The record companies lost interest. The other band members thought it was time to . . ." Lynn smiled a kind smile. "To put the instruments away." Lynn shook his head. "But Phil wouldn't have it. He coerced the other band members into rehearsing for another tour. Even when Decca cancelled their contract, Phil didn't give up. They rehearsed and rehearsed."

"And what did the other band members say to that?" asked Gilbert.

"Michelle finally got fed up," said Lynn. "She wanted a break. A good long break. To underline the point, she got pregnant. I believe they remained inactive for two years after that. Meanwhile, Phil took their rehearsal tapes to record companies and flogged them relentlessly. He got Glen to help him. Glen knew many higher-ups in the record industry. GBIA managed to get David Geffen of Geffen Records interested in the band. But before Geffen would offer them a record contract, he wanted them to go on tour to see how firm their ticket sales would be."

"I think I see where this is heading," said Gilbert.

Lynn's left brow twisted upward. "You know about Palo Alto, then?" he asked.

"Only that it was more or less their doomsday concert," said Gilbert.

"Ah . . ." said Lynn, raising his index finger. "But you don't know the details."

"No," admitted Gilbert.

Lynn's eyes grew pensive as he gazed at his coffee.

"Doomsday concert," he said. "I like that. I venture we share the same sense of cynicism, Detective Gilbert." He took a sip of his coffee. "In any case, it was . . . sad . . . particularly because it was so comical. Phil invested a great deal of money into Palo Alto. The band got on one plane, and their equipment got on another. The band arrived at Palo Alto, and their instruments went to Miami. Whose blunder was that? I don't know. Phil insists it was Glen's. Of course they couldn't go onstage without their instruments or all their other massive amounts of stage and lighting equipment."

"So what happened?" asked Gilbert.

"They had to postpone," said Lynn. "Phil drowned in an avalanche of refunded tickets. He thought fans would buy new tickets for the rescheduled show, but they never did. Glen still made a cut. He wrote the deal to guarantee an expenses clause for GBIA, so you can imagine how that made Phil feel. The rescheduled show was a bust, and that was the end of Mother Courage."

Gilbert made a note of all this in his notebook. "David Geffen backed out?" he asked.

The lawyer nodded. "David Geffen backed out. So did the rest of the band members. For good. They'd made their last try, and now it was time to lay the thing to rest. The band's breakup wasn't particularly amicable, especially not for Phil. He thought they were all . . . well . . . you know . . . whatever he said, it wasn't nice. He blamed it all on Glen. He didn't want to end his musical career. He came to me and asked me if there was any legal way he could compel the other band members to continue."

"And was there?" asked Gilbert.

"No," said Lynn. "Then he asked me if there was any legal action he could take against GBIA. I advised against it. The contract wording favored GBIA. So Phil vowed to start a solo career. He wrote a dozen new songs, and toured small clubs, and the material itself was fairly strong. He's a good songwriter. But he just didn't have the pipes. He couldn't belt it out the way Paul, Carol, or Michelle could. He tried for a record deal with a number of different labels. No one was willing to risk it. Not after Palo Alto. So he started his own label. If no one would sign him, he would sign himself."

At this point, Lynn's phone rang. He picked it up, made a few pleasant excuses to the person on the other end of the line, then gently rested the receiver back in the cradle.

"I'm not keeping you from anything, am I?" asked Gilbert.

"My wife's having trouble with the home computer again," said Lynn. "She counts on me as her savior in that regard."

Lynn scratched his tanned forehead as he decided how to continue, then moved his coffee, for no apparent reason, two inches to the left.

"Phil, of course, knew a good deal about the record business," he said, "but he didn't feel he knew enough to start his own label. He didn't feel safe going it alone, so . . . rather rashly . . . he let bygones be bygones, and got Glen Boyd in on the deal. I don't know how he explained it away to himself, all the bad feelings over Palo Alto, or if Glen finally apologized as a way to get his toe in the door on the new deal. Whatever the case, Phil sank a significant portion of his remaining savings into the label, and borrowed heavily from the bank. You think he would have learned his lesson by then. But he was desperate to resuscitate his rock-star status. Glen more or less agreed to manage the label for a token salary of one dollar a year plus forty percent of any profit. Phil went into the studio and recorded his solo album. They got initial orders for a hundred thousand copies, and sold them wholesale at ten dollars apiece. That gave them a million dollars. Glen wanted to invest that money. Phil went back to the studio to start a second record, and left Glen to find the best investment opportunities."

"Uh-oh," said Gilbert. "I think I can see what's coming."

"A crystal ball is hardly needed, Detective Gilbert. I daresay, Phil could have used one at the time. Record stores can return whatever product they don't sell for full reimbursement. A prudent label typically banks money as a reserve against these returns. Following this model, Glen should have banked half the money from those initial orders to financially guard against any of those returns. But he didn't." Lynn sighed, sat back, and folded his hands across his trim stomach. "He invested the money in Campeau." Lynn gave Gilbert an inquiring look. "Do you remember Robert Campeau, the junk-bond baron of the retail industry? Campeau stock was all the rage at the time."

Gilbert smiled grimly. "I lost five grand," he admitted.

"What a house of cards that was," said Lynn. "A big financial quicksand pit. Trendy, yes, but still a disaster. Glen sank Phil's every last penny into it. He didn't hold anything back for returns because he was convinced he would make money. Then Campeau went bust, and the label lost all its money. At the same time, it became apparent no one was buying Phil's solo effort. Think Yoko Ono, and you'll have an idea of sales. When Phil found out all his money had been swallowed by Campeau, he was furious. He had to somehow raise the money to reimburse all these record stores. And because he was paying Glen a token salary of only one dollar a year, he couldn't go after GBIA. Here's where the restraining order comes in. As lawsuit after lawsuit failed, Phil physically threatened Glen."

Gilbert grew still.

"How did he threaten him?" he asked.

"He said he would get two of his Hell's Angels friends to break Glen's legs."

"And how long ago was that?" asked Gilbert.

"Back in February," said Lynn.

"So things were said."

"It seems so. I wouldn't presume to tell you how to do your job, Detective Gilbert, but I think Phil Thompson warrants more than just a brief look, don't you?"

*   *   *

The next morning, Staff Inspector Tim Nowak, Gilbert's boss, caught Gilbert as he was coming into the office.

"Joe's already been in and out," said Nowak, a tall, thin, gray-haired man in his mid-fifties. "Some old guy was found dead in a back alley in Etobicoke."

"Does Joe want me to come out?" asked Gilbert.

"He said he'd call. Right now I thought we'd have a talk about the Boyd case." Nowak's gaze shifted. "In my office."

"Sure," said Gilbert.

Gilbert put his coffee and bagel on his desk and followed Nowak into his office. Nowak sat down. Gilbert followed suit. Out the window in the courtyard Gilbert glimpsed an odd piece of statuary, a bronze female police officer mortaring bricks. He'd never understood that particular sculpture.

"Toxicology called," began Nowak. "They looked at your drug list. Joe says you had it marked urgent."

"Right," said Gilbert. "But even if you mark those things urgent, it takes a while. Has any of it been done yet?"

"They've done some preliminary color tests, but they're inconclusive," said Nowak. "The guy had such a mishmash of drugs inside his system, it's going to take Toxicology a while to sort it out."

Gilbert's shoulders sank. "So I take it Melvin Blackstein won't rule on the possible overdose until he gets the report back from Toxicology."

"No," said Nowak. "And that frustrates me as much as it

frustrates you, Barry. Especially because Ronald Roffey from the *Toronto Star* is calling me about the Boyd case. He's actually stopped by a time or two."

Gilbert shook his head. "Shit."

"I know," said Nowak. "I'd like to wrap this one up quickly."

"How are we going to do that if the toxicology tests are going to take a while?"

"Well . . . I've sent the crime-scene photographs to Deputy Chief Ling," said Nowak. "Maybe once he sees them, he'll call the coroner's office."

"You know Mel," cautioned Gilbert. "He likes to be careful. And it takes a lot to budge him."

"Yes, but if it swims like a duck, and quacks like a duck, it has to be a duck. I wonder if he's ever heard that phrase. Maybe we can get Ronald Roffey to explain it to him. It's a big sticking point. I intend to grease the works any way I can, so that's why I've sent the crime scene photographs to the deputy chief's office. I'll be sending him regular updates as well, so keep me informed. In the meantime, we go ahead. We work with what we have." Nowak looked out the window. "That means the preliminary DNA analysis on the skin scrapings taken from under Boyd's fingernails. Joe received the report this morning."

"Really?" said Gilbert. "That fast?"

"The new digital method really speeds things up," said Nowak. "Bear in mind, the profiling is by no means complete. It'll take another few weeks to individualize it. But Forensic has done enough sequencing to tell us that the left-hand and right-hand samples came from two different people."

Gilbert stared at Nowak's much-thumbed copy of the *Cana-*

dian Criminal Code. This was indeed significant, and changed the complexion of the investigation considerably. In trying to defend himself, Boyd had gripped his attacker, and trace quantities of the perpetrator's epidermis had lodged under his fingernails. Only now there were two attackers, one coming at him from the left, the other from the right. Even more puzzling, Boyd's arm was broken. Broken after his attempt at defense? Two attackers? The Hell's Angels? Possibly. As Daniel Lynn suggested, Phil Thompson warranted more than just a brief look.

"Thanks, Tim," he said.

Nowak contemplated the gold signet ring on his left baby finger. "Boyd's a bit high-profile, isn't he?" said the Homicide staff inspector.

"Yes," said Gilbert.

"I had no idea," said Nowak. "Roffey's certainly interested. I've never followed the rock and pop scene much. I'm a jazz buff myself."

"What did Roffey say?"

"Just that the *Star's* entertainment section is running a feature on Boyd this weekend, and that he'd like to do a more in-depth follow-up piece on the homicide investigation to run with it. I think we have to be careful with this one, Barry. Roffey had that look in his eyes." Nowak gave him an inquiring glance. "You know the one he gets?"

"All too well," said Gilbert.

"Speaking of which, Joe tells me you knew Boyd." Gilbert's shoulders tightened. Nowak tapped the marble base of his pen-set a few times. "I'm just wondering if it's such a good idea . . . you know . . . you acting as the primary on the case . . . especially because you knew the man. We don't want to give Roffey more meat than we have to."

Gilbert sighed as his mood sank. "I knew him briefly twenty-three years ago," he said. "He was an acquaintance. That's all. A friend of my wife's. I haven't seen him since that time. If you want to yank me as the primary on the case, that's your prerogative, Tim. But this is just another case to me, no different from any other. I'm capable of working it, and working it fast, as speed seems to be an issue."

A relieved grin came to Nowak's face. "That's exactly what I wanted to hear, Barry."

AFTER HIS MEETING WITH NOWAK, Gilbert went back to his desk and nibbled at his bagel.

He tried to fit Phil Thompson into the existing evidence.
While it was eminently possible he might have hired the Hell's
Angels to break Boyd's arm instead of his legs, gang members
would have done a more effective job strangling Boyd. Trauma
was slight, so much so Joe thought the perpetrator might be a
woman. And Hell's Angels weren't known for their delicacy.

He took a sip of his coffee. Damn, but he was spoiled after
drinking Blue Mountain.

Then there was the blond hair. Judy Pelaez's blond hair? Or
possibly Stacy Todd's blond hair?

He concentrated on Judy Pelaez for a while, gathered some
background information on the woman from the Internet.

One web page recounted Judy Pelaez throwing a salad plate

at a waiter in Barcelona back in 1973. Another mentioned how she had trashed a hotel room in Dallas because of cold soup. So. The woman had a temper. The most telling incident was from 1979, when, in Seattle on her "Lost in Love" tour, she'd smashed Glen Boyd over the head with a guitar. Boyd got seventeen stitches, and Judy got thirty days. Gilbert saved that particular Web page, cut and pasted it into the case file. If she was capable of smashing Boyd over the head with a guitar, mightn't she be capable of strangling him with a silk scarf? The evidence, at least preliminarily, pointed that way.

He phoned the Best Western Primrose Hotel, hoping to speak to her directly.

"How may I direct your call?" asked the desk clerk.

"Judy Pelaez, please," he said.

"One moment, please."

The clerk connected Gilbert to Judy's room phone, but the phone rang ten times before the hotel guest voice-messaging system kicked in. He left a message. He thought he might as well drive over. It wasn't that far. And a surprise visit sometimes had its uses.

But first he went back to scanning the Internet.

He found a photograph of Judy Pelaez. She wore a navy blue beret. Her lips pouted seductively at the camera. She had cat-green eyes and was stunningly blond. Her broad cheekbones gave her a Slavic look, and he wondered if she might have some Ukrainian blood. She certainly had no Spanish blood, despite her last name—her first husband had been Puerto Rican. She was a willowy woman, petite, and irresistibly appealing. With such a slender frame, no wonder she hadn't caused much damage to Boyd's throat. Only how had she been able to overpower the man in the first place, unless he'd been so stoned he hadn't been able to defend himself?

Lombardo returned from his suspicious-death call in Etobicoke a short while later.

"You've been busy," said Gilbert.

Lombardo put his briefcase on Gilbert's desk.

"Traffic's getting impossible in this city," he said. As a student of feminine beauty, Lombardo immediately looked at the image of Judy Pelaez on Gilbert's monitor. "*Caramba*," he said. "What a babe."

"I know," said Gilbert.

"She makes you want to melt," said Lombardo.

"She's a lot older now," said Gilbert.

"That makes me sad," said Lombardo.

"What does?" asked Gilbert.

"That she's a lot older now, and that all beautiful women have to grow old."

"Is that just another way of saying, 'So many women, so little time'?"

"Something like that," said Lombardo. He gestured at the photograph. "When was that one taken?"

Gilbert glanced at the photograph. "Twenty-five years ago."

"I didn't think she was that pretty."

"She's a great songwriter," said Gilbert. "And a great singer. I'm going to her hotel. We have to talk to her. I thought we could do a plain-view search."

"Sure."

"And by the way, what happened in Etobicoke? Did it turn into a homicide?"

"No," said Lombardo. "The guy choked to death on a veal sandwich."

"Really?" said Gilbert.

"The paramedics tried to intubate him, but the respirator got blocked. They cut an emergency incision in his trachea, hoping they could get him to breathe. They found this big piece of veal sandwich lodged there. Plus a half-eaten veal sandwich next to his corpse. And you know what? Talk about a coincidence."

Gilbert raised his eyebrows. "Why?"

"I know this guy, just like you know Boyd."

"Really?"

"Vito Pizzale. He's an old family friend. From way back. When we first moved over from Italy. I haven't seen him in years."

"So he was a close family friend?" asked Gilbert.

"He helped my father a number of times," said Lombardo. "He was well off. He would lend money to new Italian immigrants if they couldn't otherwise get bank loans. He helped a lot of families that way. A real don, in the good sense of the word. And guess who else I saw?"

"Who?"

"Mike Strutton."

"You're kidding," said Gilbert. "From Patrol?"

"Yeah. He was guarding the perimeter when I got there."

"I haven't seen him in ages. You can always count on Mike to preserve any damn crime scene anywhere."

"And you know what he said to me?" asked Lombardo, now sounding miffed.

"What?"

"He said I was losing my hair." Lombardo fussed with his hair. "What do you think? Do you think it's looking a bit thin? I sure hope not. My hair's my best feature."

Gilbert stood up. "Let's see," he said.

He looked at Joe's hair. As he was a good deal taller than Joe, well over six feet, and Joe was a short man, he got a bird's-eye view.

"You might be losing a bit back here," said Gilbert, tapping Joe's crown.

"Really?"

"Have you ever thought about calling one of those hair club places?" asked Gilbert. "Some of them are fairly legit. I hear you have to start early and keep going if you want your hair to continue looking natural."

A panicked look came to Lombardo's eyes. "Is it really that bad? I mean, hair-club bad?"

Gilbert clicked off the picture of Judy Pelaez. "It could be worse." He didn't want to look at Judy anymore. She belonged to the boomer generation, the generation that was supposed to stay young forever, *his* generation. "I hear you told Tim I knew Boyd."

Lombardo paused. "Why?" he said. "Did he say something about it?"

"He just mentioned it, that's all," said Gilbert. "No big deal." Or was it? Gilbert couldn't decide. He had to wonder why Lombardo would tell Tim about it in the first place. "Anyway, I guess I knew Boyd about as well as you knew this Vito Pizzale. So I can't see where it matters."

The two detectives drove in one of the Luminas to the Best Western Primrose that afternoon. Situated on the corner of Carleton and Jarvis, the hotel wasn't that far from headquarters. The sun beat down like the worst of thirty-nine lashes, the mercury edged upward, and the pavement was so hot it sent ripples of heated air, mirage-like and filmy, toward the sky. Gilbert nudged the car's air-conditioning up a notch.

"Is it okay I mentioned Boyd to Tim?" asked Lombardo.

"That I knew him?" said Gilbert.

"Yeah."

"Sure," he said. "I don't care."

"Because you seem . . . I don't know."

"It was a long time ago, Joe," he said. "Think about people you knew twenty-three years ago and haven't seen since. You can barely remember them. I'm just not sure why you mentioned it in the first place."

"I mentioned it in passing."

"Yeah . . . well . . . Tim's all jumpy about this one," said Gilbert. "So I think he got all nervous when you told him I knew Boyd. I guess he thinks my connection to Boyd might blur my judgment on the case. Tim might not show it, but I don't think he's the calm man he makes out to be. I think he feels stress just like everybody else. He's just better at hiding it."

The Primrose was a nondescript tower of twenty floors built sometime in the late sixties or early seventies, of functionalist poured-concrete design, drab and unadorned. Across the street stood St. Andrew's Church, an old monstrosity from Toronto's stuffier Victorian days, now serving a Lutheran congregation of Estonian and Latvian immigrants. Maple Leaf Gardens loomed down the street. Had Judy Pelaez ever played at Maple Leaf Gardens, Gilbert wondered? If so, had she stayed at the Primrose?

He found a parking spot a block south on Jarvis. He and Joe got out and walked north to the hotel. Gilbert thought of Nina. He was anxious to get the test results back, but they wouldn't be ready till Saturday. His precious Nina. Something like this always put things in perspective. Boyd didn't matter. Tim's jumpiness didn't matter. He thought of Nina five or six times an hour, every hour, every day, hoping she would be all right.

They got Judy's room number from the desk clerk—1602—and took the elevator to the sixteenth floor. They walked along the plushly carpeted corridor. As they neared her door, Gilbert raised his hand, signaling Lombardo to stop. From inside he heard an acoustic guitar, plucked gently, with consummate skill and grace. The two detectives listened. They waited for her to sing, but she didn't. Gilbert gave the door a few soft taps. The guitar playing stopped. He heard Judy come to the door.

"Who is it?" she called.

Her voice was husky, rough, not at all the honey-toned soprano he remembered from yesteryear.

"Detective-Sergeant Barry Gilbert and Detective Joe Lombardo of Metro Homicide," said Gilbert. "Can we come in for a minute, Ms. Pelaez? We need to talk to you."

He heard the chain-lock rattle, the bolt-lock slide back, and watched the door open.

She looked up at them through tinted prescription glasses. She wore a coral-colored beret that looked as if it had been around for a while. Her hair, in contrast to the golden thick locks of her youth, was now thin and dead-looking, and escaped from her beret in a tired shade of blond, a color which, sadly, matched the shade of the hair found in Boyd's bed.

"I'm sorry," she said. "I meant to return your call."

No explanation, no excuse—as if it had never occurred to her that a homicide investigation might be a priority.

"We apologize for disturbing you," he said. He pulled out his badge and ID and showed them to her. Joe did the same. "Can we come in?"

"Sure . . . of course." She hoisted her lips in a weak smile. He saw her trademark teeth, now stained from years of cigarette smoking. "I'm working on some new material. I can interrupt that for a while."

"I'm sorry about Glen Boyd, Ms. Pelaez."

She looked away, as if she hadn't heard him.

"Would you like some peanuts?" she asked, motioning at a bowl on the table. "I can't live without them."

"No . . . no thanks."

Joe was staring at her. Gilbert knew what he was feeling. It was so often the case with famous people. You stared at them for a minute. You remembered all the photographs and television images you'd ever seen of them and compared them to the actual article. He gave her a look over himself. And yes, it was definitely her, Judy Pelaez, the megastar folksinger of two decades ago—only age had touched her in the myriad ways it touched everybody. Her petite ballerina-like figure was gone. She was heavyset on top. She held herself in a slightly stooped position, as if osteoporosis had made gains in her spine, the way it did with so many women her age. While she might have been heavyset on top, her legs were exceedingly thin. Her face no longer had its pliancy, was lined in places. She had middle-aged pouches under her eyes. Only her lips were full, sensual, and young looking. Anybody seeing her for the first time would realize, just from her lips, that she'd been an extremely pretty woman in her younger days.

She sat down—slumped would be more accurate. Gilbert took the chair opposite. Joe remained standing, glanced around, began the plain-view search, allowable under the Canadian Criminal Code. Anything within plain view was fair game as far as evidence was concerned. This kind of search didn't need a warrant.

Judy's room faced south, and through the humidity outside Gilbert saw Lake Ontario resting like a big blue plate, tranquil and calm, the antithesis of downtown's hot jumble of skyscrapers. A layer of brown smog circled the horizon. The Royal Bank Tower glowed like a gold monument to Canada's capitalist ways. Judy wouldn't look him in the eye. She sat on the edge of the couch with her hands on her thighs, uneasy, as if she were getting ready to spring any moment.

"I understand Glen Boyd was your common-law husband," Gilbert began, "and that you lived with him for ten years in San Francisco during the nineteen-eighties and nineties."

"Yes, that's right."

"And that you had two children by him."

"Yes. Morningstar and Delta."

"And that you had dinner with him on Friday night, the night he was murdered."

Her chin dipped, as if the effort to hold her head up was too much for her. She took off her prescription glasses. There. The eyes. There was no mistaking those eyes. The cat-green eyes he had seen in so many photographs. The eyes of Judy Pelaez. They grew misty. She snatched a Kleenex from the box and dabbed them.

"I'm sorry," she said.

Joe unobtrusively walked around to the back of the couch and went to the table by the window. He pretended to look at the view of the lake, then glanced at all the papers on the table.

"It's okay," said Gilbert. "I understand. I know how it is."

Many times, sympathy freely given, though meant to comfort, exacerbated tears. She cried more earnestly. She dabbed first one eye, then the other as she stared at the scanty flower arrangement on the coffee table.

"Stacy called me with the news," she said. "I'm numb. I just sit here. I can't believe he's gone." She looked up at Gilbert with hopeful eyes. "Can I see him?" she asked. She sounded curiously childlike now. "Can you take me to him?"

He hated to play the hard-ass, especially because her grief seemed genuine, but what choice did he have?

"I'm afraid that's impossible right now, Ms. Pelaez," he said. "You'll have to wait until the coroner's office gives us the okay to release the body to the funeral home." He thought of Dr. Blackstein's inconclusive autopsy report. "And there might be a bit of a delay. You'll just have to hang in there."

Her lips came together in a frustrated line. "Do you have any idea how long it will be?" she asked.

"No," he said.

Her shoulders sank. She turned, stared at the peanut bowl, then lifted a guitar pick and tapped it a few times against her skinny knee.

"I have no idea who would do this to him," she said. "I guess that's what you want to know. I fly up here every year. I try to get him to come back to his children, and convince him that I'm the one he should be with. But he never listens. He's never sensible about anything. And now look what's happened to him." She paused, thought about something, then put the pick on the table. "He told me he was seeing someone." For the first time she looked him in the eyes. Her tears dried. "You wouldn't have any idea who that might be, would you? You've been investigating. Maybe you've turned up her name. Maybe she was the one who did it."

Preposterous as he knew it had to be, he couldn't help thinking of Regina. Was Regina the mystery woman Boyd was fooling around with?

"We haven't ascertained the woman's identity yet," he said. "But rest assured, when we do, we'll be speaking to her, too."

"Because I wouldn't be surprised if she's the one you're looking for," said Judy. "If you find her, you should put her away for good."

"Ms. Pelaez, let's talk about the dinner you had with Mr. Boyd," he said. "Were you to meet him at the restaurant, or was he picking you up? What was the arrangement?"

Judy cast around for an answer, as if in her distress she couldn't immediately recall the arrangement. "I was to meet him at Scaramouche," she said.

"Scaramouche," said Gilbert. "That's familiar."

"It's north of here. I forget exactly where."

"Joe, where's Scaramouche?" asked Gilbert. As Lombardo was a regular sampler of Toronto's nightlife, Gilbert thought his young partner might know. "Have you been there?"

"It's off Avenue Road," said Lombardo. "On Benevenuto Place. It's upscale and trendy. A lot of Forest Hill–types go there." Joe turned to Judy. "Do you mind if I use your washroom?"

As was his custom, Joe was making the most of the plain-view search, widening it where he could.

She gestured distractedly toward the washroom. "Go ahead," she said.

Lombardo walked to the washroom, went inside, and shut the door.

"So you were to meet Mr. Boyd at Scaramouche," said Gilbert.

"Yes."

"And did you go there?"

"I went there . . . and I waited . . . and he never showed up." She frowned, looked to one side. "What else is new?"

"And did he make reservations? Or did you?"

"He did."

"So they were under his name."

She shrugged, an impatient jerking of her shoulders, and lifted a *Toronto Life* magazine from the table, as if she were getting bored—the way a child might get bored.

"I guess so," she said.

"And when he finally didn't show up, what did you do?"

Her frown deepened. "I called his apartment," she said. She fidgeted. "No one answered." She put the magazine down. "His voice mail was on."

"So did you leave a message?" asked Gilbert.

"I couldn't. His mailbox was full."

"So what did you do then?" he asked.

She lifted a peanut from the bowl. "I went back to our table," she said. "I waited."

"Until what time?" he asked.

"Until nine o'clock."

"Because we believe he was murdered around nine-thirty."

She grew still, as if the time of her husband's death was symbolically significant to her. "Nine-thirty," she said. "You always wonder what time you're going to die. At least I do. Everybody says they would like to die in their sleep. Not me. I'd like to die in the morning. While I'm having tea. With the radio on. And a big bouquet of roses hanging upside down by the spice rack."

Here was the lyricist Judy Pelaez, he decided, romanticizing her own death. Death seemed an apt subject for Judy Pelaez. She was the undisputed mistress of melancholy.

"So you left Scaramouche at nine," he said. "And where did you go from there?"

But it was as if she were in her own world now. She wasn't listening. She was thinking of something else. Maybe about roses hanging upside down by the spice rack. But then she snapped out of it.

"I came back here," she said with a big sigh.

"You came back to the hotel."

"Yes," she said. "I thought he might have left a message here."

Joe came out of the washroom.

"And had he?" asked Gilbert.

"No," said Judy.

"So did you try calling him again once you got back here?" he asked.

"No."

"Why not?"

She frowned. "Why should I?" she said.

"To find out what happened," he said.

"I didn't care. He stood me up. It's not the first time. He's stood up every woman he's ever loved. I'm not the only one."

Gilbert took a deep breath and stared at Judy's guitar, a Larrivée acoustic, leaning against the sofa. She had a capo strapped around the third fret.

"When do you go back to San Francisco?" he asked.

In a quiet but steady voice, she said, "After I bury my husband."

He decided there wasn't much else he could ask her right now, not until he confirmed her alibi. "We'll need to speak to you again," he said.

"If you must," she said.

She didn't get up to see them off. She simply went back to working on her new material.

Outside, on the way back to the car, Gilbert asked Lombardo if the plain-view search had yielded anything useful.

"Nothing incriminating," said the young detective. "I found

a rental agreement from Tilden. She's rented a midnight blue Buick Skylark, Ontario license plate AEDF 079. I'll put it in the file. It might come in useful later."

"Did you happen to see any perfume lying around?" asked Gilbert.

"Perfume?" said Lombardo, surprised by this.

"A bottle of *Dilys* by Laura Ashley?"

"No," he said. "Why?"

It had taken him a while, but now he remembered the scent on the scarf, one his wife wore on occasion, one of his standby gifts for birthdays and anniversaries.

"Just a gut feeling," he said.

"You and your gut feelings," said Lombardo.

"My gut feelings have helped me solve more murders than I can count, Joe," he said, now trying to quickly steer away from the perfume. It made him nervous. "We go as far as modern criminalistics can take us, and then we rely on our gut feelings. Killing's in the gut. Ask any murderer. He'll tell you he knows what I'm talking about."

CHAPTER
SIX

THAT EVENING, ON THE PRETEXT of picking up groceries, Gilbert drove to Mike Topalovich's apartment. Gilbert used the grocery pretext because he didn't want anybody in his family to know what he was doing.

Mike's building, a low-rise on Dawes Road, was in a hard-working neighborhood of new Canadians from Sri Lanka, Trinidad, and, in the Topaloviches' case, Poland. A red sun bloated to five times its normal size sank through the usual products of combustion, painting the windows of Mike's building orange.

Gilbert left his car at the curb and immediately began to sweat. High temperatures continued. He entered the foyer and discovered, much to his chagrin, that the air-conditioning was broken. No relief here. He pressed the intercom button beside number 103 and waited.

A few moments later, a gruff voice said, "Yes?"

"It's Barry Gilbert," he said. "Nina's dad. I called earlier."

"Oh, yeah. C'mon in."

The door buzzed and Gilbert went inside.

The corridor smelled of old cooking and lemon cleanser. He found apartment 103 immediately to his right. A man of about forty stood at the apartment door waiting. Tattoos covered his bare arms and sweat soaked the chest of his gray undershirt. He wore black shorts, sandals, and a gold chain around his neck. His hair was long. He had a thick mustache, smelled heavily of men's cologne, and a cigarette dangled from his lips.

"You Nina's dad?" he asked, his Polish accent thick but not impenetrable.

"Yes. Casmir?"

"Yes. Lena's out. I had her go out. She doesn't know yet. It would kill her to find out. She's at her sister's. I told her to stay there for a while. Her sister tapes the soap operas, so I think we're good for at least two hours."

A little white dog—an American Eskimo dog—pranced past Casmir's feet, jumped to its hind legs, and delicately bounced its paws against Gilbert's shins, jubilant with excitement.

"Snowflake, get down," said Casmir.

"It's okay," said Gilbert. He knelt, his arthritic knees giving him a pinch, and patted the little dog. "I like dogs. I had a German shepherd when I was teenager. Queenie was her name."

Casmir grinned. "She's a good dog," he said. "She's my angel. C'mon inside. Mike's waiting for you at the dining room table."

He followed the stocky, muscular man inside.

The smell of cigarette smoke hung in the air. The kitchen,

directly ahead of him, was a mess, with dishes stacked on all available counter space, and a green garbage bag filled to overflowing against the broom closet. Snowflake sniffed more curiously at his pant leg.

Glancing into the living room, Gilbert saw a special shelf stretching the whole length, every square inch filled with collector-item dolls, all still in their original packaging. One was dressed like a Victorian woman in a crinoline dress and a bonnet; another was in a kilt and a tam-o'-shanter; another wore a little Dutch girl's costume, complete with Middelburg cap and wooden clogs. He assumed these dolls belonged to Lena—he couldn't picture Casmir as a doll collector.

Through the kitchen, he saw the dining room, where Mike Topalovich sat morosely at the table, the wind from the ceiling fan twitching the strands of his James Deanish hair.

"You ask him whatever you like," said Casmir. His eyes grew sullen, as if he resented his son for the whole thing. "He knows he has to answer. And have a beer. It's hot in here. A beer will do you good. There's plenty in the fridge. Molson Canadian." He grinned, then parroted the famous slogan. "'I *am* Canadian!'" His eyes narrowed inquiringly. "You smoke?"

"No," he said. "But I'll take you up on the beer."

"Yeah, yeah, go ahead. They've been sitting there all day getting cold. Help yourself."

"Thanks, Casmir."

"I watch the game now," said Casmir. "Blue Jays and Kansas City Royals. We're down by two, but it's only the fourth inning." He gestured at his son. "You talk to him. You let me know when you're done. And don't let Snowflake bother you."

"Thanks."

Gilbert stepped into the kitchen. Snowflake backed away, startled.

"And Barry?" said Casmir.

"Yes?"

A troubled expression came to Casmir's face. "I'm sorry about your daughter," he said.

Gilbert's throat tightened. "I am, too, Casmir," he said.

Casmir went into the living room while Gilbert picked his way around the garbage bag to the fridge. He opened the fridge, took out a beer, and twisted off the cap. He tossed the cap into the garbage bag, spooking five or six fruit flies, then went into the dining room and sat at the table across from Mike.

Mike looked at him nervously, like he was afraid Gilbert might yell at him. The boy wore a sleeveless Toronto Raptors jersey, and, like his father, had thick, muscular arms. He was handsome, boy-band handsome, and Gilbert understood why Nina liked him—boy-band handsome was her thing right now.

Gilbert felt like shaking Mike, asking him how he could have been so stupid, and why in this age of media saturation he didn't know that unprotected sex could kill him as efficiently as a loaded revolver. But he controlled himself. He knew Mike was just a kid. At the age of eighteen, Mike wasn't about to have unerring judgment about all things at all times.

Gilbert sighed, took a sip of his beer, then looked out the grimy first-floor window at the traffic. Two little black girls— identical twins—played on the sidewalk with a couple of Barbie dolls. Out the corner of his eye, Gilbert caught Mike glancing at him.

"I'm sorry about Nina," said Mike, his voice deep, soft, unsure. "I didn't want to do this to her. I didn't know I had what I had the night we hooked up at Pascale's party."

Hooked up. That was a big catchphrase these days. And now it was being used to describe sexual relations with his daughter.

"I know you didn't," said Gilbert. He noted the boy had an earring in his left ear. "I'm not here to lecture you, Mike. I know you don't need that."

"She's nice. She's really nice."

"Mike . . . I just want to know a couple of things, that's all."

Out on the street, the Dawes Road bus swept past, swirling a few momentary dust devils in its slipstream.

"I'll help any way I can, sir."

Gilbert could see it in the intensity of the young man's eyes—he was desperate to make things right, to somehow turn back the clock, even though it now couldn't be turned back.

"Okay," said Gilbert, sitting forward, putting one hand on his knee. "So you had sex with my daughter . . . when? The end of February? That's what Nina told me. I just want to make sure she's remembering it right."

"She's remembering it right," said Mike. "It was at Pascale's party. That was the twenty-fifty of February."

"The twenty-fifth, right, that's what she said." His right eyebrow rose a fraction. "And you had sex with her just the once? She mentioned only the party, but I thought . . . you know . . . that maybe in March, or April . . . that it might have turned into a couple thing."

"No, sir. It was only the once. And I'm sorry about that, sir. I should have had better sense. I'm awfully stupid."

"Did it ever occur to you that you might get her pregnant?" asked Gilbert.

"No, sir. She said she was on the pill."

This stopped Gilbert. Nina was on the pill? Why was he always the last one in his family to know these things? He so often felt like the odd man out. He was sure Regina was privy to the news. Why not him? Then again, neither Regina nor the girls knew he was here with Mike Topalovich, and that he was trying to find out what he could about the timing of the thing as a way to possibly lessen family anxiety about it.

He took another sip of his beer.

"Okay," he said. "Let's go on. Were you having sex with other partners before you had sex with Nina?"

Mike stared at the candle sitting in the middle of the table.

"Three," he said.

"Just three?"

"Yes, sir."

"And do you know if any of those girls had HIV?" asked Gilbert.

"They're all getting tested. I don't know if they were HIV-positive at the time I had sex with them."

For the first time, Gilbert felt some hope. "And have you heard back from any of them yet?" he asked. "Are any of them positive?"

"I haven't heard back yet."

"Okay. So did you have sex with any partners *after* your night with Nina at Pascale's party?" he asked.

"One."

"One?" said Gilbert.

His hope strengthened even more. If the pre-Nina sex part-ners weren't HIV-positive, there was no way Mike could have contracted the infection from them. Which meant he would have contracted it from this post-Nina sex partner. Which meant Nina might be all right.

"Yes, sir," said Mike.

"And when did you have sex with her?"

"In March."

March. Somewhat below the wire as far as developing HIV antibodies was concerned, but, as Dr. MacPherson suggested, not beyond the realm of possibility.

"And do you know if she's HIV-positive?"

Mike's brow settled. "I haven't been able to find her, sir. My dad and I looked all over the place last week, when I first found out I was HIV-positive. She used to live two buildings down, but she's not there anymore. She's originally from Trinidad. We think she might have moved back."

Here was an obstacle Gilbert hadn't counted on, but he pushed ahead anyway.

"Do you know her name?" asked Gilbert.

"Vashti."

"That's her first name?" asked Gilbert.

"Yes, sir."

"Do you know her last name?"

"No, sir. We never found that out. She lived with a great-aunt while she was here, and her super says her aunt's last name is Parmar. But that's not Vashti's last name."

Gilbert glanced up at the ceiling where a few silken cob-
webs dangled.

"And you don't know whether she was HIV-positive?" he
asked.

"No," said Mike. "I hardly knew her. I met her at the rink. It
was . . . kind of a one-night thing."

Gilbert paused, and took another sip of his beer.

"Could you do me a favor, Mike? Don't mention you had sex
with Nina to any of your friends. She's a bit freaked out by the
whole thing. She really wants to keep it confidential."

"I won't, sir. You have my word on it."

"And could I get the telephone numbers of the other girls
you had sex with? The ones before . . . you know . . . before Pascale's party." He took out his notebook. "I'm going to have to
phone them."

Mike looked away uncomfortably. Snowflake sprung to the
boy's lap but he pushed her off.

"No, sir. I can't do that."

Gilbert's face stiffened. "Why not?"

"Because they're just like Nina, sir," said Mike. "They don't
want anybody finding out."

Gilbert paused. Mike had a point. It wasn't right that
Gilbert should ask Mike to safeguard Nina's confidentiality, then
insist he do the exact opposite with the other girls. As much as
he felt he had the right to be inflexible when it came to Nina's
welfare, he knew he had to give in on this point.

"Okay," he said. "Fine. But it's really important Nina's
mother and I learn their test results. You've been Nina's only sex
partner, so there's no way you could have caught it from her. And

if those girls before Nina weren't HIV-positive, it means you caught it from Vashti. If you caught it from Vashti, it means Nina is clean. So we would really like to find out." He took out his business card and handed it to the teen. "Here's my number at work. I've written my home number on the back, too, and you can call me there if you absolutely must. But I'd prefer you to call me at work."

Mike looked at the card. "You're a homicide detective?" he said.

"Yes," said Gilbert

"Wow. That's neat."

"I'm proud of my job," he said. He pointed at the card. "Could you call me? When you find out their test results?'

"Yes, sir, I'll do that."

"And if you hear anything about Vashti?"

"I'll call you straight away, sir." He looked at Gilbert's card again. "I was thinking I might become a police officer."

"It's a good job," said Gilbert. "There's always something new. You never get bored. And the benefits are good."

Mike's eyes grew pensive. "Now I don't think I'll ever get the chance," he said.

Gilbert had to agree. Nothing stole a future away faster than an HIV infection.

The next day passed without any significant development in the Glen Boyd case. Gilbert called Phil Thompson's home, left several messages, but Phil didn't return any of his calls.

Thursday passed in much the same frustrating way. He

checked in with the Crime Scene Unit. Boyd's apartment had been gone over with special forensic vacuums, and the cataloguing of all myriad fibers, dirt samples, and other minute detritus was well underway, there for when and if he needed it.

Lombardo spent much of these forty-eight hours in Computer Support trying to help them crack Boyd's passwords.

"One set of encryption codes leads to another," Lombardo complained to Gilbert.

Ronald Roffey from the *Toronto Star* came by on Thursday afternoon. He was a man in his late forties with longish brown hair and a nose that had a curious twist to the end, like it might have been broken.

"Ron, I've got nothing to add to what I already told you on Monday," said Gilbert.

"So in other words, you're stumped," said Roffey.

Gilbert frowned. "The investigation's ongoing," he countered. "The coroner hasn't ruled conclusively on the autopsy yet."

"Can you at least give me a copy of the autopsy report?" asked Roffey.

"That autopsy report belongs to the coroner's office at present," said Gilbert. "And the coroner's office isn't ready to release it at this time."

"But you're still willing to admit that there was trauma to Boyd's throat, and that one of the possible scenarios is strangulation."

"Yes."

Things didn't start moving again until he got a call from Ted Aver, the former Mother Courage drummer, on Friday.

"I'm calling from a telephone booth," said the drummer, "and I'm being watched. Meet me in Jean Sibelius Square at seven o'clock tonight. Do you know where that is?"

"Over in the Annex somewhere, isn't it?"

"At Brunswick and Wells, just south of Dupont."

Gilbert hung up. He stared at the paperweight made of bullets on his desk, perplexed by the call. Ted being watched? It sounded a little dramatic. Watched by whom? Was the man paranoid? Or was there a real threat? He glanced up from his paperweight where he saw Detective Bob Bannatyne, his old partner from Fraud, a thirty-two-year veteran of the force, now also a homicide detective, doing paperwork. One way or the other, he had to meet and talk to Ted.

Accordingly, he found himself on a bench in Jean Sibelius Square—really more a park with a small playground for kids—at seven o'clock that night. Why the city named a park after a twentieth-century Finnish composer of symphonic music he wasn't sure—it seemed an odd choice. The sun, a hot red ball, peered over the three-story duplexes to the west. The air was heavy with humidity, and the leaves in the maple trees drooped.

Fifteen minutes later, a man in a wheelchair appeared. Even though the man wore sunglasses, Gilbert recognized him instantly as Ted Aver. From this distance, he saw that the top half of the drummer's body hadn't changed at all, was still strong and muscular. Gilbert glanced at the moms and nannies minding young children in the playground. A few, ever-vigilant, looked at Ted, but he doubted if any of them recognized the former rock star. Though world-famous at one time, Ted hadn't been anywhere near the limelight for the past two decades. These twenty-something moms didn't know Mother Courage at all, were more acquainted with the current crop of boy bands and adolescent divas.

Gilbert waved to Ted. Ted spotted him and waved back. Gilbert got up, thinking Ted might want help. But Ted was athletic, had a hot-rod of a wheelchair, with the wheels slanted out, and he wore racing gloves. He made his way up onto the dipping wheelchair-accessible curb with ease, and headed over to the bench at a good pace. As Ted got closer, Gilbert thought to himself, here was yet another famous person, one he recognized well. Here was the characteristic Ted Aver square jaw and cleft chin, the heavy brow, and the hair—for the most part still brown, cut in bangs over his forehead, shoulder-length, in old rocker style. Here was the man he had even met once a long time ago, when Regina had been chums with Michelle Morrison. Despite that, Ted obviously didn't remember Gilbert at all, and that was just as well. Gilbert wanted to remain anonymous for the sake of the investigation.

"Detective Gilbert?" said Ted.

"Hi."

Gilbert reached for his badge and identification.

"Don't show me your badge," said Ted, looking around nervously. "Just be cool. I don't want anyone getting suspicious. Sit down, will you? You look like a cop. Christ, do you ever. Sit down."

Gilbert sat down. "Sorry," he said.

"It's all right."

Ted took out a package of cigarettes, French Gauloises, shook one out of the pack, stuck it in his mouth, and lit up. The smoke, blue and thick, whirled around his head and dissipated into the hot, humid air.

"What a fuck-up," he said. He contemplated Gilbert serenely.

"What is?"

"Glen."

Over in the playground, a child started to cry.

"You obviously know something about Glen's murder or else we wouldn't be here," said Gilbert.

Ted took a huge drag on his cigarette, attempted a few smoke rings, but there was just enough breeze to rip them apart before they were fully formed.

"We never had this meeting," said Ted. "I want to be a protected source, or whatever you guys are calling it these days, because if this ever gets back to the wrong people, I'm fucked." Ted peered at him quizzically. "Are you looking at anybody specifically yet?"

"I can't really disclose . . . you know how it is."

Ted raised his hand. "Sure," he said. "Say no more."

"And rest assured, your anonymity will be protected."

"I'm giving you a tip," said Ted. "That's *all* I'm giving you. I won't go to court for you. I won't testify for you. I won't do anything but point you in the right direction. Because if word gets out I'm involved in this, I'm really screwed."

He glanced around the park one more time, relaxed a bit, then turned and stared at Gilbert for a moment or two.

"I deal with these . . . these people sometimes. I do business with them. I'm a businessman. I don't know if anybody's told you, but I've done well since the breakup of the band. Better than any of the others. And that's because I know how to be flexible. Part of being flexible is dealing with a wide range of people. I'm a legitimate businessman, Detective Gilbert, and I only deal with legitimate businesses. But some of the people I deal with, they run both legitimate *and* illegitimate businesses. The deals *I* do with them are legal, aboveboard, bread-and-butter, middle-of-the-road, law-abiding deals. But sometimes I hear things about their other deals, their *illegitimate* deals. It's none of my concern. I keep my mouth shut." His face reddened. He looked away. "But this is Glenny we're talking about." His voice now sounded torn. "And I want to see the fuckers put away as much as you do."

Gilbert leaned forward. "So you think you know who killed Glen Boyd, then?" he asked.

Ted lifted his thumbnail to his mouth and nibbled for a second. "Glen and I deal with the same people. I'm a partner in a laminating business with them. He buys product from them. Drugs. An outfit from Barranquilla. Middling cocaine merchants trying to carve a niche here in Toronto. Three guys, young guys, real cowboys. They have connections to the Ramayá brothers in Cali."

Gilbert remembered the unopened packet of cocaine on Boyd's bedside table.

"Do you have their names?" he asked.

Ted took yet another drag on his French cigarette, hesitating, like he was really afraid of these guys.

But finally, he jumped right in.

"The ringleader is Oscar Barcos. He's the one who answers to the Ramayás. Then he's got two partners, Francesco Deranga and Waldo Munoz. I know for a fact that Glen owes these guys money, a lot of money, nearly a hundred grand. Problem is, Glen can't raise it. GBIA's always in a cash-flow crunch. But Oscar doesn't care about any accounts-receivable log-jam bullshit. To further complicate things, Oscar's getting nervous about the operation up here in Toronto. He thinks someone has compromised him, he's not sure who. He thinks maybe Glenny. A lot of his street-level guys are getting busted. He told me he may have to leave for a while. But before he does, he wants to tidy up loose ends. Glen's one of his biggest loose ends. So he gave me a message to give to Glen. This was a week ago Monday, five days before Glenny was killed."

"And what message was that?" asked Gilbert.

Ted Aver shrugged, his well-developed shoulders flexing like a body-builder's as a fragile and guilt-ridden twist came to his brow. "Pay up or die," he said. "And I know Oscar meant it. He's a real executioner, that one."

ON SATURDAY MORNING, GILBERT LIFTED the *Star* from his doorstep and went to the kitchen to read it. Regina made coffee and pancakes. He flipped to the entertainment section—a section as foreign to him as the dark side of the moon—and found the feature article on Glen Boyd.

He scanned through the many inches of column. He learned that in the 1990s, Boyd had expanded his business beyond the rock and pop arena to include classical and jazz acts, and also things as diverse as monster-truck rallies and bikini contests. The feature mainly focused on his rock and pop days, though. Several photos accompanied the article.

Here was a picture of Boyd standing outside Maple Leaf Gardens with rockers Steve Tyler and Joe Perry of the Boston mega-band Aerosmith. Here was another from the 1970s with members of the Diodes, Canada's top New Wave band, outside the legendary El Mocombo rock club. Another showed Boyd with reggae god Bob Marley. Standing with them was Daniel Lynn, Bob Marley's countryman and Boyd's lawyer. A final photograph showed Boyd as the quintessential hippy standing onstage at Woodstock in 1969—he could have been that freak who had warned all those flower children about the bad brown acid that had been floating around.

Sidebarred to the left was Ronald Roffey's follow-up: INVESTIGATION STALLED AS POLICE CONTINUE TO SUSPECT FOUL PLAY.

"For the love of . . ." He gave the paper a whack with the back of his hand.

Regina turned from the stove. "What's wrong?" she asked.

"Roffey's screwing us again," he told her.

She came over and had a look at all the photographs of Glen Boyd. She grew still. She raised her hand to her mouth, then returned to the stove.

He stared at her.

"Reggie?" he said.

She flipped a pancake. She did not, would not, turn to him. He put the paper down, got up, and went over. He put his hands on her shoulders and peered around her hair. Her eyes brimmed with tears. He tried to live it down. It was okay. He was in *his* kitchen. He was with *his* wife. And Boyd was now dead.

"I'm sorry about Boyd," he said.

She nodded, but still took a few moments to get herself together. "This is so damn silly," she said.

She grabbed a paper towel from the vertical dispenser on the counter, dabbed her eyes, and wiped her nose.

"You loved the guy," he said.

"I know . . . I know . . . but I love *you* now." She poked one of the pancakes with the spatula. "It's just . . . such a waste. Why would anybody want to kill him?" Gilbert wasn't about to make matters worse by going into the details of his investigation, how Boyd had a lot of enemies. "He was too young," she said. "And . . . he . . . he should have married someone . . . someone who would have knocked some common sense into him."

"He had his chance with you," he said. "He should have recognized it as a golden opportunity."

She turned to him swiftly and put her hand on his cheek. "Barry . . . he never had a chance. Never. Never."

She kissed him on the lips. He slipped his arms around her. It quickly turned into a movie kiss, the big romantic kind, and just as he was thinking they were going to have to go "read in bed" while the girls watched TV, Jennifer walked in.

"Do you guys have to do that in the kitchen?" she asked. "It's not pretty, you know. People over fifty should be arrested for stuff like that."

Gilbert frowned. "You won't feel that way when you're fifty," he said.

"Mom, are you crying?"

"Allergies," said Regina. "They're driving me nuts. I have to get Dr. MacPherson to give me something stronger than Allegra."

The telephone rang. Gilbert picked it up, and, speak of the devil, who should it be but Dr. MacPherson himself.

"We got the results back from Nina's first test," said the doctor.

Gilbert's hand tightened like a vise around the receiver. "And?" he said.

"They're negative," said the doctor.

"Negative?" said Gilbert, the word leaping from his mouth.

He covered the receiver with his hand. "Nina's first test is negative."

Regina dropped the spatula, raised her hand to her mouth yet again, and sat down in the nearest chair, her eyes once more filling with tears. Jennifer jumped up and down, bouncing, bouncing, and bouncing in silent glee.

"So that's the first hurdle then," Gilbert said to Dr. MacPherson.

"Yes. Let's not get too excited yet, though. It's definitely good news. But as I told you before, the rate at which people develop the HIV antibodies varies. Maybe she just doesn't have enough of them in her system yet to trigger the test. We'll get her tested . . . when did you say you were going to the cottage?"

"Actually, that's changed," said Gilbert. "We're now going up the second week of July instead of the first week."

"Then let's get her tested the first week of July. That's . . . Tuesday the third. The lab is open till seven o'clock on Tuesday nights. It should be convenient for you if you're working that day."

When Gilbert hung up, he put his hand on Regina's shoulder. "I guess we should go tell her," he said.

"Maybe she's still sleeping," said Regina.

"No, she's lying in bed listening to her Discman," Jennifer informed them.

Father, mother, and daughter climbed the stairs. Nina's door was partially closed. Gilbert pushed it open with a gentle shove.

Nina was sitting in bed, knees up, listening to her Discman—Shakira, it sounded like—and flipping through the most recent issue of *Cosmopolitan* magazine, a magazine she now subscribed to. She looked up and grew still. She took off her earphones.

"What?" she said.

"Dr. MacPherson called," he said.

She tensed. "So what's the verdict?" she said.

"You're negative," he said.

She flopped back in bed, overcome with relief. He hated to see this. He felt like crying, that's how much he hated to see it, that his daughter should have to live through this much fear, the greatest fear of all, the fear of death, at such a young age. Regina came in behind him. Nina got out of bed, went straight to her mother, and grabbed her as if for dear life.

"We'll beat this thing, honey," said Regina. "You just watch."

Nina then turned to Gilbert with wide eyes. She went to him. She put her arms around him and pressed her face tightly to his chest.

"Hi, Daddy," she said.

"Hi, Nina."

They would sail through the next test with flying colors. And if he didn't find out about Vashti or Mike Topalovich's other partners before the third test, they would sail through that one, too.

And all this would be just a brief horror show that Nina would someday forget.

That same evening, he watched *MuchMusic* with Nina. Phil Thompson was on, live from the Hard Rock Café in New York City, a release party for Phil's new solo CD, *Phil Thompson Unplugged*, a lavish affair sprung for by, yes, Geffen Records.

"Can you tell me a little about your new CD?" asked the veejay. "What makes it so different from *Livin' with Her Mama*, your first solo effort, or any other Mother Courage record?"

Phil shrugged. "It's unplugged," he said.

"Yes, right, but the actual music."

Phil thought about it. His long hair, parted in the middle, framed his narrow face.

"This is material I've been working on for the last ten years," he finally said. "I've taken some chances with this stuff. It's not the old Mother Courage stadium rock. I've been working on my vocals, trying to expand my range, and to individualize my stylings. I've been training with a vocal coach for the past five years. I feel confident about my own singing on this album. Much more than I did on *Livin' with Her Mama*. And the musicians I worked with on this album are second to none. They contributed a lot."

"So what's up next for you?" asked the veejay. "Any plans for a tour?"

"Yes," said Phil. "I'll be flying back to Toronto on Monday for more rehearsals. Then we'll be taking it on the road for a twelve-city tour. If ticket sales are strong we'll add another ten dates."

A little more blah, blah, blah, and the veejay let Phil go.

"Party on," the veejay told Phil.

Phil grinned, but it was a perplexed grin, as if he wondered why the veejay wasn't giving him more airtime.

"Thank you," he said, and turned away, narrowly dodging a tray of drinks a waiter carried by.

At least Gilbert now knew why Phil hadn't returned his calls. He'd been in New York all week.

The church, a small one, stood half-hidden behind three blue spruce trees on a tiny street in Moore Park. Phil Thompson lived in this church. The church was now renovated and converted into his residence.

Gilbert sat in his unmarked car on Monday afternoon outside Phil's unusual domicile. He waited for Phil to come home from the airport. Phil's home still looked like a church, despite the renovation, and had probably served a small parish back in the 1880s before the city had encroached this far north.

Even though Gilbert had the air-conditioning in his car on full, it wasn't doing much good—he felt the heat right through the car's metal body. He also felt tired. These days, it got to be two or three o'clock in the afternoon—like it was now—and he felt like having a nap. He closed his eyes. That was better. He knew he was slowly turning into an old man.

He woke with a start fifteen minutes later as he heard a car door slam outside. He opened his eyes and saw an airport limousine parked in front of the converted church.

The driver, in a chauffeur's uniform, opened the trunk and lifted a suitcase out for Phil Thompson. Phil Thompson stood at the curb fishing money out of his wallet.

Here was yet another famous person, perhaps the most famous Mother Courage band member of all. He was tall, six-and-a-half feet, as skinny as a lamppost, and still wore his dark hair long, down to his shoulders, and parted in the middle. He had a

Jesus-like beard and wore expensive Ray-Bans. He was dressed in an impeccably tailored suit, a white shirt, and a Western-style string tie.

Phil paid the driver, lifted his suitcase, and headed up the walkway, disappearing behind the trio of blue spruces. The airport limousine drove off, swirling the dried maple fruit all over the road. Gilbert waited a few minutes, then got out of his car and approached the church.

He followed the walkway up through the spruce trees and around to the side of the church, where he found an oaken door, lancet shaped. He climbed the broad stone steps and rang the doorbell.

A moment later Phil Thompson peered through the long narrow window next to the door. The guitarist opened the door. Gilbert pulled out his badge and ID.

"Philip Thompson?" he said.

"Yes?" said the musician.

"I'm Detective-Sergeant Barry Gilbert of Metro Homicide. I'm investigating the death of Glen Boyd. Could you answer a few questions for me?"

Phil paused, not long, only a second, but Gilbert's feelers automatically went up. Then, in an instant, Phil turned into a perfect gentleman, and a solicitous grin came to his face. He swept his arm in greeting toward the interior of the church.

"Sure," he said. "Come on in. It's hot out here. Come into the cool."

Gilbert followed Phil inside. Obviously Phil didn't remember him at all from the many backstage passes Michelle Morrison had given Gilbert and Regina way back when, and, as with Ted Aver, that was just as well.

They went into the sanctuary, now a huge rehearsal space. The peaked ceiling rose thirty feet in the air, was paneled with cedar, and had three ceiling fans spaced evenly along its length. Two guitars, drums, a bass, keyboards, a double bass, a mandolin, a banjo, a steel guitar, and a saxophone lay scattered about on various stands amid numerous amplifiers, mixers, and other recording equipment. The legendary brand names asserted themselves: Fender, Marshall, Zildjian, Ludwig, Gibson, and Selmer.

"Have a seat," said Phil. "I'll get you a cold drink. On a day like this, you could probably use one."

"A Coke would be great," said Gilbert. "Thanks."

"Sure."

Phil retreated through what had once been the transept door, now just an open archway drywalled over, painted pale olive.

Gilbert glanced around as he waited.

Like Glen Boyd, Phil Thompson also had a vanity wall. The wall was filled with photographs, gold records, and platinum records, all in neat black frames. He walked over to the wall and had a look at the photographs.

One showed Phil with his arm around Stacy Todd somewhere up in the French Alps. Another showed a teenaged Phil Thompson in a Vancouver record store having Jimi Hendrix sign a copy of *Electric Lady Land* for him. One captured Phil jamming with Jeff Beck at Guitar Summit '99. Another shot had Phil walking hand in hand with Stacy Todd along a beach somewhere in the Caribbean, possibly Jamaica, his long hair in dreadlocks. Did Phil have a thing for Stacy Todd then? Or were they just friends?

Phil came back to the sanctuary with a couple of canned Cokes.

"That's my 'History at a Glance' wall," he said, giving a Coke to Gilbert.

"I didn't realize you had so many gold and platinum records."

"All our albums made it to gold. Two actually made it to double platinum."

"That's impressive."

"Thanks. You were a fan?"

Gilbert grinned. "I still am."

Phil nodded. "It's appreciated." He sat in a rattan chair and opened his own Coke. "Now . . . about Glen Boyd. I don't mean to rush you, but I'm totally bagged. I've really got to get some sleep."

"Okay, sure." Gilbert glanced at some sheets of paper on the table, scrawled with writing, all of it illegible, but looking as if it were in verse form. Lyrics? "We've been digging around." The faint breeze from the ceiling fans cooled his forehead. "We've been talking to a few people." He now looked at the stained-glass window at the end of the sanctuary—a blue, white, and green Lady-of-the-Lake affair, with a young woman in a flowing gown stepping off a small boat into some reeds. "Shaking loose whatever there is to shake loose." He took a sip of his Coke, put it on the table, and arched his back, easing the ache from his long sit in the car. "And we've learned that you and Glen Boyd . . . over the past number of years . . . well, ever since Palo Alto, as a matter of fact . . . that you haven't exactly been on the best possible terms with each other. We also have a restraining order on file."

Again, the hesitation. But there was nothing suspicious about the hesitation this time. He could tell Phil was tired. Answering a cop's questions at this point was more of a chore, something he had to get through before he could carry himself off to bed.

"Let me put it this way, Detective Gilbert," he said, his voice quiet, polite. "Glen wrecked my band, the only thing I ever loved. Then he gypped me out of my life savings by blowing it all on high-risk stock. Under those circumstances, no, we're not on the best terms. As for that restraining order, yes, I uttered threats, I lost my temper, I blew up. When people lose their tempers, they say things they don't mean. I'm generally a civilized man. I don't lose my temper often. But that time I did. And I regret it. I apologized profusely to Glen. But Glen got dramatic about it, like he does about everything, and had Danny Lynn file that restraining order for him. It was more to make a point. That's fine. Glen's allowed his tantrum. As to the instructions of that restraining order, I've obeyed them to the letter. I haven't been anywhere near GBIA since February." Phil glanced at a scythe leaning against the grand piano, an odd implement to have hanging about the rehearsal space. "If you ask me, Glen needs hundreds of restraining orders. Not just one. He should sandbag GBIA with them. He should entrench himself like the Kaiser's army with them."

"And why's that?" asked Gilbert.

"Because he's got hundreds of enemies," said Phil. "I'm not the only one."

The guitarist leaned back in his rattan chair. He looked to one side, his face slack, his eyes narrowing, his Adam's apple bobbing a time or two.

"I rather suspected it wasn't just you," said Gilbert.

"No," said Phil. "Let me tell you the way it works. Glen makes money out of people's dreams. That's his business. He takes the dreams of young musicians and turns them into money. He looks for a kill, and gleans the best scraps for himself. I blame myself for trusting Glen with my dreams. But he was trendy at the time. He had a high profile. If you were on Glen's list, at least back in those days, you were a name. Not anymore. Now it's dog shows and circus acts for Glen."

"The article in the paper this weekend mentioned that," said Gilbert.

"I know," said Phil. "I read that article. Back in the seventies it was just bands. Talk to Ian Mackay of the Diodes. Or John Fleck of The Zap. Some of these bands were so badly gypped by Glen, they had to fold, just like Mother Courage did. Bye-bye to all their dreams. He gypped the Kyoto String Quartet. He gypped the Lights of Italy Bikini Contest. He even gypped the St. Vladimir Ukrainian Boys' Choir. He nickeled and dimed them to death. He circles and circles, like a vulture, waiting for the best rip-off he can find. And the dreams of his clients be damned."

Gilbert took down the names of these other bands and organizations.

"Okay, that's fine," he said. "I understand he wasn't a particularly ethical businessman. I suspected as much. But I have to narrow things down. That's why I'm here. To eliminate possibilities. In particular, the possibility of Phil Thompson as a suspect."

"I understand," said Phil. "The minute I heard he got killed, I knew someone would knock on my door. The restraining order more or less guaranteed that."

"I have to check it out," said Gilbert. "Sorry."

"No, that's okay."

"So on to the usual questions?"

"Sure."

"We'll start with alibi," said Gilbert. "In fact, we'll finish with alibi, too. I can see you're tired, and alibi is all I'm really interested in right now."

A line came to Phil's forehead. "So . . . when was it? Last Saturday?" He nodded. "Right. Last Saturday I was on a plane to New York."

"No, it was last Friday," corrected Gilbert. "Friday the first. At about nine-thirty."

Phil thought again. "I was here," he said. "Getting ready to go. Packing and stuff. I was in bed by ten."

"Was anybody here with you?" asked Gilbert.

"No."

"Did anybody call?"

"No."

"Hmm."

"That's the best I can do for you," said Phil. "Sorry."

"No . . . no. That's fine. Do you know anybody who might want to kill Boyd?"

"Practically everybody who knew him."

"Yes, I realize that. But . . . anybody specifically?"

"I haven't talked to Glen since February. I spoke to Ted, though. Ted Aver. Ted told me Glen was mixed up with some guys from Colombia. I have no idea what that's all about, but it might be worth checking into. And it doesn't surprise me he would get himself killed. He was always dumb about the impact he was making on people, always rubbing people the wrong way, especially recently." Phil shook his head. "He's lost touch with what's appropriate. No wonder he makes so many people angry. I half suspect it's because he's never been able to clean up his act."

"No?"

"No. He's never kicked his habits the way the rest of us have. I still have the occasional bout with the bottle, once a year or so." Gilbert remembered the suspended license report on Phil. "But Glenny does it daily, both drugs and alcohol, and when you're fifty-seven, your body can't take it. Your mind gets all fucked up. When you're under the influence all the time, whether it's drugs or alcohol, it's hard to see things the way they really are. I'm sure he said something to these Colombians to make them mad. And you don't want to make Colombians mad. At least not Colombians in that line of work. But Glen thinks he can get away with anything. He always has."

Like stealing my wife away to France, thought Gilbert, and again wondered if he could be objective on this case.

"Do you know these Colombians?" asked Gilbert.

"No. Ted just mentioned them in passing. The White Lady is a thing of the past for me. Unfortunately, not for Glen. It's too bad, because I think Glen had a real talent at one time. But the

White Lady screwed him. I wish he and I could just go back. I wish we could find out where it all went wrong, and mend all our broken bridges, and just start over again. I had some real good laughs with Glenny. We all did. I wish things never got sour between us."

Gilbert thought he'd better wrap it up.

"I saw you on TV the other night," said Gilbert. "The release party for your new CD."

"Yes."

"Good luck with that."

"Thanks," said Phil.

"You told the veejay you were going on tour," he said. "When's that going to happen?"

"We're rehearsing till the end of July, taking a week off, then heading out the second week of August. Our first date is August tenth in New York City."

"I don't know how long my investigation will take, but I may need to talk to you again."

Phil nodded. "I'll have my publicist send you the concert list. She'll include our hotel phone numbers."

"Thanks," he said. He took out a business card and handed it to Phil. "Call me if you have any more thoughts about Glen."

Phil slid the card into his shirt pocket. "Sure," he said. "But I try not to think about Glen. I find it only irritates the hell out of me."

On this, thought Gilbert, they were of like minds.

UNDERCOVER NARCOTICS AGENT AL VALDEZ, a Canadian of Mexican descent, sat in the Homicide office with Gilbert and Lombardo the following Wednesday. He had long hair, a beard, and a mustache. He was young, in his late twenties, and wore baggy ghetto-style pants, a Chicago Cubs sleeveless sweatshirt, and a baseball cap on backward—gang attire, in keeping with his undercover job.

"Barcos is a vicious bastard," Valdez told them. "You see this scar?" he asked, holding out his arm for inspection. Gilbert saw a scar two inches long. "He cut me with a knife. Just on a whim. Just to see how I would react. He thought it was funny. He had a good laugh about it. I had to go to Emergency for nine stitches. I didn't find it funny. I wouldn't be surprised if he's the one who killed Boyd."

"What about Deranga?" asked Gilbert. "What's he like?"

"Frank's equally capable. I was with him when he broke the kneecap of that street-level guy in Moss Park I told you about. A young guy, couldn't have been more than eighteen, just a kid. Frank used a water-filled aluminum baseball bat. He says the water gives it extra torque, really adds power to the swing. I wanted to stop him, but what could I do? I couldn't blow my cover. So, bang, we crippled this guy, and we just left him there. If Frank can do that, he can easily strangle Boyd."

"And is Waldo Munoz the same way?" asked Lombardo.

Valdez shook his head. "No. You don't have to worry about Waldo. He's their money guy. He cleans it all up for them and sends it down south. He's a nice guy. He wouldn't hurt a flea. He actually writes poetry. It's the other two you have to worry about."

"So why has Narcotics suspended your operation?" asked Lombardo.

"Because Barcos is on a witch-hunt," said the undercover agent. "I've been rolling up his network one dealer at a time. Now he's suspicious as hell, and he's ready to shoot just about anybody. I have a wife. I have a baby girl. Joyce took me off. She says Barcos needs time to cool down."

Gilbert remembered what Ted Aver had said, how Barcos thought someone, possibly Glen Boyd, had compromised the Toronto operation. In fact, it had been Al Valdez.

"He's as unpredictable as a wild animal," continued Valdez. "Joyce and I both know that, so we scaled back to surveillance-only for the time being. If you two guys end up arresting him, take the uniforms along. I'd even get the K-9 unit. It takes an animal to fight an animal, and believe me, he'll put up a fight. He's the kind of guy who will shoot you in the foot just for looking at him the wrong way."

Over the next day, Lombardo organized a witness canvas of Queen Street West. Gilbert was glad Joe was doing most of the legwork, ducking into arty boutiques, trendy restaurants, and corner convenience stores. Gilbert's arthritic knees were giving him a hard time this week.

"He's showing Al's surveillance photos of the Colombians to the local retail and restaurant people on Queen Street," Gilbert explained to Staff Inspector Nowak. "We're hoping someone might have seen them on the night Boyd was killed."

"It's a long shot," said Nowak, "but I guess you have to try."

Long shot or not, the effort produced results by Thursday afternoon in the way of a convenience store security video.

"Jay's Smoke and Gift," said Lombardo, shoving the tape into the machine as he and Gilbert sat down to watch. "On the corner of St. Patrick and Queen. A nice old Korean guy runs the place. He remembers Barcos and Deranga distinctly. Especially Deranga's jacket. Rhinestones all over the place."

"Good work, Joe," said Gilbert.

Lombardo ran the tape.

Barcos and Deranga came into the store. The image was black and white, a bit blurry, but the suspects were still recognizable as the two Colombians. Jay, the old Korean guy, didn't look too happy to see them, smelled trouble the minute they walked in.

Oscar Barcos was short, and couldn't have weighed more than a hundred-and-twenty pounds. He had dark curly hair and big square-rimmed glasses. His mustache was no more than stubble, not a mustache at all, just a shadow of whiskers.

Francesco Deranga was of average height with extremely broad shoulders and a thick chest. He had a body builder's physique. His dark hair was cropped close to his scalp. He was clean-shaven, and he looked one or two years younger than Barcos. He wore that jacket. Rhinestones all over the place. The rhinestones were like tiny islands of light on the pale material. Definitely something one would expect to find on that stretch of Queen Street, where outrageous fashion was the rule.

Barcos went up to the counter and bought a pack of cigarettes. Deranga stood by waiting. Another customer, a bald guy in his forties, looked at skin mags at the magazine rack. Deranga gave him a glance. The guy unfolded the *Playboy* centerfold.

The evidentiary value of the tape lay in the clock readout in the bottom right-hand corner: June 1st, Friday, 9:17 P.M., roughly thirteen minutes before Boyd was strangled.

"How far is GBIA from this smoke shop?" asked Gilbert.

"Two blocks," said Lombardo.

Barcos paid for his cigarettes and the two Colombians left the store.

"This looks promising, Joe," said Gilbert. "Barcos and Deranga look like they might be our guys."

And that was a relief because he really wanted to clear this one quickly.

"At least it explains why we have two different DNA patterns for the trace epidermis found under Boyd's fingernails," said Joe. "One belongs to Barcos, and the other belongs to Deranga."

Gilbert tried to piece the events of the evening into a likely sequence.

"They leave Jay's Smoke Shop around nine-twenty, they get to GBIA at nine-twenty-five, they rough Boyd up, break his arm, then strangle him with that scarf around nine-thirty, maybe a little later." Gilbert grew hopeful. His brow creased. "The only thing I can't figure out is the fresh packet of cocaine we found on Boyd's bedside table."

"What about it?" asked Lombardo.

"If they were going to kill him," said Gilbert, "why would they sell him a fresh packet of the stuff, and then just leave it there afterward?"

Lombardo shrugged. "Maybe it was already there," he said. "Maybe he bought it from somebody else, since his credit was shot with the Colombians."

Gilbert was doubtful. "Maybe," he said. He peered more closely at Lombardo. "There's something different about you today. You've done something."

"No," said Lombardo. "There's nothing different."

But his partner was acting self-conscious.

"You've definitely done something," said Gilbert. "Something with your hair."

"Oh, that," said Lombardo. "I parted it on the other side. You don't notice the bald spot at the back so much. Plus Virginia likes it better parted on this side."

"Virginia?" said Gilbert. "Virginia Virelli, from Patrol?"

"Yeah."

Gilbert shook his head. "I knew it was only a matter of time."

"She's a nice girl," said Lombardo. "I like her. She knows how to dance."

Gilbert glanced at his hair. "Let's see," he said.

"Pardon?"

"I want to see if parting it this way hides the bald spot better."

"Okay."

Lombardo leaned forward and showed Gilbert his hair. Gilbert had a look.

"Actually, I think it hides it better when you part it on the other side," said Gilbert.

Lombardo looked up at him, his eyes wide. "Really?" he said. He started fishing in his pocket for his comb.

"Yeah."

Lombardo shook his head. "I told Virginia that, but she said she didn't think so."

"It just goes to show you, Joe."

"What?"

"Always trust your partner first when it comes to your hair. At this stage of the game, Virginia's going to say anything you want her to say. It won't matter what side you part your hair on, she's going to say she likes it."

Regal Road, a tree-lined street of modest but well-kept homes in Toronto's West End, curved steeply up from Oakwood Avenue, south of Little Italy, and close to the small Hispanic community at Dovercourt and Hallam. The houses, built in the late 1920s, were of redbrick, and terraced their way up the hill stepwise, one after the other, until they reached Regal Road Elementary School, a dour-looking building plunked amid a treeless expanse of macadamized playground.

Barcos lived in an attractive if small dwelling, a story and a half, with a green-shingled roof shaded by lofty American beech trees. The big front porch was cool and deep, had cushy old furniture, and a canary cage hanging from a hook screwed into the cream-colored ceiling slats. Tall cedar hedges lined either side of the yard.

Gilbert got out of the car and checked over the DNA court order—they needed a baseline sample from Barcos to compare it to the skin samples underneath Boyd's fingernails, and, on the basis of the Smoke and Gift videotape, had obtained a warrant from Justice Dave Lembeck a couple hours ago.

Lombardo, sitting in the passenger seat, radioed their location to Dispatch. Dispatch in turn alerted units in the area in case Barcos decided to give them trouble.

Gilbert leaned over and peered at the public-health nurse, a squat, fiftyish woman of Irish descent, who sat in the back, ready to take swabs from the suspect's mouth.

"Fran, you might as well wait until we make sure he's here," Gilbert told her.

"I'll make myself comfy," she said, and took out a *Reader's Digest*.

Gilbert and Lombardo walked up to the house. Gilbert was impressed with the lawn and garden. The grass was clipped to golf-course length, as thick and lush as a carpet, unmarred by any crabgrass or dandelions. The flowerbeds were planted with tasteful arrangements of daylilies, monkshood, and Canterbury bells, exhibiting the care and attention one might find in the flowerbeds of Toronto's various botanical gardens.

As they neared the porch, a woman, twenty-two or -three, emerged from the house's cool dark interior. She possessed a keen Latin beauty. Her eyes were like perfect emeralds set in the teakwood darkness of her unblemished face. Her body had the alluring curves of a Spanish guitar. Her hair was like black silk.

Lombardo stopped dead in his tracks. "*Caramba,*" he murmured.

"Hello?" she called, in a Colombian accent. "Can I help you?"

"We're here to see Oscar Barcos," said Gilbert. "Is he home?"

"No," said the woman. "He's working many hours these days."

Her accent was exotic and musical.

"Are you his wife?" asked Gilbert.

"No. I'm his sister."

"What's your name?" asked Lombardo, out of the blue.

"My name is Magda," she said.

"I'm Joe and this is Barry."

They didn't identify themselves as police officers. Now that Barcos wasn't here, what was the point? To tell Magda or any other family member they were police officers would only warn Barcos. They didn't want him running.

"You are his friends?" she ventured. "He has so many friends, I can hardly keep track of them all."

She looked at Gilbert innocently, sweetly, and he wondered if she had any inkling of the true nature of her brother's business.

"No, he wouldn't know us," he said. "But it's work-related." That, after all, wasn't a lie. "Could you tell us where he is?"

"He has many concerns, sir," she said. "Where he is at any given moment I cannot be certain. And when he comes home, sometimes I'm at work. Only Mama sees his comings and goings because she is here all the time. She looks after his house."

Gilbert glanced at the house. "Tell her I've never seen such a clean house."

She smiled, taken with the compliment. "Thank you," she said.

"Your garden is beautiful, too," said Joe, getting in on the act.

Magda's smile disappeared, as if she didn't like Joe at all. Gilbert didn't see this reaction often, but every once in a while, Joe rubbed a woman the wrong way.

"My mama knows how to nurture these small things that grow," she said.

Her voice was prim, civil, and curt. Sometimes the real beauties just didn't get Joe.

Gilbert saw that Lombardo was trying to think of something to say, but, uncharacteristically, just stood there, tongue-tied, growing red in the face.

"Do you have a card . . . Mister . . . Mister . . . Barry?" asked Magda.

"No," said Gilbert. "I'll call Oscar at the laminating plant. Do you think he'll be there now?"

"He often is," she said. "But he races around town like a

Nascar driver, now that he has his Porsche. From one end to the other, it doesn't matter to him, he loves to drive that car, no matter where."

Gilbert saw Magda had a real affection for her brother. He was about to say good-bye when a summer breeze wafted the scent of her perfume to his nose.

"What's that perfume you're wearing?" he asked.

She smiled demurely. "That is Laura Ashley," she said. "A scent she calls *Dilys*."

"It's nice," he said.

"Thank you," she said.

As they walked back to the car, Gilbert turned to Lombardo.

"What's wrong with you?" asked Gilbert.

"She didn't even look at me," said Lombardo. "It must be my hair."

"Joe, it's not your hair," said Gilbert. "Contrary to what you think, not every woman's going to look at you, and it doesn't necessarily have anything to do with your hair." Then he faked a proud but modest grin. "Now, with someone like me, it's different. They're going to look at me no matter what. I could be as ugly as the Elephant Man, and they would still look at me. It's my charm."

"At least you have all your hair."

"Joe, you can't even notice it. I wish you never ran into Mike Strutton. Mike always has to say something. I remember that about him from Patrol."

"And what's with the perfume again?" asked Lombardo.

Gilbert shrugged casually. "Like I say, I go with my gut feeling. I smelled perfume on the scarf around Boyd's neck."

"And you recognized the scent?" said Joe. "This *Dilys,* or whatever it is?"

"My wife wears it," said Gilbert. "And now Magda wears it, too. And that just made our case against Barcos a hell of a lot stronger. The scarf probably belongs to Magda."

Having failed to locate Barcos or the other Colombians at the laminating plant, Gilbert got his next lead on them from Detective-Sergeant Bob Bannatyne, his old partner from Fraud. Bannatyne called him at one-thirty in the morning at home.

"This could be good news or bad news," said Bannatyne. "It depends on what you're doing with the Boyd case."

Gilbert sat up in bed, coming alive at the mention of Boyd's name. Far in the distance he heard the rumble of thunder. Regina stirred beside him.

"Where are you?" he asked Bannatyne.

"In Mississauga," said Bannatyne. Mississauga was a suburb in the extreme west end of Toronto. "In front of a place called Club Lua. A Latino dance club. Deranga and Munoz are lying out front with bullet holes in their heads."

Gilbert's shoulders tensed. "Really?"

"I thought you might want to know. I'll wait for you, if you want to come out. Deranga's wearing the rhinestone jacket you were telling me about. Who the fuck did he think he was? Roy Rogers?"

"Don't touch that coat."

"I'm a double-breasted man myself, Barry."

"And come to think of it, that's not our jurisdiction," said Gilbert. "That's Peel Region. What are you doing out there?"

"They want our help. They know Joyce and Valdez were working on these guys. They think we might be able to assist."

"I'm coming right out."

"Hurry up. It looks like it's going to piss buckets any second."

"I'll get there as fast as I can."

He got dressed, climbed into the family's Ford Windstar, and drove up the Don Valley Parkway to Highway 401.

Driving west toward Mississauga, he saw heat lightning flicker in the distance. All the hot weather was finally going to break. A storm was definitely on the way.

He passed the cloverleaf at Allen Road, the basket-weave at Keele, and had just reached Highway 400 when rain hit the minivan like a hundred snare drums beating all at once. He eased his foot on the brake as visibility dropped drastically. He turned on the windshield wipers.

Lester B. Pearson International Airport came into view. A 767, its tailfin lit with the crown of Royal Dutch Airlines, sailed over the freeway a few hundred meters up, coming in for a landing, its headlight piercing through the rain with laser-like intensity, its jet engines adding to the roar of the storm.

Gilbert skirted the south side of the airport along the 401 and exited onto Dixie Road. He passed the Gateway Postal Facility, as well as the 12 Division Peel Regional Police Station, and soon came to the Rockwood Mall.

At the south end of the mall stood Club Lua. Seven radio

cars were parked haphazardly outside the club, five of them with their lights flashing, one of them up on the sidewalk.

He drove across the nearly empty parking lot and eased to a stop outside the crime-scene perimeter. He got out of his Windstar, and was instantly wet in the pelting summer deluge. He took his badge and ID out and showed them to one of the uniforms standing guard. The uniform, wearing a big yellow rain slicker, lifted the police tape and let him through.

Deranga and Munoz lay outside the entrance to the club, each now covered in an orange tarp. Bannatyne, along with a detective from Peel Region, talked to a group of young club-goers, taking statements under the club's huge stainless-steel portico. The back of Bannatyne's brown raincoat was lit by the pink neon starfish and the green neon palm trees in the club's plate-glass window. Bannatyne glanced over his shoulder and saw him coming. The sixty-year-old detective said a few words to the other detective, and greeted him halfway.

"That was fast," he said.

"There was hardly any traffic," said Gilbert.

"I hate rain," said Bannatyne. He motioned at the water rushing down the gutter at the curbside. "There goes our goddamn crime scene. Not that it's going to take a rocket scientist to figure it out. We have seven witnesses. Barcos shot his own best buds."

"Barcos did?" said Gilbert. "Shit." He glanced at the victims. "Al said he was a maniac."

Bannatyne raised his stubby index finger. "A homicidal maniac," he corrected.

Gilbert sighed. "Christ," he said.

"You want to have a look at them?"

Gilbert glanced at the bodies. A kind of no-man's-land aura emanated from them, as if some invisible death force separated them from the living. Rain puddled in the folds of the orange tarps. A couple of young guys. Gone, just like that. Their mothers would be sad.

"Might as well," he said. He nodded toward the other detective. "He's the primary from Peel?"

"Yeah. Steve Ludmore. A real nice guy. I'll introduce you once he's finished talking to his witnesses. I filled him in on the Boyd case. I hope you don't mind."

"No, not at all."

They walked over to the bodies of Francesco Deranga and Waldo Munoz.

Bannatyne pulled the orange tarps back.

Deranga had a single gunshot wound to the left temple. His bronze-colored face was spattered with blood, the blotchy congealed patterns reminding Gilbert of a Rorschach inkblot test. His short hair was gummed up with blood.

Munoz, a much slighter man, had taken one in the face through the cheek just below his right eye, the skin all puffy and discolored around the wound, powder burns evident all over his face—a close-range shot. The man's glasses rested askew on his nose. His lips were parted, revealing long yellowish teeth, the front two overlapping.

Here was Oscar Barcos's handiwork. With Al Valdez unraveling the Toronto network, had Barcos at last seen enemies everywhere? Did Barcos finally come to doubt even Deranga and Munoz?

"Seen enough?" asked Bannatyne.

"They all look the same when they're shot in the head. I just feel sorry for them. They're so young."

Bannatyne gazed at the corpses, as if recognizing their youthfulness for the first time.

"Yeah . . . well . . . crime's a young man's game. What do you expect? Let's sit in my car until Steve finishes up. I hate all this rain. I can feel it right through my shoes, even though I sprayed some of that rain-proofing shit on them."

They walked through the rain to Bannatyne's car, one of the newer unmarked Impalas, and got inside. Bannatyne pulled out a big white hankie and wiped his face and hands. He then pulled out a pack of Players, withdrew a cigarette, and lit up. He took a big drag. Gilbert opened his window a crack. He hadn't smoked in years.

"Does it bother you?" asked Bannatyne.

"No," he said. "Go ahead."

"You gave it up, didn't you?" said Bannatyne.

"A long time ago," he said. "Regina insisted." Gilbert stared out the rain-specked windshield at the nearest patrol car. "I'm just wondering if you and Steve could do me a favor, Bob."

"Sure."

"We have skin samples from underneath Boyd's fingernails. We think one of the samples might be from Deranga." He motioned toward the dead Colombians in front of the club. "So if you could, bag some blood or hair from him so we can make our comparisons. That's why I really drove all this way. To get a DNA baseline."

"Not a problem," said Bannatyne.

"Will you be searching the Barcos residence?" asked Gilbert.

"Definitely."

"Because we think the other sample might be from him."

"I'll bag whatever I can find once I get the warrant," said Bannatyne. "A hair or whatever."

"Thanks," said Gilbert. "We haven't been able to find him."

"And I imagine it's going to be a lot harder now that he's shot his own best buds. He's going to be running."

Rain drummed off the roof of the car and made tiny silver splashes on the hood. Bannatyne took another drag on his cigarette and let the smoke drift from his mouth in a thick white stream, sniffing a bit of it up through his nostrils. A troubled look came to his face.

"Have you told Joe about Boyd and Regina yet?" he asked.

Gilbert looked away. He gazed at the tarp-covered bodies, saw the blood seep from under the orange canvas onto the sidewalk. "No," he said.

"Are you going to?" asked Bannatyne.

Gilbert didn't answer.

Bannatyne sighed. "Barry . . . come on . . . you've got to tell him. He's your partner. When you and me were partners back in Fraud, we told each other everything. And Boyd and Regina . . . Christ, Barry, it tore you apart. You know it did." Bannatyne tapped the ash on the end of his cigarette into the ashtray. "I know you're a good detective. I know you're objective.

But Boyd was the worst thing that ever happened to you. And you should let Joe know. He's a bright young guy. He'll cover for you if you start making dumb mistakes. Do yourself a favor. Let Joe know. Before you start fucking up on this thing royally."

ON MONDAY, GILBERT TOOK LOMBARDO to lunch at Erl's Bistro, curiously spelled, Erl, without the "a," just south of the Provincial Parliament Buildings on University Avenue. They found a table next to the fountain on the outdoor patio. Though Friday night's deluge had cooled the city for the weekend, temperatures were rising again, and even here, on the shaded patio, it was warm.

They ordered salads, sandwiches, and beer, and over the next half hour Gilbert told Lombardo exactly what had happened between Regina and Boyd all those years ago.

"They finally flew to France and lived together for nine months," said Gilbert.

This stunned Lombardo. He stared at Gilbert, didn't even get distracted by the pretty waitress walking by, sat back in his chair, and let his fingers slide from his beer.

"And she slept with the guy and everything?" said Lombardo.

"Yeah."

"And you were married at the time?"

"Yeah. Six years. Nineteen-seventy-eight. We married so damn young. She wasn't settled down."

Lombardo lifted his fork and tapped it a few times against the table. "Somehow I can't picture Regina . . . I mean, she's so responsible. It seems so out of character. She's always struck me as the steady, moral type."

"She was young."

"And you didn't have any kids at the time?" asked Lombardo.

"Jennifer was still three years away. We were married for ten whole years before we had Jennifer. Jennifer doesn't know it, but she saved our marriage. She made us survive, Joe."

Out on the sidewalk, a child, clinging to his mother's hand, dropped an ice-cream cone and started to cry.

"I know some guys," said Gilbert, "if their wives did the same thing to them, they might have said game-over." His throat tightened. "And several times I came close to it, Joe. But I love her. The whole thing hurt like hell, it nearly killed me, it was the worst thing that ever happened to me, but I just couldn't bring myself to give her up. So I suffered through it, hoping she would come back to me. I knew Boyd's style. Women were as interchangeable as spark plugs to him. I knew sooner or later he would get another one. And don't go blaming Regina too much. Times were different back then. There's never been anything like those times, before or since. The nineteen-seventies. You were a kid at the time. But for people in my generation, it was like . . . like . . . "

Gilbert struggled to define the period.

Lombardo grinned. "Like the dawning of the Age of Aquarius?" he said.

Gilbert gave him a sour look.

"Don't joke about it, Joe," he said. "It might seem quaint now, but at the time . . . I had hair down to my shoulders. Regina wore hip-hugger bell bottoms, paisley shirts, and a peace-sign amulet. We were big music fans. We went to lots of concerts together. We saw Fleetwood Mac, the Eagles, Bob Dylan, the Stones twice, and Creedence Clearwater Revival. We saw Led Zeppelin, the Doobie Brothers, Joni Mitchell, Pink Floyd, and Santana. In our first apartment we had beaded doorways, black-light posters, and burned incense to cover the smell of pot. And if we didn't have any pot we smoked banana peels. Dinner was typically twelve scented candles flickering on the shelf, the fondue pot simmering on the table, and the latest Frank Zappa album on the stereo. It was crazy. We had parties all the time. Or we went out dancing. I couldn't imagine me dancing now. Not with my knees the way they are."

"You smoked pot?"

"Joe, back in the seventies, everybody smoked pot. Even cops. Everybody was experimenting. Everybody was trying new things. And Regina was extremely impressionable. All the old morality went out of style overnight. We had one credo. If it felt good, do it. The world was full of wackos, and she met a lot of them when she went to teacher's college. That place seemed to have more than its fair share of wackos. Then there was Michelle

Morrison, and we were always getting free tickets to see Mother Courage whenever they played in town. Boyd was always hanging around somewhere, trying to get into Michelle's pants. But even back then, Michelle was with Pat Kelly, so Boyd didn't stand a chance. Michelle introduced Regina to Boyd. I should show you a picture of Regina when she was twenty-eight. She was a knockout."

An image of Regina came to mind, her face flushed as she walked naked down the pathway at the cottage, her blond hair long and parted in the middle, a bracelet of Hindu brass bells tied around her ankle. How could she have ever denied him? Even now, he felt a great hollowness inside whenever he thought about it.

"So after Michelle introduced them, Regina and Boyd started seeing each other?" asked Lombardo.

"Yeah," said Gilbert. "This was just about the time I made detective in Fraud. Bannatyne was my partner. You know how Bob is. Everything is the job. We worked like hell. A lot of extra hours every bloody week. Regina was a supply teacher at the time, so she had tons of free time."

"And no kids yet," said Lombardo.

"No kids yet," echoed Gilbert.

"And times were different back then," said his partner, now sounding like he was making a sincere effort to understand Regina's behavior.

"You could sleep with anybody you liked, and no one was supposed to get heavy about it. It was all part of the new thing. Free love, and all that. I came home early one day. I had the flu. I was running a fever. Bannatyne sent me home. And there they were, Regina and Boyd, in bed together, smoking Panama Red out of a hookah pipe. It just about killed me."

"Then she was off to France?" said Lombardo.

"Three days later. I don't know what kind of poison Boyd filled her head with, but let's face it, I was a cop, and a cop to a counterculture poster-boy like Boyd . . . I imagine he thought the amoeba was the higher form of life."

Lombardo had nothing to say, just sat there, his shock now milder. The fountain, really more a waterfall sliding over a piece of sheet-glass into a collecting pool, bubbled with the promise of many languid summer days to come. The waitress passed by, lifted their dirty dishes onto her tray, and retreated toward the bar.

"But it's over now," said Gilbert, in a quieter voice. "It happened a long time ago. And times are different now. I like these times better. Regina's the best wife any guy could have. It's not easy being a cop's wife. But she's the sweetest, most loving, caring person in the world, and she's a great mother. I hate what Boyd did to her—to *us*—but I'm glad I stuck with her. It was the best decision I ever made."

"So how did it . . . you know . . . how did it all end?" asked Lombardo.

"She phoned me from Aix-en-Provence. Boyd had a place there at the time. She said she didn't want to live with him anymore, and that she'd made a mistake. So she came back. I'd never seen her so miserable. She was so skinny. And pale. Her teaching career came to a dead stop. She didn't know what to do with herself. She was really depressed, and the doctor put her on something, an antidepressant, but that just made her sicker. She cried a lot. Half the time I'd come home from work and I'd find her crying in the kitchen. I made a lot of macaroni salad in those days because that's practically all I knew how to make. Regina wasn't up to cooking. We ate a lot of takeout. At least I did. Regina hardly ate anything at all. She took a whole bottle of aspirin one night. I don't know what she was thinking. The aspirin wasn't going to kill her. But she took them anyway, and they made her sick, and she had to spend a week in the hospital. I'll never forgive Boyd for what he did to her. We came so close to losing it, Joe. So damn close. It makes me shudder to think of it."

Lombardo glanced out at University Avenue where Philips Demolition tore down the old Bell Wing of the Toronto General Hospital. Some sparrows fought over bread crumbs on the sidewalk. A homeless man sold copies of the homeless weekly, *Outreach*. A woman with a perfect hourglass figure walked by but Joe didn't even notice.

"I got to ask you," said Lombardo, "as one detective to another, do you think you can work this one? Do you think you *should* work this one? All this . . . this business with Boyd and Regina . . . it was a big thing in your life, I can tell, and I just want to make sure you can work the investigation."

Gilbert took a sip of beer, a German one that tasted sweet as it went flat in the warm air.

"Joe . . . if I didn't think I could work it, I would have told you a long time ago. But I'm okay with it. Bannatyne advised me to tell you about Regina and Boyd, so that's what I did."

"Bannatyne knows?"

"He was my partner at the time." Gilbert glanced at Lombardo's hair, thinking he had done something else different with it. "We're short-staffed right now, what with summer holidays around the corner, and I don't want to have to stretch any of the other guys further than they're already stretched. I don't want to have to stretch you. This one's going to be a dunker. You know it, I know it, and Tim knows it. Ten to one the Colombians did it. I bet we get a match on Deranga's DNA by the end of the week. And once Bannatyne finds a hair in Barcos's house, we'll get a match on him as well. Done. Finished. A dunker."

"Somehow I don't think it's going to be that easy, Barry. You got to remember Blackstein and the toxicology report. Deputy Chief Ling called him, but so far it hasn't done much good."

"You've got to phone Blackstein more than once if you're going to make him budge. Ling will call him again, especially if Ronald Roffey starts kicking up a fuss. By the way, you've done something to your hair again."

"I've combed it back," he said. "You see? Like this."

Joe demonstrated by swiping his palm straight back from his forehead.

"I don't know, Joe," said Gilbert.

"No, it's good," said Joe. "Virginia says it makes me look mysterious. And it covers that bald spot back there."

"Joe, you can hardly see that bald spot to begin with. You know what I think about you combing your hair back like that?"

"What?"

"It makes you look like the Godfather. Comb it normal, and forget about it, Don Corleone."

By Thursday, the first day of summer, a day so hot it broke records going back fifty years, the Centre of Forensic Science positively matched the skin scrapings under the fingernails of Boyd's left hand to DNA found in blood taken from Francesco Deranga's corpse.

"From the broken arm?" asked Lombardo.

"From the broken arm," confirmed Gilbert.

Furthermore, a thread taken from Deranga's distinctive rhinestone jacket matched one found among the vacuumed materials taken into evidence.

"This is all we need," said Gilbert.

Lombardo looked doubtful. "So we're going to write a warrant on a dead man?" he asked.

"At least we don't have to waste time looking for him."

"I think we should run it by Tim first," said Lombardo. "You got his e-mail?"

Gilbert frowned. "I got his e-mail." He shook his head. "Damn that Roffey. The *Toronto Star* should fire that guy."

"He was here again this morning," said Lombardo.

"I know. I saw him in the lobby."

"He was in Tim's office for twenty minutes. Tim actually spoke to me afterward."

"And what did Tim say?" asked Gilbert.

"That, yes, he wanted Boyd done fast, but that he wanted him done right as well. There can't be any mistakes on this one. That's why I think we should hold off on pegging Deranga as the killer until we talk to Tim. I think he's there right now. Why don't we go check?"

Gilbert paused. He was usually the patient one. Lombardo was the one who always rushed things. Maybe Bob Bannatyne was right. Maybe he needed someone to cover his back for him on this one after all, a good partner who would make sure he didn't do anything stupid.

"Okay, let's go," he said.

They went to the staff inspector's office. They found Nowak at his desk going over some work.

"We just received the report on the Boyd skin scrapings from the Centre of Forensic Science," Gilbert said. "The sample from his left hand is a DNA match to blood taken from Deranga's corpse in Mississauga. We also found a fiber from Deranga's coat in Boyd's apartment. I think we've got enough to move on this, Tim. Deranga's our guy. We should get Justice Lembeck to make a posthumous ruling on Deranga's culpability. Then all we have to do is have Patrol pick up Barcos as an accomplice, and we'll be finished and done with this thing."

The computer-savvy Nowak called up the case file with a few clicks of his mouse, glanced it over, then looked out the window, where the air was heavy with a haze as thick as cheese.

"I don't know, Barry," he said. "It seems a bit easy to me."

Gilbert had to give that a moment. Was he truly rushing this then, simply because he was uncomfortable with Boyd and Regina after all these years? He had to think, and think objectively. Think outside himself, and beyond the squalid memories. See the thing from a professional perspective, become a homicide cop and *only* a homicide cop. Yet even as he cleared his mind and looked at the thing from an objective standpoint, he still believed the evidence pointed to the two Colombians. He pushed ahead, despite the staff inspector's uncertainty.

"Tim, it's perfect," he said.

"Not really," replied Tim.

"Why?" said Gilbert.

"Because the skin from the right hand hasn't been identified yet."

"It belongs to Barcos," said Gilbert. "You watch. Bob will bring back a hair from the guy's house, and that'll be it, case closed."

"Yes, but you yourself said we still don't have Barcos. And until we have Barcos, and have determined that the other skin sample belongs to him, I'm not willing to go to Lembeck to get a posthumous ruling on Deranga, not when Roffey's just waiting for us to make a mistake. The other thing I'm worried about is the timing of the thing. I'm not convinced by it."

"What's wrong with the timing?" asked Gilbert. "We have the tape from Jay's Smoke and Gift."

"And that's good," said Nowak. "That's strong circumstantial evidence. But it's not definitive. Nine-seventeen is not nine-thirty. And we can't be absolutely certain Barcos and Deranga went to GBIA after they left the smoke shop. Our strong speculation is that they did, but the proof's not a hundred percent conclusive. I would like the evidence to be conclusive in this particular case. I expect it to be conclusive in *every* case, but I reiterate, in this particular case more so because of the media attention involved."

Gilbert sighed, frustrated by his boss. "Ted Aver said the Colombians threatened Boyd. 'Pay up or die.' That's an exact quote. Phil Thompson told me Boyd was mixed up with these Colombians as well. We find Deranga's skin under Boyd's fingernails. We find a thread from that crazy jacket. We have a videotape that puts Barcos and Deranga five minutes away from the crime scene in and around the time of the murder. I don't see what's not to like about it. This is the kind of case a Crown prosecutor loves to get. I say we ship the whole works to Justice Lembeck and have him sign off on it. At least on Deranga. Then we'll concentrate on nabbing Barcos."

Nowak remained calm. "I won't deny the case looks particularly strong against the Colombians. And yes, we should do everything we can to apprehend Barcos quickly." He clicked through a few more screens of the case file. Lombardo shifted uncomfortably. Gilbert felt he was missing something here. Nowak finally lifted his finger in the air. "But if we send it to Lembeck right now, he's going to take a look at the autopsy report."

"So?"

"He's going to wonder why a big guy like Deranga hardly left a mark on Boyd's throat."

"And then we tell him Barcos was the guy who killed Boyd, while Deranga stood by. Barcos is a shrimp. Him strangling Boyd explains the lack of trauma to Boyd's throat. You saw the videotape. He probably has trouble opening a jar of peanut butter. Either way, they both go down."

"What about Phil Thompson's restraining order?" asked Nowak.

"I'm sure once we bring Barcos in and get him talking, we can eliminate Phil as a suspect. Phil's a musician, not a killer."

"And what about Judy Pelaez?" asked Tim.

"She was at Scaramouche waiting for Boyd to show up the night Boyd was killed. She's already told us that."

Lombardo piped in. "Actually . . . Barry . . . I forgot to tell you. I checked the Scaramouche thing out. None of the waiters remember seeing Judy at the restaurant on the night of the murder. So you never know."

Gilbert turned to Lombardo. "Really?" he said. "Are you sure?"

"I talked to the maitre d'. I talked to the manager. They said Boyd had a reservation, but no one showed up. The maitre d' said he finally had to give the table to another party."

Gilbert's airtight case against the Colombians now glimmered with doubt.

"Why would she lie to us?"

Lombardo shrugged. "Who knows?" he said. "I personally don't think she did it, but I could be wrong."

"We'll have to talk to her again," said Gilbert. He shook his head in deepening frustration. "Still, I have this gut feeling it's Barcos and Deranga."

"And you're probably right," said Nowak. "But there's no hurry in taking the thing over to Dave Lembeck just yet. Bob Bannatyne's already got an existing warrant on Barcos for the double homicide at Club Lua. Why write another warrant when we're going to arrest Barcos anyway? There's no point. That doesn't mean we won't make Barcos our number-one priority. Like you say, Barry, with Barcos in custody, we might eliminate the other suspects."

"We can offer him a deal on the double homicide if he comes clean on Boyd," said Gilbert.

Nowak raised his brow. "That's good," he said. "I like that. Bob's not going to like it, and Peel will probably hate it, but I'll try and smooth it out one way or the other."

"Good," said Gilbert, feeling both uncomfortable and relieved that he had forced a square peg into a round hole. "We go for Barcos. We use Bob's warrant. We hold off on sending the case to Lembeck until Barcos is in custody. The minute we have him, I'd like that stuff to go right over to College Park." He changed tack, tried to soften his urgent tone. "Now . . . what's been done about finding him? Bob was in and out so fast this morning, I didn't get a chance to talk to him."

"Patrol has been announcing the posting every morning at roll call, and every evening when the night shift comes in," said Nowak. "Peel Region is doing the same. We haven't found Barcos at home or at any of his businesses, so we're fairly certain he's running or hiding. I'm working on a Canada-wide posting. That should be ready by tomorrow. By the start of next week, we'll have postings not only in the U.S. and Mexico, but in Colombia as well, in case he decides to go back home. Al Valdez says that's the likeliest scenario." Nowak clicked off the case file on his computer. "And Bob Bannatyne's spoken to the sister."

"Magda?" said Gilbert.

"It didn't go so well," said Nowak. "Bob's heavy-handedness sometimes backfires on him. He says she was completely ignorant of her brother's criminal enterprises, and extremely upset by the discovery."

Gilbert winced. "I should have told Bob about that," he said. "When we went to get our DNA swab from Barcos, I got the sense Magda didn't know what her brother really did for a living."

"Bob said she was inconsolable. Either that, or she was putting on a big act."

"That was Bob's interpretation?"

A grin came to Nowak's face. "You know Bob," he said. "If Magda has any idea where her brother is, she's not letting on."

"Maybe I should go talk to her," said Lombardo.

This was so transparent, Gilbert nearly laughed.

"Leave it to me," he said. "I got more of a response out of her when we went to take the swab. I'm sure I might make some headway if I just go easy on her."

ON MONDAY MORNING, AS GILBERT ate breakfast at the kitchen table before going to work, the telephone rang. He got up from the table and answered it. It was Mike Topalovich. Mike had news about his three pre-Nina sex partners.

"Two of them came back clean," he told Gilbert. "They're not HIV-positive. They were my first two partners out of the three."

"What about the third?" asked Gilbert.

In the background, Gilbert heard Snowflake barking.

"I don't know, sir," said Mike. "She's disappeared, just like Vashti. She's gone on holiday or something. Her telephone just rings and rings. Me and my dad drove by her house the other night and her house was dark."

"What's her name?" asked Gilbert.

Mike hesitated. "Carolyn," he said.

"And she was the last of the three, the one immediately before Nina?"

"Yes. I think it was Valentine's Day. We were getting all romantic."

At least this narrowed it down to either Carolyn or Vashti.

"Have you spoken to any of Carolyn's friends?" asked Gilbert.

"We spoke to her neighbor, a guy named Eldon. He says he doesn't know where they've gone. The house hasn't gone up for sale. The furniture's still there. You can see it if you look through the window. But Eldon says he hopes they're gone for good. He doesn't get along with them. He says they're really noisy. I know Carolyn likes to play her music loud. My dad and me gave Eldon our phone number, and he said he would call us if they came back. We told him it was really important."

Gilbert thought for a moment.

"Thanks, Mike," he said. "How are you doing . . . are you doing okay?"

Mike paused. "I'm okay, sir," he said.

"You're a good guy, Mike. Thanks for helping me out like this."

"If I could go back and do things differently, sir, none of this would have happened."

"I know, Mike," said Gilbert. "I know."

Lombardo was waiting for him when he got to the office later on. His partner's expression was somber, his brow set, his mouth slack, his dark eyes evasive.

"Let's go to the police museum," said Lombardo. Joe glanced around the squad room at the other detectives. "I need to talk to you."

"The museum?" said Gilbert.

"There's never anyone there this early."

They left the Homicide Office. Lombardo grabbed a legal-sized envelope from his desk as they went.

They walked around the third-floor gallery overlooking the atrium, and headed to the elevators on the opposite side.

"What's going on?" asked Gilbert.

Lombardo looked around nervously. "Let's just wait till we get to the museum, okay?" he said.

The police museum, a public-relations showcase on the first floor of College Street headquarters, featured old photographs, an ancient police car, different guns, and overviews on mounted display boards of the more notorious cases the force had solved in its long colorful history. Original furniture and equipment from a 1920s dispatch office—mahogany stuff that looked pinched from a gangster movie set—stood against the wall. Air-conditioning wafted icy air from ceiling vents.

As Joe had predicted, no one was there. The two detectives leaned against the old dispatch office railing.

"So?" said Gilbert.

Lombardo lifted the legal-sized envelope. "We finally broke into Boyd's computer," he told Gilbert. "I've printed some of his e-mails. I thought you better have a look."

"I don't know why you had to drag me all the way down here to look at his e-mails," said Gilbert.

"Boyd had some unexpected e-mail correspondents." Lombardo stared at him steadily, allowing the envelope to sink to his side. "Your wife was one of them."

The air-conditioning now seemed frostier. His first thought was: *Why?* Regina had absolutely no reason to correspond with Boyd. But then he realized he was in the police museum, far from prying eyes, and that Joe had brought him here for a reason.

Gilbert reached for the envelope.

"Let's see," he said.

"Barry, it's not good."

His voice hardened. "Could I see the envelope, please?"

Lombardo surrendered the envelope.

Gilbert withdrew the e-mail printouts. He read them in growing disbelief.

One was dated the eighth of February, sent to Regina's e-mail address at school.

Regina: Meet me this Wednesday for lunch at the Queen Mother. We have a lot of catching up to do. I'll always remember Aix. Glen.

Lombardo sighed, put his hands on his hips, walked away, and stood next to the organized-crime display. Here was another e-mail from March, this one sent from Regina to Boyd.

Glen: I would greatly appreciate your discretion in all this. Should word ever get back to Barry, I wouldn't be able to see you again. Reggie.

Gilbert's heart sank. His blood felt constricted around his ankles, wrists, and throat. Here was another one, Boyd to Regina, from March Break, when Regina had enjoyed the week off.

Reggie: I've had such a marvelous time these past few days. Having you all to myself has greatly restored my spirits. When can I see you again? GB.

Regina's response came the next day.

Glen: I've already told you. All you've got to do is call. Like the old James Taylor song. RG.

He glanced at Joe.

"That's it?"

Lombardo sighed. "It's not just the e-mails, Barry," he said. "It's the scarf, too. The murder weapon."

Gilbert saw two bicycle police roll up in the courtyard on mountain bikes.

"What about it?" he asked.

"It's a Villa Bolgheri, handmade in Tuscany, not that common. I spoke to the Canadian distributor, Forzieri's. They told me only three stores in Toronto sell it. One of them is Neck and Neck, in Hazelton Lanes. I brought the scarf to Neck and Neck. That's where our scarf came from. The manager could tell from its number. I had him go through his credit-card slips. Regina was the one who bought that scarf, Barry. I've got the charge-card slip right here."

Lombardo took a wrinkled Visa slip out of his shirt pocket and showed it to Gilbert. Gilbert looked at Regina's signature.

"She certainly likes to shop at Hazelton Lanes," he said. "But just because she bought the scarf doesn't mean she had anything to do with Boyd's murder, if that's what you're getting at. I mean, come on, Joe, this is Regina we're talking about."

Lombardo raised his hands. "I wasn't even thinking that," he said. "All these e-mails tell us is that she's had contact with Boyd. No doubt for completely innocent reasons. She forgot her scarf down there, Barcos and Deranga found it, and they used it to strangle Boyd." Joe scratched the back of his neck. "Even so . . . we can't . . . there's no way we can just bury this, Barry. It's got to go into the case file."

"I have no objection to that."

"And speaking of the case file . . . I don't see the perfume anywhere."

Gilbert felt his face redden. "I haven't put it in yet."

"Well . . . just as a matter of procedure . . ."

"I know . . . I know . . . I'll put it in."

"Good. I think we have to go by the book on this one."

"So Tim knows about these e-mails?"

Lombardo nodded. "That's why we have to make such an effort to be aboveboard."

"Fine by me," said Gilbert, his voice hardening. "We'll put the scarf in. And we'll put the perfume in, too."

The two detectives gazed at each other.

"Are you all right?" asked Lombardo.

"It's a bit of a shock, Joe," he said.

"I thought I was going to have a heart attack when I saw those e-mails," said Lombardo. "But then I realized she's probably got a perfectly reasonable explanation."

Gilbert lifted the sheaf of e-mails. "Is that it?" he asked. "Are there any more of these?"

"We don't know," said Lombardo. "We haven't searched all Boyd's e-mail folders yet." Lombardo motioned at the e-mails. "God knows what kind of filing system he uses, but it's taking us a while to figure it out."

"I'm sure it made perfect sense to Boyd. He makes up his life as he goes along."

"He's got encryption software tangling up everything," said Joe. "You should see the techno-nerds in Computer Support. They've never had so much fun. They've got a nickname for him now."

Gilbert's response was half-hearted. "What are they calling him?" he asked.

"The Evil Genius."

"Huh."

Gilbert looked at the e-mails again, then glanced at Lombardo, who had a worried look on his face.

"There's something else, isn't there?" said Gilbert, his voice flat, resigned.

"Tim . . . he wants . . . you know . . . he just wants the file . . . to add up neatly."

"I already told you, we'll put the scarf and the perfume in."

Lombardo's eyes narrowed and he shifted uncomfortably. "Actually, it's more . . . it's just that you and Regina . . . on the night of the murder . . . you were at the Royal Alex . . . and he . . . you know, the way you lost each other. He wants that worked out."

"Worked out how?" But then Gilbert understood, and something squeezed inside him. "Oh, c'mon, Joe."

"He's being careful, Barry, that's all. That's the way Tim is. He used his duck phrase again. He said it was quacking like a duck . . . you know . . . the scarf, the perfume, and you guys at the Royal Alex . . . but he was willing to admit that it wasn't really walking like a duck. At least not yet."

"At least not yet?" said Gilbert. "Joe, that's got to be the most ridiculous thing I've ever heard."

Lombardo sighed. "If you could just tell him . . . you know . . . that Regina went home . . . tell him about Nina's friend who has HIV . . . so he won't think Regina went over to GBIA."

"I'll do that."

"Or maybe have Nina speak to him personally."

"That won't be necessary." Gilbert had to protect Nina's confidentiality.

"Okay."

Gilbert gazed at a fifty-year-old ballistics microscope.

"Tim's just going to have to take my word that Regina was nowhere near GBIA on the night of the murder," he said.

"And I'm sure your word is all it will take," said Lombardo.

To work after these revelations proved impossible for Gilbert.

He called Regina at East York Collegiate Institute, where she worked as an English teacher.

"Could you meet me at home for lunch?" he asked.

She hesitated. They didn't often meet at home for lunch. "What's wrong?" she asked.

"I can't talk right now," he said. "We'll talk at home."

"Is it about Nina?" she asked.

"No, nothing like that," he said. "Just meet me at home as close to noon as you can."

He fidgeted at his desk while he waited for the lunch hour to come. But as the lunch hour was still a long way off, and as he simply couldn't sit still at his desk another minute, he left headquarters, pent up with nervous energy, and went outside to see if he could get rid of some of it by walking around.

He headed up Bay Street, only dimly conscious of how hot it was, not really concentrating on where he was going, just walking, trying to alleviate some of his anxiety. He hiked north to the Polo Center, glanced up at the building, thought of Daniel Lynn, then spied in the distance, west on St. Joseph, the shaded expanse of Queen's Park. The shade looked inviting. He could kill some time sitting in the park for a while. It would give him a good chance to think. And to calm down.

He walked along St. Joseph and crossed Queen's Park Circle to the park.

Lofty maples rose sixty feet high. After last Friday's rain, the grass under the trees was lush and green.

He walked to the middle of the park where a bronze statue of King Edward VII, Victoria's son, stood amid its own bed of impatiens. The king rode a bronze horse. Gilbert found a bench, sat down, and looked up at the trees. He took a few deep breaths, and caught a whiff of hot dogs from the hot dog vendor down the way. A woman in a tight track outfit practiced tae kwon do by a tree. She looked good, and she knew she looked good, and she wasn't fooling Gilbert in the least. Exhibitionism took many forms, as he well knew from working in the Sex Crimes Unit years ago.

He thought of Regina. He knew he could trust Regina. They'd gone through so much together. A gray squirrel jumped onto the bench and approached him boldly. He wished he had some bread crumbs for the little guy. Regina would have her reasons, and they would be good reasons, and her reasons would explain away all this ridiculous anxiety.

He spent another hour in the park. He bought an iced tea from a roadside vendor. He walked slowly back to headquarters, his mind going round in circles.

He signed out one of the Luminas and drove home. He brought the printed e-mails with him.

The Windstar was in the drive—Regina was in the house already. But when he went inside, he couldn't find her anywhere.

Jennifer sat in the den reading the latest John Grisham novel.

"Is your mother anywhere around?" he asked.

His twenty-year-old looked up from her legal thriller.

"You're both home?" she complained, as if she resented having her privacy invaded. "What are you *both* doing home?"

"We're having lunch together," he said.

Jennifer went back to reading. "She's in the backyard," she said. "Fighting the war of the weeds."

He went into the kitchen, opened the sliding glass doors, and stepped out onto the cedar deck. Regina, wearing a straw sun hat and canvas gardening gloves, stooped over the garden, diligently digging away at fescue and crabgrass. The temperature was punishing back here. A cicada whirred in the birch tree. The Galloway teens and some friends talked about something or other next door by the pool. The smell of chlorine, not unpleasant, sweetened the air. A hornet landed on the barbecue, a brief touchdown, then flew off, sinister and dark in the bright sunshine.

He walked quietly over the grass to Regina. The garden glowed with the last of the irises and the first of the poppies. In the back bed near the compost, Regina's young tomato plants grew up through their metal frames. Regina turned. She got up. Her fair face was flushed with heat.

He stopped.

"Hi," he said.

"Hi," she said.

She grinned, but it was an unsure grin. She rubbed her nose with the back of her gloved hand. A bag of Miracle-Gro sat on the grass next to her.

"Well?" she said.

"I found out about you and Boyd," he said.

She stared at him across the sunlit yard from under the shade of her hat brim.

"I thought you might," she said.

She gave him a weak shrug, then waited. He lifted the envelope of e-mails and handed it to her.

"Here," he said, approaching her, dimly noting that the grass was speckled with white clover like stars in a green sky. "Your e-mails. At least what we've found of them so far."

Regina took the envelope, pulled out the e-mails, and

glanced through them quickly. Her lips came together, the same way they sometimes did when she marked test papers at the kitchen table. She flipped through each e-mail a second time, speed-reading them in that way she had, then handed them back to Gilbert.

"I didn't want to upset you," she said.

"What do you mean?"

"He called me. Back in January. He was in bad shape." She gestured at the e-mails. "If you think there's something more than just friendship in those e-mails, you can rest easy. I should have told you. But I knew how much it would upset you."

"Why would he call you?" asked Gilbert. "After twenty-three years?"

She glanced to one side where a bumblebee hovered like a speck of gold above one of her white peonies.

"He was in bad shape," she said. "He needed someone to talk to."

Gilbert frowned. "So you went to see him?"

"Barry, I had to. There's nothing more pathetic than a fifty-seven-year-old drug addict. I do drug counseling at the school. I thought I could help him. Until I realized he was beyond help."

"If he needed help, he should have gone to a rehab center. Or to his doctor."

"I urged him to do both," she said. "He said he would, but he never did. I understand now that he just wanted my attention. I really wanted to help him. I was so shocked when I saw him. He looked about eighty years old. I never knew drugs could mummify a person like that."

This, then, sounded characteristic of Regina. She was a

source of succor to a lot of people, himself included. Boyd had tapped into that, not because he ever planned to stop drugs, just because he wanted some of her female attention. When someone called for help, she was there, no questions asked. He believed her story, every word of it.

"You could have trusted me with this," he said.

"I didn't want to upset you," she said.

This, too, was characteristic of Regina. She went to unbelievable lengths to spare anybody the smallest upset.

"You still should have told me," he said. "I'm here to share your burdens. And Boyd's a big one."

She looked away. "I know what he did to you," she said. "I didn't want him touching you in any way ever again. I thought I would see him once or twice, try to do what I could for him, and that would be it. But Glen gets so needy. Once or twice turned into a half dozen times. When I found out he was murdered, I knew it was just a matter of time before you discovered what I'd done. And I was dreading it. Several times I came close to telling you. But then I always held back, thinking I could somehow spare you."

He shook his head. He knew he had to tell her about the scarf, that it was more than just the e-mails, and that a whole silly set of coincidences had inadvertently put her, at least technically, on their list of suspects.

"Sometimes life has a way . . ." But he didn't finish because he saw Regina was really upset. "It's okay," he said. He stroked her cheek with the back of his hand. "This is just one of those things."

"I don't know how he could have destroyed himself so badly."

He remembered Boyd's corpse, the eyeliner around his eyes, his wrinkled face, the track marks on his arms, the painted toenails, a man prematurely aged by abuse, and that pricey Italian scarf around his neck.

"You're missing a scarf, aren't you?" he said.

"Pardon?"

"A fancy Italian scarf you bought in Hazelton Lanes in February."

At first she was puzzled, but then a look of incredulous horror came to her face as she realized what he was talking about.

"You're kidding," she said. She gave the garden a fretful glance. "Shit."

"Don't worry about it. I'm going to smooth it over."

"I'm sorry, Barry."

"Don't worry."

"It's going to be awkward for you," she said.

"Tim just wants to . . . you know . . . with all the press attention, he doesn't want any surprises."

She glanced hopelessly at the fescue. "Do you want me to phone Tim?" she asked. "I'll speak to him, if you want. I hope he seriously doesn't think I had anything to do with Glen's murder. I was wondering where that scarf went. Let me call Tim."

"No, it's all right," said Gilbert. "I just thought you better know. I'll smooth it over. I'll tell him you were trying to help Boyd, and that should be enough."

GILBERT VISITED THE PRETTY HOUSE on Regal Road the following day to speak to Magda Barcos about her fugitive brother.

They sat on the back deck. The back garden was a perfect floral showcase. The flower beds to the left grew festively with poppies and irises. Five pygmy fruit trees shaded the weed-free grass. A garden shed, made of white and green aluminum, girded by two compost bins, stood off to one side. Hydrangea climbed the fence.

Mrs. Barcos, a stout widow dressed in black, came out the sliding glass doors with a tray of lemonade and a bowl of grapes. Magda sat there rigidly, back erect, knees together, fists clenched on her lap.

"*Esto te calmaria a ti y a tu amigo,*" said Mrs. Barcos.

"*Gracias, Mama,*" said Magda.

Mrs. Barcos paused, glanced at Gilbert, then turned back to her daughter as she put the grapes and lemonade on the table.

"*Esta todo bien?*" she asked.

"*Sí, Mama,*" said Magda. "*Todo esta bien.*" A strained grin came to Magda's face. "*Mama, porque no vas adentro? Esta muy caliente para ti.*"

Mrs. Barcos paused. She obviously sensed all was not right. "*Sí,*" she said. "*Sí.*"

The old Colombian woman went back into the cool interior of the house with a look of extreme reservation on her face. Magda turned to Gilbert with the suddenness of a bird and gave him a sweet but nervous smile.

"Is my brother going to be all right?" she asked. "That other detective . . . Ballantine."

"Bannatyne," corrected Gilbert.

"He was so mean."

Gilbert shrugged. "He's a bit old-school," he said. "He likes to shake things loose fast." Gilbert cast a covert glance toward Mrs. Barcos's retreating form. "Your mother doesn't know yet, does she?"

Magda's green eyes narrowed in distress as she pursed her lips. "No," she said. She flexed her delicate shoulders forward, as if she were cold. "And it is my sincere wish we keep it from her as long as possible."

Though her impulse was noble, Gilbert knew it was ultimately futile. No doubt Magda characterized her brother differently than Al Valdez did. A wasp flew in from the garden, hovered above the grapes, then banked into the sunlit yard.

"Detective Bannatyne says you . . . that you were shocked," said Gilbert.

Her distress deepened.

"I don't believe half the things Detective Bannatyne told me," she replied, her lower lip curling. "My brother's not a monster. He looks after us. He's given us a new life in Canada. We are happy. We have money. We have nice things."

Gilbert sighed. What he had here was a mountain to move. Clouding the mix was his own personal goal of wiping the Boyd case off the board as fast as possible by putting Barcos behind bars quickly.

"I believe Colombia uses the Napoleonic system of justice," said Gilbert. "A suspect is guilty until proven innocent. It works the other way around here. In Canada, a suspect is innocent until proven guilty. Your brother's been accused of some crimes, but that doesn't mean he's guilty, despite what Bob Bannatyne says. As far as I'm concerned, Oscar's innocent. I'll believe he's innocent until twelve jurors tell me otherwise. In the meantime, he's at considerable risk. He should turn himself in before he gets hurt. Do you have any idea where he is?"

She gazed at the grapes on the table. "No," she said.

He again sensed her innocence, realized it wouldn't even occur to Magda to lie to him, but he chipped away at her anyway.

"He hasn't called here?" he asked.

"No."

"When was the last time you saw him?" asked Gilbert.

"A week ago. Or maybe ten days ago. Before that storm. In any case, he hasn't called here. I haven't seen him. I've phoned everywhere I can think of, even back home, but he's nowhere to be found." She turned to him with a frantic look in her eyes, and gripped the arm of her wicker chair. "I'm worried about him. I wish he would call home. Mama's nerves have never been so bad. He's usually good about calling."

Tears collected in her eyes. She wiped them away. God, he hated this, to see her suffering like this, and to have to disillusion her so unflinchingly about her brother. He could see Magda loved her brother unconditionally. It didn't matter to her if he was a murderer.

"Do you think he might call you?" he asked in a softer tone.

"I hope he does," she said.

"Because if he does . . ." He lifted a glass of lemonade, the glass beading with condensation, and took a sip. "You should urge him to surrender. He's only going to make matters worse for himself if he runs or hides."

"Yes, of course, I will try to make him understand this," she said. "But Oscar has a temper. And he's stubborn. And reckless. And he always thinks he's right."

Gilbert let her sit a bit. A robin landed on the bird feeder, but when it saw them, it flew away, and observed them from a safer perch on top of the garden shed.

"I would hate to . . . to see him hurt," said Gilbert. *Let the gentle manipulation begin,* he thought. "I would hate to think he would try to fight the police. There's no way he could win. And if he tried to fight us with a firearm . . . well . . . that would be foolhardy." Gilbert took out his card and gave it to Magda. "Here's my number." He flipped the card over. "And here's my home number. Call whenever you like. If you hear from him, and if you think you can get him to surrender peacefully . . . because I know it would break your heart . . . and your mother's heart . . . if he somehow tried to fight it out with police and

wound up getting hurt, or maybe even shot. If he wants to surrender to me personally, then, sure, we can do it that way. All I
want to do is see him home safe again. I'll do everything in my
power to make sure he doesn't get hurt if you can get him to
cooperate with me."

Lombardo dropped by Gilbert's house unexpectedly on Wednesday
night while Gilbert, Regina, and the girls were having a barbecue
out back.

"What are you doing here?" asked Gilbert. He glanced past
Joe's shoulder. "And who's in your car?"

"Virginia," said Lombardo. "I'm taking her to the Molson
Amphitheater to see Matchbox Twenty."

"Matchbox Twenty?"

"They're a band, Barry," Lombardo said. "Virginia lives only
five minutes from here. I thought I'd stop by to give you some
good news. Also to get you to sign this."

Lombardo handed him a document.

"A consent-to-search?" said Gilbert.

Lombardo chuckled. "I don't actually plan on searching your
house, Barry. Tim just wants it in the case file as a kind of . . .
backup. In case anybody ever looks at our paperwork. It's got to
add up. We've got to show that we've at least looked at Regina."

"Don't you think that's going overboard?"

"Tim's the boss," said Lombardo. "We've got to humor him."

"Okay, but I think . . . it's really a bit much."

"What can we do? You've got to sign it. Tim says so."

"Tim's going to yank me from this case, isn't he?"

Joe shrugged. "I don't know. But the further we go, the less promising it looks."

Gilbert shook his head. Every so often, with Tim running things, he didn't feel like a member of a special club anymore. He signed the consent-to-search and gave it back to Lombardo

"Why didn't you just wait till tomorrow at work?" he asked.

"Because I was in the neighborhood, I had it in my brief-case, and because I've also got something else to show you." Lombardo pulled out a parking receipt from the Toronto Parking Authority, vouchered in a Ziploc bag, and waved it in front of Gilbert's face with a smile. "You know where I found this?" he asked.

"Where?"

"Inside Judy Pelaez's rented Buick Skylark."

"And how did you get inside Judy's Skylark?"

"With a slim-jim," he said. "How else?"

"No, I mean . . . legally."

"Her lying to us about Scaramouche was enough probable cause. Justice Lembeck signed a warrant on the car for me."

Gilbert examined the receipt. He read the big words: LEAVE ON DASH—THIS SIDE UP. The expiration date was the first of June at 10:30 P.M. The time of issue was at 7:46 P.M. The street was McCaul Street, just around the corner from Glen Boyd Interna-tional Artists. All over the city, automated ticket dispensers, which printed dashboard receipts like this one, were replacing the old coin-operated parking meters. And now this dashboard receipt was evidence. Judy Pelaez had parked two blocks away from the crime scene in and around the time of Boyd's murder.

"Joe, this is great."

"Do you mind if I use your can?" asked Lombardo. "I really got to go."

"Go ahead. But can I ask you a question?"

"Sure."

"Why did you cut your hair so short? I've never seen it so short. People who get their hair cut that short usually do it for one reason. They have lice."

Lombardo frowned. "I don't have lice," he said. "I got it cut because now you can't even notice the bald spot at the back. I look like a regular guy."

"You look like a skinhead, Joe."

"No, seriously, Virginia likes it. She can't stop rubbing her hands all over my head."

"You should have left it alone."

"Barry, I had to do something. I'm going bald."

"You *are* bald, Joe, now that you have that haircut."

While Lombardo was upstairs in the bathroom, Gilbert walked into the living room and flipped through Jennifer's CDs. He found the CD he was looking for, *Mad Season*, by Matchbox Twenty. He studied the CD artwork. A chubby little man dressed in blue ballet slippers, a Roman toga, and an orange cap with rabbit ears walked a toy peacock on a leash. The artwork was sur-real, in a way much of the old psychedelic album art had been surreal back in the late nineteen-sixties. Things hadn't changed that much. Kids today thought they were so hip. But the univer-sal backbeat, loud guitars, and screaming vocals had been around for a long time.

He heard Joe come downstairs. Gilbert went into the hall. He held up the CD.

"See?" he said. "I'm not as square as you think."

Lombardo gave him a doubtful look. "That's not your CD," he said.

"Sure it is."

"It's Jennifer's," said Lombardo.

"How do you know?"

"Because I bought it for her last Christmas."

"Well . . . I listen to it," Gilbert said.

"When do you ever listen to it?" asked Lombardo.

Gilbert let the CD sink to his side. "Whenever she puts it on and I'm forced to."

Lombardo grinned. "See you tomorrow, old-timer," he said.

Gilbert knocked on Judy Pelaez's hotel room door. The peephole darkened. The chain-lock rattled, the bolt slid back, and the door opened.

"Did you find out?" asked Judy.

His eyes narrowed. She wore men's clothing several sizes too big for her: off-white pleated pants, a mauve blazer of 1980s vintage, and a yellow T-shirt that was faded from too many washings. She wasn't wearing her glasses and her eyes were puffy. He wondered how many crying jags she'd suffered through since coming to Toronto.

"Did I find out what?" he asked.

"Who the other woman was?" She seemed annoyed that he

wouldn't instantly know what she was talking about. "The one Glen was having his fling with."

He felt sorry for her. She'd been driving herself nuts with jealousy all this time. "No," he said. "Not yet."

She peered at him more closely. "What are you looking at?" she asked.

"Your clothes," he said.

She looked at her clothes, obviously pleased with them. An odd grin came to her face, like Gloria Swanson's grin in *Sunset Boulevard*.

"These are Glen's clothes," she said. "I wear them sometimes. Especially when I'm feeling blue. They make me feel close to him."

"Oh," he said, not offering comment, but recognizing this quirk as another sad symptom of her unhealthy obsession with Boyd. "Can I come in?"

"Are you through with his body?" she asked. "Can I bury him yet?"

She said this as if she had an unquestionable right to his body, as if it were not only the body of her former husband but also her personal property.

"No," he said. "We're not through. Like I said, the coroner's run into a snag, and it's going to take longer than usual."

Her face grew grave, but she finally nodded. At least she seemed to understand that the process had to be careful. She stepped out of the way and he came inside. She looked tired.

"I just want to go home," she said. "I want to see my children. How much longer will I have to wait?" She closed the door.

"I've already contacted a funeral director. We're making arrangements. It's going to be big. Glen knew a lot of people. The media have called me about it. They're eager to cover it."

Gilbert sighed. "I was originally hoping we might get it wrapped up by the end of next week," he said. "But I suspect it might take longer now. And I'm afraid you haven't been entirely honest with us either, Ms. Pelaez."

Judy grew still. The corners of her lips sank. Those famous lips hadn't aged, he thought again. They were still full and enticing, the lips of a woman who had once been a superstar but who was now just sad and lonely, and torn apart by a man who had ruined her life.

"Since you obviously think you know something, Mr. Detective," she said, "why don't you explain it to me?"

"We spoke to the manager and the maitre d' at Scaramouche," he said. "They told us you never showed up."

Her eyes widened. "I don't think so," she said. Her irritation was palpable; he could see she wasn't particularly fond of restaurant people. "I was there, and every one of the hired help saw me." No, she didn't like restaurant people at all—the derision in her voice proved it. "It's not my fault that dumb-ass maitre d' can't remember me."

He remained unswayed. "You have a famous face," he said. "I'm sure if he saw you, he would remember you. You're Judy Pelaez. People know you."

"I was wearing sunglasses and a hat. And people don't know me that well anymore. Especially young people. That maitre d' had to be all of twenty. He knows Christina Aguilera better than he knows me."

"Even with sunglasses and a hat—"

She raised her hands, stopping him. "I'm sorry, I was there. Whether you believe me or not is beside the point. I was sitting at the third table down. Go back and tell the maitre d' that. See if he remembers me then."

He pulled out the vouchered parking receipt and showed it to her.

"We found this in your car," he said. "It's a parking receipt from the night of June first. Care to explain it?"

It took a moment, but she finally deduced the implication of the parking receipt.

She rested her hand on the dresser beside the door. The sleeve of Boyd's mauve blazer lifted. He saw a tenser bandage around her left wrist. The detail stuck, and he filed it away. A petite woman like Judy Pelaez would have had to use a lot of force to cause even the minimal trauma around Boyd's neck, and she might have injured her wrist in the attempt.

"I was still at Scaramouche," she insisted, as if she now wished to continue their previous altercation as a way to avoid a new one.

He sighed. He wished she'd stop being so flighty and defensive.

"Judy . . . why don't you just tell me the truth? We want to eliminate you, that's all. We don't want to waste unnecessary effort on you. We want to catch your husband's killer quickly. You'll go home sooner. Back to Morningstar and Delta."

She moved around, walking as if in a dream, and sat on the sofa. She gazed sightlessly at some blank music paper on the table. She looked so small in Boyd's clothes.

"I'm not lying," she said, her voice now softer, her tone hurt, as if she couldn't understand why he was being so cruelly persistent with her. "I was at Scaramouche. But I didn't come back to the hotel, like I told you before. That part was a . . . a fib. I didn't think it mattered. I didn't think you'd go snooping in my car. I forgot about that parking receipt. I . . . I didn't want to confuse the issue . . . because I . . . I couldn't see the point." She gave him a withering glance. "I didn't want you to waste unnecessary effort on me," she said, mimicking him perfectly.

He came over and sat in the chair opposite the sofa. "You have to tell us the truth, Judy . . . no matter how confusing or . . . or pointless it might seem to you." He took out his notebook. "So you left Scaramouche and you drove to GBIA at what time?"

The color rose to her face and she looked as if she were about to snarl.

"What does it matter?" she said. "This was to be our reconciliation dinner. This was going to be our big let-bygones-be-bygones dinner. This dinner was where we were both going to happily agree that the only thing left for us to do with the twenty or so years we had left was to grow old together. We talked about that over the phone. He said that's what would happen. I thought this time he was really telling the truth. And then he stood me up. Not only that, he's having a fling with another woman. I should have known not to trust him. I should have stayed in San Francisco with Morningstar and Delta. Now he's gone and gotten himself killed. What a bastard."

Gilbert tried again. "What time did you leave Scaramouche?" he asked.

"How should I know?" she said. "I don't look at my watch every second. I sometimes don't even wear a watch. I hate watches."

"Was it around eight o'clock?" he ventured.

"Around that," she said.

"So you left Scaramouche, parked on McCaul Street, and then you walked over to GBIA?" he asked.

"Yes."

"What time did you arrive there?" he asked.

"You tell me. You've got my parking receipt. Isn't there a time on that?"

"What did you do once you got to GBIA?" he asked.

She smiled suddenly. Her quick changes of mood, seemingly orchestrated for effect, disquieted him.

"I *wished* I would have strangled him," she said, her voice strangely perky. "If anybody had a right to strangle him, I did. Never mind the big things. It was all the little things he did to me. Over the years. Grinding me down." The perkiness left her voice and she now sounded serious. "I *should* have strangled him. I should have stabbed him, or shot him, or taken an ax to him. But I didn't. I just yelled at him. How lame can you get? Yelled at him like I always do. He hardly listened to me this time. He was distracted about something. He kept on going into the office and looking out the window. I asked him if he was expecting someone, like that other woman, and he said no, and then told me he wished I would just go away, that he had things to do that night that didn't involve me." Her face reddened. "Can you imagine? After he had invited me all the way from San Francisco for our reconciliation dinner. It was more than I could stand. I picked up the phone and threw it at him. After that, I stormed out of there. Old lame Judy thinking she was making a point."

GILBERT SAT WITH NINA THE following Tuesday evening in the waiting room of Dominion Medical Laboratories. They were here to get her second test done. The waiting room was crowded, and Gilbert realized it would be a while before Nina's name was called. He had his arm around her. Nina pressed her cheek against his shoulder, something she hadn't done in a long time. The waiting room television played the *MuchMusic* station. Five black dudes rapped suavely, gesticulating with fork-fingered hands, wearing big baggy pants, medallions on gold chains, and backward baseball hats—the whole South Central L.A. uniform.

"You all right?" he asked Nina.

He could tell things were getting to her, just sitting here, hoping her name would be called next.

"I'm nervous," she said.

"You're going to beat it," he said.

"How can you be so sure?" she asked.

"Because I'm your father, and I know you're going to beat it."

"I don't get your logic."

Everything had to make sense to Nina, or she unabashedly challenged it.

"There's no logic," he said. "It's just a gut feeling."

She sighed. "You've been a cop too long, Dad. I'm getting sick of your gut feelings. Is Dr. MacPherson going to call us at the cottage when he gets the results?"

"Yes," he said. "He has our number up there."

"What if it turns out to be positive?" she said.

"It's not going to be positive. It's going to be negative. You wait and see."

"I'm not so sure," she said.

The five black dudes on the TV finished. Who should come on next but Phil Thompson—a new video from *Phil Thompson Unplugged* called *Old Dance Partner*.

"Check it out," said the veejay. "Phil Thompson in a mellow mood on his new CD, grasping for gold. That's right, *Unplugged* reached certified gold status last week, a first for Phil since *Another Party Girl* back in 1979."

"I don't believe it," said Gilbert. "It's Phil Thompson."

Nina peered at the TV. "Who?" she said.

He listened to the song. Phil Thompson had returned to his roots—that fundamental building block of all good rock and roll, the acoustic guitar. The insistent way he played the guitar gave the song a catchy rhythm. Nina nodded her head to the beat. Phil's great height gave him a presence on video many recording artists might envy. The video's visual mood of nostalgia, enhanced by the use of a yellow camera filter, fit the song perfectly. Phil, dressed in a suit, his hair long and flowing, danced in classic ballroom style, maneuvering a beautiful young woman in a gypsy dress around a honky-tonk dance floor with the ease and grace of a latter-day Fred Astaire. Gilbert was glad to see a man in his fifties looking so spry. It gave him hope.

"He's kind of dreamy," said Nina.

With that, Gilbert knew Phil had as good as sold a hundred thousand records. Nina was never wrong when it came to pop singers. If she thought Phil Thompson was dreamy, then a million other seventeen-year-old girls would think he was dreamy, too. That meant they would be down at record stores buying his new solo effort sooner rather than later. And that meant Phil Thompson was definitely on the comeback trail.

On Friday, the day before Gilbert went on holiday, he sat at his desk going through some of his other cases, making sure he wasn't leaving any loose ends before traveling north. He was alone. All the other detectives were either at lunch or out working cases. Two o'clock in the afternoon, and the city slow-cooked in the humid heat. The weatherman said the mercury would rise even higher. Gilbert couldn't wait to head north so he could leave all this heat behind. He wanted to go home early, but Nowak wanted to meet with him at three. He was anxious about the meeting. After signing a consent-to-search for his own home, he felt he was on shaky ground.

George Monaco, from the mailroom, a middle-aged Filipino man with prematurely silver hair, came in with a trolley full of mail.

"Busy?" asked George.

"All the time," said Gilbert.

George lifted a parcel off his trolley. "I got one for you, man." He handed the package to Gilbert. "I don't know," he said. "Smells like coffee." George's smile got bigger. "Like, wake up and smell the coffee, man."

"Thanks, George," said Gilbert.

"No problem, man."

George wheeled his trolley away.

Gilbert smelled the package. It indeed smelled like coffee. It was marked ATTN: HOMICIDE, C/O DETECTIVE BARRY GILBERT, in block capitals, with a return address of Mavis Bank, Jamaica, W.I. Gilbert figured it out a moment later. Blue Mountain coffee. From Daniel Lynn's uncle in Jamaica. He was really starting to like Lynn. He opened the package. The package was red, with gold lettering. The Jamaican flag and the Union Jack crisscrossed at the top. Gilbert took a long lingering whiff of the package. He was going to try and enjoy the smell of that coffee as much as he could. Especially because it was probably going to be the high point of his day.

Lombardo came in five minutes after he got his coffee. The young detective glanced around the Homicide Office.

"We alone?" he asked.

Gilbert motioned at all the empty desks. "Everyone's out doing things," he said.

Lombardo grabbed a chair and sat down. His face was stiff

and unflinching, the way it got whenever he had bad news to convey.

"You know that blond hair we found in Boyd's bed?" he said.

"Yes?"

"We found a match."

"Judy Pelaez?"

"No," said Lombardo. "Regina Gilbert."

Lombardo let that bomb explode for a while. The shock waves reverberated. Gilbert had to give it several seconds before it settled. He pulled his thoughts together. Bomb or not, he didn't lose faith in his wife, never believed, not once, that she was anything but faithful to him, even with the presence of her blond hair in Boyd's bed. Hairs got all over the place. Regina's hair in Boyd's bed could have had any number of explanations. Regina was his wife. She was his religion. And he would believe in her always.

Then it dawned on him—a *match*. A match would need a comparison hair.

He figured it out instantly.

"The consent-to-search," he said. "When you went up to my bathroom."

Lombardo nodded guiltily. "I'm sorry, Barry," he said. "I had to. Tim pressured me."

"Shit," said Gilbert.

The corners of Lombardo's eyes creased, his lips drew back, and he seemed to struggle for words.

"I'm a bit caught in the middle here, Barry," said Lombardo, "in case you haven't noticed."

"As soon as we find Barcos, this case will be closed."

Lombardo took a deep breath and sighed. "Funny you should mention Barcos. The skin under the fingernails of Boyd's right hand?" he said.

"It belongs to Barcos?" said Gilbert, his brow rising with hope.

"No," said Lombardo.

"Really?" Gilbert was disappointed. "Who does it belong to?"

"We don't know yet. But it doesn't belong to Barcos."

Gilbert glanced out the window sullenly. "This is bullshit, Joe," he said.

Lombardo rubbed his hand over the nap of his now extremely short hair and looked toward the front of the office with an expression of supreme helplessness.

"Don't you think . . . that with this particular case . . . you know . . . the emotional baggage, and all."

"I'm fine with it," said Gilbert.

"I don't know, Barry . . . this blond hair."

"Hairs get all over the place," said Gilbert.

"I know, but—"

"Why shouldn't one of Regina's hairs be down there?" he asked. "We know she was down there to help him with his . . . his problem. She told us so, plus those e-mails spell it out. I see no reason to be surprised by the comparison result, or to even think it suggests a smoking gun."

"Yes, but when you add the blond hair to everything else . . . the scarf, the perfume, you losing her at the Royal Alex . . ." Lombardo's lips drew back. "Regina's a major roadblock in all this. That's why we're having a meeting with Tim at three. To talk about Regina."

Gilbert's eyes narrowed. "You're going to be at the meeting, too?" he said. "I thought it was going to be only me and Tim."

"Ling's been after him on this one."

"Tim doesn't have to worry about Regina," insisted Gilbert.

"I know, but he said this new evidence is diagrammatic of Regina's culpability. His exact words."

"Diagrammatic?" said Gilbert. "That's the word he used?"

"I thought it was weird, too."

Gilbert stood up, his chair rolling back with force. He slid his hands into his pockets and walked to the window.

"It's not a duck, Joe," he said. "It's not even diagrammatic of a duck."

"Try to put yourself in Tim's shoes," said Lombardo. "He's got to be concerned about how all this looks. Technically, Regina's a suspect. And if someone like Roffey were to sniff that out, even though we all know Regina would never hurt a flea, it wouldn't look good, especially because you're the primary on the case. That's what Tim's got to think about."

"I think he's wasting his time."

"He wants the paperwork to add up, that's all," said Lombardo.

Gilbert swung around, his hands coming out of his pockets in a gesture of supplication.

"We haven't even got the toxicology results back yet," he said. "That's paperwork. And okay, the skin doesn't belong to Barcos. So we have to positively identify it, and that's more paperwork. Paperwork we should do before we even think of looking at Regina in any serious way."

"Tim knows that," said Lombardo. "And in fact he's ordered a comparison-DNA test of the skin against Regina's hair so we can rule her out."

"Christ, Joe. I can't believe this."

"Tim just wants all the pieces to fit together so there won't be an uproar when the case goes to trial."

"This is bullshit. Judy Pelaez had a big fight with Boyd that night. I bet that skin belongs to her. If we're going to run a comparison test against Regina, we have to run one against Judy as well."

"It's already been requisitioned," said Lombardo. "I found some hair in her rented car."

"So when we run the sample against Judy's hair, that'll be it. We can leave Regina alone."

Lombardo's face sank. He looked positively woebegone. "Actually . . . there's something else . . . Tim wants me to show you this . . . Ling's seen it, and he's really concerned about it."

His young partner got up, walked over to his desk, lifted a manila folder full of papers, and came back.

Gilbert's eyes narrowed apprehensively. "What's that?" he asked.

Lombardo sat on the edge of Gilbert's desk, opened the manila folder, withdrew a half dozen sheets, and handed them to Gilbert.

"These are additional e-mail printouts," said Lombardo. "We hacked through more of Boyd's e-mail folders. Read the top one. The rest of them really don't say much. But this one . . . I don't know, Barry. Regina sent it to Boyd on May thirtieth, two days before Boyd was murdered. Go ahead. Read it."

Gilbert read the short missive out loud. " 'Glen. I'll do any-thing—*anything*—to stop you from telling my husband about Marseilles. RG.' "

Gilbert looked at Lombardo. Distress spread through his nervous system like hemlock through Socrates. "Marseilles?" he said. "What the hell is Marseilles?"

"It's a city in France," said Lombardo.

"I know . . . but what does she mean by it? Marseilles. She never said anything to me about Marseilles. What the hell is she talking about?"

Lombardo gazed at the other sheets.

"I read through all those other e-mails looking for clues," he said. "I found a few more mentions of Marseilles, but nothing that really told me what she meant by it, or what, if anything, might have happened there." Lombardo weaved a bit, like a boxer in the ring, something he occasionally did in a difficult sit-uation. "So I had to use a different approach." He swung his hand toward the phone. "I had to track down people who knew Regina from way back when, people who might know something about Marseilles. You told me about Michelle Morrison. So I tracked Michelle Morrison down and talked to her."

"You talked to Michelle Morrison?"

"She's got this beautiful flower shop downtown."

Gilbert nodded, even as the hemlock advanced further through his body. "Stacy Todd told me she was in the flower business."

Lombardo nodded. "Anyway . . . I asked her about Marseilles." Lombardo looked at the e-mails again and shook his head. "At first she was reluctant to tell me anything. But when I explained how she might make matters worse if she kept it to herself, and how she actually might end up hurting Regina, she took me to her office and told me what I needed to know." Lombardo tapped the manila folder a few times. "This is so awkward . . . this is like . . . your own personal business. And I wish I didn't have to be mixed up in it, because I know it's going to hurt you, and I don't want to hurt you, Barry. But Tim asked me to brief you about it before we had our meeting, so I guess I'm going to have to . . . and . . . well . . ." Lombardo looked him in the face, a belligerent curl coming to his lip. "Regina made a trip from Aix-en-Provence to Marseilles with Boyd in September of 1978 to have an abortion."

Every so often the tone of the street crept into Lombardo's voice, what they called *Ital-Inglese* in Toronto's old Calabrian districts. Rough, boomy, and aggressive, Joe's voice conveyed the essential fact, and the essential fact was like another dose of hemlock to Gilbert.

He sat down, leaned forward, rested his elbows on his desk, and put his head in his hands. He felt like this was his own personal Cuban Missile Crisis.

"And it was Boyd's child?" he asked.

"It was Boyd's child," said Lombardo. "I didn't want to tell you, and I told Tim that, but in the context of this e-mail, he insisted I had to. He's the boss. You can see she was trying to protect you . . . but the way she did it . . . it doesn't look good, does it? Especially when we look at all this other crazy evidence.

She was willing to do anything to stop him from telling you about Marseilles. *Anything*."

"Joe . . . I just want to crawl under a rock."

Gilbert didn't feel sorry for himself. He felt sorry for Regina.

He remembered how broken Regina had been when she'd returned from France: skinny, drawn, and as pale as parchment. He recalled how she hadn't left the house for a whole month, how she had never smiled, and how she hadn't even had the energy to walk up and down the stairs. He remembered her overwhelming sense of hopelessness, and the crying jags that would go on for hours. He would never forget how he would sometimes wake up in the middle of the night and find her sitting on the edge of the bed, staring at nothing, unable to sleep. Regina loved children. Never mind the great unsettled abortion debate. Politics aside, aborting a child was against Regina's nature, and he now believed that Boyd had coerced her somehow, talked her into it against her will. No wonder she had returned from France in such bad shape. The guilt she must have come home with!

Joe offered some support. "I hope you and Regina . . . you know . . . I hope you can work this out."

"We leave for Kipawa tomorrow," he said. "We'll have a lot of time to talk. And Joe, it's not going to shake us apart. Our marriage is the strongest thing we have, and we're both smart enough to know it. I just wish she would have come to me sooner about this. I wish she would have realized she could have spoken to me. And this e-mail." He tapped the sheet. "I wouldn't call it a stellar example of her better judgment. As you say, it supports all this other crazy evidence."

* * *

Nowak entered the Homicide office at a quarter to three with his small, sleek attaché case carried primly at his side. He walked directly into his office, looking at neither Gilbert nor Lombardo. Lombardo was answering some of his voice mails. Gilbert tried to work, but was too upset to concentrate. He took a few deep breaths, but it didn't help. He wasn't mad at Regina. Or angry at Boyd. Rather, he was annoyed with himself because, all professional pride aside, he hadn't detached himself enough from his feelings about Boyd to run an unbiased investigation.

Fifteen minutes later, at exactly three o'clock, Nowak leaned out his door.

"Barry?" he called. "Joe?" The staff inspector ran his schedule with military precision.

The partners rose and went into Nowak's office.

Nowak gestured at the two chairs.

"Have a seat," he said.

The detectives sat down. Nowak took his own chair and glanced at his computer screen. He rubbed his thin lips with his index finger, his thick wedding band gleaming in the overhead fluorescent lights, then turned to Joe. A calm grin came to his face.

"You told him?" he said.

Lombardo nodded. "I told him."

Nowak looked at Gilbert. The staff inspector's expression softened.

"You okay?" he asked.

"I'm still working through it," said Gilbert.

Nowak nodded, put his elbows on the edge of his desk, interlocked his fingers, and leaned forward, his eyes seeming to sharpen to fine points as he gazed at Gilbert.

"You go on holiday tomorrow, don't you?" he said.

"Yes, I do," said Gilbert.

"And you're gone for . . . how long?"

"A week."

"To Lake Kipawa?"

"Yes."

Nowak nodded reflectively. "It must be nice up there," he said. "I've never been to that part of Quebec. I have my cottage here in Ontario."

"It's everything you want a lake to be," said Gilbert.

"And you take the girls fishing?"

"Jennifer's okay with it, but Nina doesn't like the worms."

"I try to get my boys to come with me," said Nowak, "but I guess they're getting sick of the old man." His eyes grew pensive. He got back to business. "Seeing as you're going on holiday, Barry . . . and because the Boyd case is becoming . . . I don't know—" He turned to Joe. "A liability? Would that be the right word, Joe?"

Lombardo, put on the spot, shrugged vaguely. "I guess so," he said.

Gilbert already knew what was coming. "You're going to yank me, aren't you?" he said.

Nowak paused. He let his interlocked fingers drift apart, allowed his lips to separate in a patient and disappointed smile, and tapped his black desk blotter a few times.

"Barry . . ." The staff inspector cast for words. "I have no choice. I have to." He leaned back in his chair, a few lines creasing his otherwise habitually smooth forehead. He looked out the window where the air was shot through with a damp and choking haze, then turned to Gilbert with a practiced it's-not-my-fault look in his eyes. "I tried to keep you on it as long as I could . . . but now . . . under the circumstances, I just don't see how I can."

"I'm perfectly capable of solving this case, Tim," said Gilbert. "You don't have to yank me."

"Yes, but your wife's a suspect."

"Only in the technical sense," said Gilbert.

"What other sense is there?" asked Nowak.

"You know what I mean. My wife would never kill anyone. Sometimes it's not a duck, Tim."

"Yes, I know that, Barry," said Nowak. "And everyone knows your wife would never kill anyone. But there's a certain suggestive semblance in the evidence. I've talked it over with Deputy Chief Ling, and he agrees with me . . . that the evidence is diagrammatic of a certain . . ." Nowak shook his head. "Put it this way. Ling wants us to take a close look at Regina. And he feels we can't do that if you're the primary on the case. Ling wants results, and he wants them fast, particularly because Roffey and the *Star* can't leave it alone. Ling knows what Roffey might write if he finds out about your wife. We can't have a primary investigating a case where the primary's wife is actually a suspect, even if she's only a suspect in the . . . the technical sense. That's my rationale for yanking you. It has nothing to do with your competency. I know how much you value what you do. You're one of my best detectives. So don't think me yanking you is a reflection of what you've done on the case so far. It's not. It's just that when Ling and I looked at it . . . I mean, put yourself in our shoes. You've got a victim like Glen Boyd, a well-known and even international figure in the entertainment industry. Then you've got Ronald Roffey barking like a dog around our heels."

"We don't have to tell Roffey a thing," said Gilbert.

"We have to tell him something eventually. If we don't, he's going to dig, and Ling would just as soon avoid that."

"I wish the *Star* would fire that guy," said Gilbert.

"They're not going to fire him," said Nowak. "He's too good at unearthing compromising facts. And there are a lot of compromising facts in this case, all having to do with Regina. There's that e-mail about Marseilles. There's the blond hair, the scarf, and the perfume. And I know she went directly home from the theater on the night of the murder, but no one can conclusively verify that. So in the interests of doing what's best for the case, I really have to pull you, Barry. I have to minimize the risk of any fallout."

Gilbert stared at the Homicide Golf Open trophy on Nowak's desk.

"So what do you want me to do?" asked Gilbert. "Who's going to be the primary on the case now?"

Nowak and Lombardo looked relieved.

"Give all your stuff to Joe," said Nowak. "He and Gord are going to work on it. You'll be on regular rotation when you get back."

"Thanks, Tim," he said. He tapped his knee a few times. The others waited.

"Is there something else, Barry?" asked Nowak.

Gilbert wanted to protect Regina.

"Are we still going after Barcos?" he asked.

Because if he could manipulate the case, even from the outside, as a way of deflecting the investigation away from Regina, then at least he had to try. He wanted to spare Regina any unnecessary pain.

"Of course," said Nowak. "Barcos is high on our list. I'm sure he's our guy, even though we haven't got a match on the skin from the right hand on him."

"Okay. Good. And are we still going to offer him a deal on Deranga and Munoz if he's forthcoming about Boyd?"

Nowak turned to Lombardo. "Joe? Is that your game plan?"

"I've talked to Bob, and he's willing to go for it."

"Thanks, Joe," said Gilbert. "The case is yours. And Tim . . . I understand. I know you had to do this. I don't like it, it bugs the hell out of me, but I know you had no choice. I just hope we can get this thing over and done with quickly. Regina doesn't like thinking about Boyd and neither do I. If you have to talk to Regina, try to be sensitive about it." His throat tightened. "Especially if you have to talk to her about this Marseilles business. In hindsight, I can see it just about broke her to pieces. So let's make an effort to bury this one fast. Okay?"

ON THE HILL BEHIND THE cottage, where the cedar and silver birch eked out a meager existence in the small pockets of soil scattered over the scarred Precambrian granite, Gilbert and Regina, finally alone, talked things over. Wild blueberries and strawberries winked at them from under ferns and fireweed. Regina's plastic yogurt container was half full of wild blueberries.

Now that Gilbert had sketched it all in for her, she wouldn't turn his way, kept her back to him, her head protected by a straw hat and mosquito netting. The hill sloped to Lake Kipawa. Lake Kipawa sang its summer song—motorboats going back and forth to the marina. He stared at his wife's back. She wore a pink shirt, blue jeans, and the hiking boots from L.L. Bean he'd given her last Christmas. No, she wouldn't turn. The mention of Marseilles had paralyzed her. He hated to see it. It was as if some essential piece had crumpled inside her. She now looked small, vulnerable, ready to blow away in the next strong wind.

She dropped the container full of blueberries and they scattered down the hill—dark little racers, some tumbling smoothly over bare patches of prehistoric rock, others losing themselves in the grass and lichen. A kingfisher flew by, its crest feathers disproportionately large to its body, a streak of blue, black, and white in the sunny air. Regina sat down—suddenly, precipitiously—as if her legs couldn't support her anymore.

She cried. Her shoulders jerked. The black flies landed on her back, but were quickly repelled by Deep Woods Off. A wretched little sob escaped from somewhere underneath all that mosquito netting. Boyd, after all these years, could still hurt her. He grew more determined than ever to find Barcos, even though he wasn't the primary on the case anymore. Once they found Barcos, they could throw him to the Crown like a Christian to the lions, and Regina wouldn't have to worry about the old black mark in their lives anymore.

Gilbert heard the breaking of twigs and the rustling of leaves in the forest up the hill. He glanced over his shoulder. Something was up there. He feared it might be a bear. For one reason or another the Province of Quebec had canceled the bear hunt this spring. He'd been hearing that sound up there for the last fifteen minutes. For the first time in a long time he was actually worried about bears.

"And now you're more in the case file than ever," he said.

She still couldn't answer. He took a few steps toward her but stopped. He felt her *otherness*, the sense that, after all, she was a separate and unique person, not just his wife, not just the mother of his two children, but a singular entity, apart from him, someone he could ultimately never know, and who he could never really help.

"I tried to spare you this," she said at last. "I should have left Glen alone. I should have recognized the poison in his eyes the minute I saw him, but it was too late. I should have known he would just end up hurting us again. But I'm like a silly moth who flies too close to the fire. He was so pathetic. I had to help him."

Gilbert sat on the ground next to her. He saw a small green snake weave silently through the grass. Over the astringent scent of insect repellant, he caught a whiff of her perfume, *Dilys* by Laura Ashley.

"I don't know if Tim is seriously considering building a case against you or not," he said. "Tim is more or less doing what Ling tells him to do. And Ling wants to take a close look at you. So that's what Tim's doing."

But it was as if she hadn't heard him. "Marseilles . . . Marseilles," she said, chanting the name with despondency. "It was the worst thing that ever happened to me. I can't help thinking of that poor small child, and what I did to it. I can't believe I let Glen talk me into it. I should have refused. I should have come home all strung out and pregnant . . . and hope . . . hope that you would have taken pity on me as well as on that baby. If only I'd had the courage . . . and the common sense."

She couldn't go on. He put his arm around her. He heard some more rustling in the forest up the hill and glanced over his shoulder. What *was* that? Whatever it was, it was starting to get on his nerves. A huge oak tree, anomalous to the region, stood on top of the hill. The noise was coming from behind that tree. Was it really a bear? Were they about to be attacked? The thing rustled again. Regina stopped crying and looked over her own shoulder, her blue eyes growing apprehensive behind the mosquito netting.

"What was that?" she asked.

He turned around and looked toward the cottage, which sat on a knoll by the lake a quarter-kilometer away, its silver aluminum roof spotlight-bright in the sunshine. Given the distance, a bear would easily outrun them if they made a try for the cottage.

"I don't know," he said. "But I sure wish they hadn't canceled the bear hunt this year."

"I can hardly come out here now," admitted Regina.

He listened some more. He didn't hear anything.

"I think it's gone," he said.

Regina's shoulders eased. He pulled her nearer.

"It's okay, Reggie," he said.

"I'm sorry, Barry," she said, her voice torn. "I never . . . I just didn't want to . . . I didn't see the point of ever telling you because I thought it would just end up . . . hurting us. My mind was such a muddle in those days. Having an abortion was nearly a badge of feminism . . . and all the things I was reading at the time . . . Gloria Steinem, Germaine Greer, Marilyn French . . . as if my life wasn't dramatic enough already. I thought it would be okay. But it really killed me. It made me turn my back on all that counterculture stuff. All I wanted to do was come home and be a wife and a mother."

Gilbert sighed. "I can't help thinking that I'm . . . you

know . . . that I'm your second choice. That if things had worked out with Boyd, you and I would be leading entirely different lives right now, and the girls would never have been born."

"No," she said, and said it so firmly Gilbert had to believe her. "I eventually saw the . . . the shiftiness in his eyes . . . and it dawned on me that I'd somehow been duped into thinking I was the only one he cared about. He was compelled—absolutely compelled—to look at every woman who walked by. And what's odd about it, he doesn't even necessarily like women. I'm convinced he's a die-hard misogynist. There's a bad vibe with him as far as women are concerned. In my case, I got the sense, near the end, that it was more a power trip than a love thing. Having sex with him was always . . . I don't know . . . I couldn't help feeling humiliated in some way. There was always this . . . this what-a-little-fool-you-are look in his eyes . . . as if he'd somehow outsmarted me by having sex with me. Sex with Glen was scary at times. I feel so much better when I'm having it with you."

"Boyd's a real sick puppy," commented Gilbert. "Did he try anything when you saw him . . . you know, in the spring?"

"He pawed me a few times, but I pushed him away. I guess that's when my hair got in the bed."

"You always hear about his reputation as a womanizer," said Gilbert.

"I wish I'd known about it when I went to France with him."

"He really tried to paw you?"

She sighed, lifted her mosquito net, and wiped her eyes. "We had a bit of a scuffle. He was trying to kiss me. I lost my balance and I fell to the bed. I don't know why he even bothered. He's half in love with Stacy Todd."

"Really?" he said. "You wouldn't know it. His murder didn't phase her at all. When I took her to the office, it was business as usual."

"No," she said. "He had a thing for her. He told me as much. He said a few suggestive things to her while I was there, but I guess she's gotten in the habit of ignoring him."

"What a poor guy," he said.

More rustling came from behind the oak tree on top of the hill. They both turned. It sounded big. Two dragonflies sped down the hill as if they were fleeing from the thing. It got louder. It got closer. Gilbert rose to his feet and lifted a rock, preparing to use it as a weapon, now wishing he had his 9mm Beretta from work with him. He felt himself tensing. Bob Birch across the bay said he'd seen several bears at the dump this year, more bears than he'd seen in the last thirty-two years.

"I think it's a damn bear," said Gilbert, incredulous.

A sudden wild foraging came from behind the oak tree.

Regina sprang to her feet. "Oh my *God*," she said. "Is it a bear?"

A moment later, a red squirrel jumped delicately out from behind the oak tree, stood on its hind legs, stared at them, and twitched its fluffy tail playfully. Gilbert frowned and let the rock drop to the ground. Regina's shoulders sagged in relief.

He glanced at her.

"I'd like to know one thing," he said.

"What's that?" she asked.

"What ever happened to the red squirrel hunt this year?"

She grinned. Then laughed. And all her *otherness* disappeared.

On Friday, after a week of earnest and successful marital repair on the shores of bright Kipawa, Gilbert was just changing into his bathing suit to join the girls for a swim when the cottage telephone rang.

"Barry Gilbert here," he said.

"Hi, Barry. It's Dr. MacPherson."

"Oh, hi . . . hi. How are you?"

"Are you having good weather up there?" asked the doctor.

"Sunny and hot," he said. "Perfect swimming weather. And the blackflies aren't too bad this year, either."

"Good. I'm glad to hear it. Unfortunately I have some rather bad news for you. Nina's second test came back positive for HIV."

Gilbert felt his chest contract. The beer he'd drunk earlier felt unsettled in his stomach. His palms grew moist. A hummingbird swooped into view outside the screened window, hovered at the nectar-style bird feeder, dipped its slender beak into one of the feeding holes, sipped, then darted back to the lowest branch of a nearby white pine. He heard the sound of a chain saw in the distance.

"Are you sure?" he asked.

"Well . . . there's a small possibility the test might have come back as a false positive."

"What's a false positive?"

"It means she could be negative, but because of the

reported one-percent margin of error on the test, it came back positive."

"So her chances are one in a hundred then?"

Nina's chances had to be better than one in a hundred, he thought.

"Probably a little greater than that," said Dr. MacPherson. Far in the distance, *Sûreté du Québec* game wardens boated toward a choice walleye spot, aiming to apprehend some unlicensed fisherman. "The manufacturers claim these tests are ninety-nine percent accurate . . . but that's just a claim. I don't buy it for a minute. I won't get too technical. There's a whole science in the way they predict the reliability of these tests, with numbers and figures involving your basic risk population, superimposed against patients who might show abnormal proteins for other reasons besides HIV." Already the doctor was losing Gilbert, but he listened as intently as he could, and tried to understand. "Then you have to look at the whole thing in the framework of positive predictive value," continued Dr. MacPherson. "When you do all that, I'd say Nina's chances are closer to one in twenty-five." A breeze rustled the branches of the white pine outside, and the hummingbird flew away. "Not good, but definitely better than one in a hundred."

Gilbert felt his heart beating faster. His mouth was now dry and sour from the beer.

"So what do we do?" he asked, hoping the doctor would pull some miracle solution out of his bag of medical tricks. "Should we pack up and come home for another test?"

"The lab closes early on Friday," said Dr MacPherson.

"What about tomorrow?" asked Gilbert.

"They're not open on Saturday. Not during July and August. And a few days aren't going to make a difference anyway. Bring her in on Monday. I'll write another requisition, and we'll have her tested then."

After Gilbert hung up, he stood by the wall-mounted phone for several seconds, a cool sweat forming on his brow. His throat felt tight. He wondered if he should spare Nina the news until they got back to Toronto on Sunday night. Why wreck her weekend, and her final two days up at the cottage? No. He should tell her now. He had to tell her the truth no matter how much it might hurt, give her a chance to get used to the idea before she got back to town. Let her have whatever reaction she was going to have, take the next two days getting herself in reasonable shape, then go to the doctor's office and the lab on Monday.

He left the cottage and walked down the path to the dock. Regina and the girls were already in the water. A wooden foot-bridge made of pressure-treated timber led to an island off the east point, part of the property, small but picturesque. A dozen pine, cedar, and birch trees grew on the island, and a few granite boulders, left there by glaciers thousands of years ago, were embedded into the pale-green ground moss. Regina and the girls floated on noodles—bright tubes of highly buoyant synthetic material—just off the south point of the island.

"Could you guys come out for a sec?" he called. "I have something to tell you."

"Why don't you come in?" called Regina, her smile happy and unsuspecting. Then she caught the worried look on his face, and her smile disappeared. She turned to her daughters. "Come on, girls," she said. "Let's get out. Dad has something to tell us."

They swam to the island, climbed out of the water, and walked across the footbridge. They came up the path to where he stood beside a lichen-covered boulder. Regina looked at him more closely. Her face sank. He could tell she knew what was coming. From across the bay, Bob Birch started his rudder-steered eighteen-footer and began heading across, perhaps on his way to the marina.

"I just got a call from Dr. MacPherson," he said. He turned to Nina, feeling helpless, wanting to do something for his daughter, but knowing it was out of his hands. "I'm afraid the news isn't good. Your second test came back positive."

A strange look came to Nina's face. She went pale, her pupils lost their focus, and she looked at him as if she didn't know who he was. Gilbert remembered this from his diabetic brother Howard. Howard would sometimes faint when his glucose levels did something unexpected. Bob Birch motored closer and closer, steering the boat around the far side of the island.

"She's going to faint," warned Gilbert.

He grabbed on to her and steadied her just as she lost her footing. Her legs went all rubbery, and her eyes rolled back into her head, and he had to grab on to her tighter so she didn't collapse to the ground. Regina rushed in to help. Bob Birch came out from behind the island and saw them all standing there beside the big boulder. Nina continued to collapse, and they carefully laid her on the ground, her skin getting covered with old brown pine needles.

Bob waved, even though he looked somewhat perplexed by what was going on.

Gilbert waved back, the old social forms of the lake taking over no matter what, practiced since the summers of his boyhood, when his father had owned the place, automatic and instinctive, even though his daughter had just been handed a death sentence.

On Saturday night, their last night there, Gilbert sat out on the island, his back against a boulder, his bare feet stretched over a lip of granite that sloped gently into the lake. He faced east, across the lake. In and amongst the pine-covered islands he heard a loon calling, its voice timeless, tragic, and ethereal. To the north, where the salmon hues of sunset faded in the skies above the Ojibwa reserve, a last few fisherman trolled for lake trout in their small boats before calling it a day.

He heard the cottage screen-door open, then bang shut on its spring-loaded hinges.

"Barry?" called Regina.

He cocked his head over his shoulder.

"I'm out here," he called. "On the island."

He turned east again, where high among the highest hilltops across the lake he saw the red light of a fire tower winking off and on, ever watchful of the endless cedar, birch, and pine. He heard Regina walk across the footbridge. She climbed onto the island. Her flashlight beam searched him out. She maneuvered around the big boulder and sat down on the granite beside him.

"Is she asleep?" he asked.

"Finally," said Regina. "Jennifer's in bed with her. They're sleeping together."

"Good. She needs all the comfort she can get. It must be hard when you're so young."

"I gave her a couple of those old Sominex. The ones that have been in the medicine cabinet forever. I don't know if they're still good, but she took them with a glass of warm milk, and it seems to be doing the trick."

"She's exhausted," said Gilbert. "Her nerves are shot. She needs sleep."

He put his arm around his wife and drew her closer. They, too, were exhausted. They hadn't slept much, not more than a couple of hours since receiving the bad news from Dr. MacPherson yesterday.

He looked out at the lake. The bugs weren't too bad. The record-breaking heat in June had killed most of them off early. Bats skimmed and dove above the calm lake.

"Are we okay now?" asked Regina. "You and me?"

He sighed. "I just wish Boyd had never happened," he said, "that's all. I accept it, I live with it, it's over and done with, but I still wish it had never happened."

She leaned her head against his shoulder. "When I was over there . . . in Aix-en-Provence . . . and living with him in that little stone place he had . . . I met a woman . . . God, there were so many women around, and who knows how many of them he slept with." The loon called again. "Her name was Renate Dresler, and she was a music student at the *Hochschule* in Vienna, and she and I . . . we became good friends. I don't know whether she slept with Glen, but I imagine she did. She was part of his coterie." The sky got darker, and the stars grew more brilliant. "Renate was a sweet girl. She was a real support to me. She came to Marseilles with us. She held me after the doctor did what he had to do. Glen buggered off somewhere, to a café by the harbor. Renate was the one who listened to me when I told her Glen was the biggest mistake of my life, and how I would always look back on this time with a lot of bitterness. And you know what she said to me, and what I've been wanting to tell you all these years, but have never had the nerve?"

"What?"

"*Jemand wer nie bitteres geschmeckt hat weiss nicht was süss ist.*"

Gilbert raised his eyebrows. "What on earth does that mean?" he asked.

"It's an old Austrian proverb," she said. "It means 'He who has never tasted what is bitter does not know what is sweet.' And you're sweet, Barry. In every sense of the word." A satellite drifted across the sky, a speck of grace against the filmy dross of the Milky Way. "I'm only sorry it took someone like Glen to make me realize that."

WHEN GILBERT GOT BACK TO work on Monday, he couldn't concentrate. He tried working on some cold cases, but kept thinking how Regina was taking Nina to Dominion Medical Laboratories that morning.

He glanced around the squad room. Detectives Jim Groves, Jay Birnbaum, and Lisa Hemmings worked at their desks. He glanced at Joe's desk. Lombardo looked as if he hadn't been in yet. Gordon Telford's PC was on, his screen-saver rotating pictures of his wife and kids, but the man was nowhere in sight. Gilbert felt like talking to someone, but saw that the few detectives in the squad room were too busy to talk. He couldn't work. He needed something to clear his mind.

He got up and headed for the cafeteria. Another coffee. That's what he needed. And maybe a Danish. To hell with his diet. He needed a caffeine-sugar fix, something to boost his energy and sharpen his focus.

In the cafeteria, he sat by the window. College Park, an elegant shopping-condo complex where some of the justices had their offices, stood across the street. He couldn't get his mind off Nina. She was bright, quick to laugh, and always eager to help people. She was creative, always making things. For instance: the soap carving of Cleopatra's head, complete with Egyptian headdress, up at the cottage last week. His throat tightened. He didn't want to believe that he might lose her. His eyes misted up.

Just as he was reaching for a napkin, Lombardo came over with a tray full of breakfast. Lombardo caught him with the napkin. Damn. He had to pull himself together.

"Joe . . . hi . . . how are you doing?"

Lombardo stared at him. "Are you all right?"

He shoved the napkin aside. "Fine," he said. He gestured at the chair. "Sit down."

Lombardo hesitated, then slid his tray onto the table.

"I'm glad I bumped into you up here," he said. He sat down. "Where we can . . . you know . . . talk by ourselves. How was your vacation?"

"Good. We had a great time."

He peered at Lombardo. His young partner's brow was set. He was obviously troubled about something.

"What's wrong?" asked Gilbert.

Lombardo unfolded his napkin and put it on his lap.

"Ling forced Nowak to hand the Boyd case over to the Crown Prosecutor's Office last week while you were away," he said.

Gilbert paused. Obviously the paperwork didn't matter that much after all if Ling was going to force them to give the case half-baked to the Crown.

"Isn't that a bit premature?" asked Gilbert.

"Nowak had no choice," said Lombardo. "Ling wanted him to do it."

"And who did he give it to?" asked Gilbert.

"Marie Barton," said Lombardo.

Gilbert considered the choice. "She's good," he said. "She's tough. But I hope she'll have the good sense to hold off until you and Gord have a chance to iron out some of the wrinkles. Or at least until we catch Barcos."

Lines formed at the corners of Lombardo's mouth, and he looked more troubled than ever.

"That's just the thing, Barry," he said. "She's not going to hold off. She's going to go full-steam ahead. I was talking to Vicky Fountain about it . . . my old legal assistant friend from over there?"

"Vicky. I remember her. How's she doing?"

"She's doing good."

"And what does she say about it?"

"Well . . ." Lombardo looked out the window and tapped the table a few times. "She says Marie's trying to build a case against your wife." Lombardo let that sit, reached for the salt, and sprinkled some on his scrambled eggs. "I told Vicky to tell Marie to hold off, but she's the Crown, and she's got all this evidence, and she thinks she can build a snug little ship against your wife." Lombardo faced Gilbert. "I think Ling's office has been in touch with the Crown." Lombardo's eyes narrowed. "You don't look too surprised. I thought the news would flatten you."

Gilbert's lips tightened. "I had a chance to think about it up at the cottage," he said. "I was afraid this was going to happen. Not that Marie has much of a chance in securing a conviction against Regina, but I sure hope we can stop it before it goes to trial. Regina and I can't afford it, for one thing, not with Jennifer's tuition fees. And for another . . . I want to spare Regina the upset. Boyd really hurt her. That whole Marseilles thing . . . we thrashed it through up at the cottage . . . and it was really hard on her." Gilbert gave Lombardo an inquiring look. "Does Tim know about Marie's plans?"

"Yes," said Lombardo.

"And has he talked to Marie?"

"He's talked to her." Lombardo put the salt down and raised his palms in a gesture of helplessness. "And he's asked her to hold off, but . . . I think Ling's office is telling her to go ahead anyway." Lombardo shook his head. "So Vicky says Marie is . . . you know . . . that she's working on it. I don't know how quickly it will result in a warrant or an indictment against your wife, but with the deputy chief's office in the picture, I imagine it won't take much more than a week. Two at the most."

Gilbert took a deep breath and looked out the window. Below, a double-decker tour bus drove by, crowded with tourists. A few seagulls fought over an old pizza crust someone had dropped on the sidewalk.

"So in other words, we have a week to find Barcos," he said.

"Or to nail Judy," said Lombardo.

"Or to maybe even take another look at Phil. Whichever way we work it, we have to work it fast. We have to give Marie something she can . . . think about . . . something she can use to maybe start building a case against one of the other suspects. Because if she's really going to go ahead with Regina . . . they'd have to drag up all that ancient bullshit . . . they'd have to go into Marseilles . . . and that would kill Regina."

Lombardo lifted his fork, moved his eggs a centimeter or two, but didn't immediately eat them.

"I know you're not supposed to be working the case," said Joe, "but I'm not going to tell anybody if you want to go ahead and . . . you know . . . develop something . . . independent from me and Gord. She's your wife, Barry. I know you really want to do something. If I were in your shoes, I'd be the same way."

A strained grin came to Gilbert's face. "Thanks, Joe," he said. "It feels funny not working with you."

"Yeah . . . yeah, I know. Gord's a good guy, though. He's not Barry Gilbert, but he's a good guy."

"A great detective," commented Gilbert. He took a deep breath, looked at his Danish, but now had no appetite for it. "Joe . . . you and Gord . . . you really got to . . ."

Lombardo raised his hands. "We'll do everything we can, Barry," he said. "We're not going to let any of this touch Regina."

Gilbert slipped out at eleven o'clock and walked to the University Avenue Courthouse, where Marie Barton had her office. She was one of several Crown attorneys who shared the same secretary. The secretary wasn't there so Gilbert slipped past the reception area and walked down the corridor to Marie's office. Her door was partially open. He stuck his face inside. She was sitting at her computer, going over some work.

She looked up. She was in her late thirties, wore glasses, had short dark hair and a cherubic face, a plump but energetic woman who was a dynamo in the courtroom.

"Uh-oh," she said, her tone amiable but cautious.

"Marie, what's going on?"

"What are you doing here, Barry? You really shouldn't be here. You should stay away from this. You're just going to make matters worse."

"What else am I supposed to do?" he said. "You're building a case against my wife. I'm not going to sit by and do nothing."

"Barry, I wish I could talk to you about it. But I can't. This is a high-profile case. I'm sorry. I'm just doing my job."

"You can't possibly believe that Regina killed Boyd."

"All I see is the evidence," she said. "And the evidence doesn't look good. The evidence is strong. The evidence is compelling. It's my job to present it in the most convincing way I can. That's what I do, Barry. I can't do anything else."

"Yes, but you should really hold off. Joe has several other leads he's working on. And if you go ahead now, it will really hit Regina and me hard."

Marie shook her head. "I'm sorry, I can't hold off. I've been asked to fast-track this any way I can. Not only by your own trials division, but also by my boss. And I'm afraid that's what I've got to do. My advice to you is to find an attorney that specializes in this kind of thing. And if it's any consolation, I honestly hope I lose. I hope the court finds Regina innocent. But right now, she's the best case I have, and I've been told to present it as soon as possible. That means the two of you should prepare yourselves as well as you can. I think it's only a matter of time before the police arrest her."

Carol Reid, the squad secretary, took messages for off-duty or vacationing detectives, nine to five, Monday through Friday. If the calls weren't urgent, she immediately typed them up as e-mails and zinged them electronically to the recipient's in-box.

Gilbert, when he got back from Marie Barton's office, booted up Outlook and saw several such messages relayed by Carol. One was a phone message from Magda Barcos. *Please call.* The call had come in while he'd been down at the courthouse.

He glanced nervously around the squad room. Jim and Jay were gone, Lombardo was in the copy room faxing something, and Lisa Hemmings, still at her desk, phone to her ear, was giving the bad news to next-of-kin about a murdered loved one. He lifted his phone and called Magda. Three rings later, she answered.

"It's Detective Gilbert," he said. "You called."

In the background, a large tropical bird squawked. "Tico, quiet!" she said. "Just a second. I have to go to the other room." He heard her press the receiver to her palm and move to the other room. A few moments later, when she spoke again, the bird, still squawking, was a lot further away. "Thank you for returning my call," she said.

Her voice was tremulous, and he could tell she was agitated.

"What's up?" he asked.

"I've been talking to my brother," she said. Considering Marie Barton's plans for his wife, this was just the news Gilbert wanted to hear. "He called early this morning. He wants to meet me tonight." Her voice got choked up. "He misses me." She paused. "And I want to do what is right by the law so he won't get hurt."

He glanced over his shoulder. Joe was still in the copy room. He wasn't sure if he should tell Joe about this or not. Joe wasn't going to tell anyone if he developed his own leads, but at the same time, Nowak had officially yanked Gilbert from the case, and to go ahead and work on it in the face of that would unquestionably be an act of insubordination. To tell Joe about Magda's call would make Joe guilty of insubordination by association. He couldn't tell Joe, at least not right now, not if he wanted to spare Joe any fallout.

"So you want me to . . . you know, like we discussed . . . you want me to be the one to take him into custody?"

"Yes. I know you won't hurt him. If you come by yourself . . . and you explain things to him . . ." He heard her take a deep breath, as if she were trying to get control of her feelings. "You know how to put things so well. He will listen to you. He will understand that it is no good to fight. And then he will surrender to you and he won't get hurt."

He grabbed his FROM THE DESK OF BARRY GILBERT pad and a pencil.

"So when tonight?" he asked. "Did he . . . like . . . you know . . . give a specific time?

"Ten o'clock."

"And he knows . . . that I'm coming?"

In the background he heard Mrs. Barcos trying to quiet the big bird in Spanish.

"No . . . not yet. But when I meet him . . . he will . . . I will talk to him, and he will . . . he has always listened to me. He knows that I am right most of the time. He will understand that he has to give himself up. I will explain to him that you won't hurt him."

Gilbert realized that Magda was still naïve as far as her brother was concerned.

"Are you sure it's going to work?" he asked her.

She didn't seem to understand that Barcos wouldn't listen to reason. Barcos would run. Barcos was a live wire. Gilbert didn't want to go it alone. But he couldn't take Joe. He thought for a moment. . . .

He would take Bob Bannatyne. That was perfect. Bannatyne had a reason to come. Bannatyne was hunting Barcos for the murders of Deranga and Munoz anyway. And if Bannatyne was in on the case, Gilbert would have a legitimate reason to call Mike Strutton in Patrol to get some backup units in place.

"I know that sometimes he is reckless," said Magda, as if she felt she had to make a case for her brother. "But I know he will listen to me. When I talk to him, and tell him that you're not going to hurt him . . . when I tell him how worried our mother is . . . I know he will do the sensible thing."

Gilbert didn't see the point in shattering Magda's illusions just yet. He would let her brother do the job later.

"So . . . did he give a place?" he asked.

"Hillcrest Park," she said. "Do you know that park?"

He sifted through his encyclopedic knowledge of Toronto. "I think so," he said. "At Christie and Davenport. Up on the hill."

"Yes," she said. "You park on the street. I will sit on a bench and wait for him. He knows I will be sitting on the bench close to the wading pool. When he sees me he will come over and sit on the bench next to me. I will be so happy to see him. I will tell him how bad Mama's nerves are, and how she is so worried about him. I know he will listen to me. When I have convinced him, I will wave you over. He will surrender to you. He will not fight you." In a woeful tone she added, "You won't even have to bring your gun."

The innocent trust she had in her brother made him nervous. If what Al Valdez said was true, he was going to bag a lion tonight. A few sweet words from Magda weren't going to make a difference.

"Then I'll see you tonight," he said.

"Yes," she said, relieved. "I will see you tonight. And thank you. Thank you from the bottom of my heart."

She thought she had it all figured out. But she was living in a dream world.

It didn't matter.

As long as she got Barcos within a hundred feet of himself and Bannatyne, they would do the rest.

He drove to Hillcrest Park that afternoon. He wanted to familiarize himself with the terrain.

The day was sunny, hot, and the lilac bushes around the tennis courts undulated prettily in the balmy breezes that buffeted the hill from the city below. Lawn sprinklers shot streams of water over the thirsty grass.

The park couldn't have offered a better arrangement for tonight's takedown. A rectangle, it was fenced in on three sides, with only the north end, along Hillcrest Avenue, fully open. They would block Barcos in from the north, then.

Gilbert walked south over a large flat grassy area. He finally came to the edge of the hill. It overlooked Davenport Road. He could see the whole city spread out below, the skyscrapers downtown rising in a jumble of ever higher monoliths to the landmark towers of the financial district four miles away. Down the hill, cars and trucks traveled east and west along Davenport Road. A chain-link fence, anchored in a stone embankment, blocked access to the street. Barcos would have to climb this challenging barrier if he decided to flee south. Even better, the hill itself was choked with knee-high weeds, and such a tangle would slow Barcos down. Add to that the three-dozen spindly black locust trees shading the hill. Barcos faced a punishing obstacle course. In the dark, Barcos would likely run into one of those trees. Barcos had made a big mistake choosing Hillcrest Park to meet his sister.

Still, the two exits at Christie and Turner bothered Gilbert. A long series of steps led diagonally down to each exit at opposite corners. If Barcos managed to find his way to either exit, he might get away clean. And if he got away clean this time, there wouldn't be a second chance. So Gilbert couldn't let that happen. Barcos was going down tonight, no matter what. With Marie Barton building a case against his wife, the stakes were too high for any other outcome but a capture.

Back at headquarters, after finishing a few things in the

office, he caught Bannatyne in the underground parking lot as he was going home and told him about the takedown.

"I thought I'd gift-wrap Barcos for you," said Gilbert.

Bannatyne, red in the face from all the heat, smoothed his thinning gray hair over his damp brow.

"I'll give you this," said his sixty-year-old colleague, "you're a persistent buggar."

"So are you in?" asked Gilbert.

On one of the lower parking levels, someone was revving an engine again and again.

"Of course I'm in," Bannatyne said gruffly. He gave Gilbert a wink. "It's my case, isn't it?"

"Thanks, Bob. I appreciate it."

"It'll be just like old times, only more so."

"Why more so?"

"Because if what Al Valdez says is true, Barcos is going to make it fun for us."

"I've already thought of that," said Gilbert. "I've talked to Mike Strutton in Patrol."

"And he's game?"

"He'll have units ready and waiting."

"It should be easy then."

"We still wear vests, though. And we take our weapons."

Doubt flickered in Bannatyne's eyes. "We'll take our weapons," he said. "But those vests are so damn hot."

Gilbert gripped Bannatyne's shoulder and gave it a comradely shake. "We're not cowboys, Bob," he said. "We're detectives. This guy's a pistol. Strutton would have a conniption fit if we showed up in shirtsleeves."

*   *   *

When Gilbert told Regina that Marie Barton planned to build a case against her, she turned off the electric frying pan, let the pork chops sizzle untended, and sat on one of the kitchen chairs. She raised her thumb and finger to her brow, closed her eyes, and rubbed gently. She looked up at Gilbert, her eyes distressed.

"What next?" she asked.

"You don't have to worry," he said. "Me and Bob Bannatyne are going to nab the real killer tonight. Barcos. I told you about him."

Her eyes widened. "But I thought you were off the case," she said. "And I thought Barcos was a wild man. Are the two of you going to pick him up yourselves?"

"It was the only way it could be arranged," he said. "Remember? What I told you about the sister?"

"First Nina, then Marie Barton, and now you're going one-on-one with a known killer."

"There's no other way, Regina. And if it helps, I'm just the guy who's baiting Barcos. Patrol will be there to move in once I've got him hooked."

"It still sounds dangerous."

"I've got to do it," he said.

"You can just refuse," she said. "I don't care what happens to me. They can put me in jail, for all I care. As long as my family is safe."

He walked up to her and put his hand on her shoulder. He heard the girls watching television in the den. Regina seemed to sag under his touch, like the strain of everything was too much for her.

"This is just a bad patch, Regina."

"Be careful. I don't want to lose you."

"I've got to do it," he said. "I'm not going to let them arrest you. The lawyer's fees . . . and all that crap from way back when . . . that would just put more of a strain on the family. I'm going to end this, Reggie. And I'm going to end it tonight."

GILBERT AND BANNATYNE SAT IN Gilbert's Ford Windstar later that night next to Hillcrest Park. The lights shone in the tennis courts, and a quartet of club members played doubles. A half-dozen teenagers loitered around a picnic table by the playground. A last rosy smear of daylight reddened the sky. Some eleven- or twelve-year-olds swung on the swings, straining the rusty old danglers to their limit. A big half-moon, the color of orange sherbet, hung in the hazy evening sky.

Gilbert looked toward the bench by the wading pool. The bench was still empty.

Bannatyne checked his Beretta Nine. "I'm glad we got these," he said. "Those old revolvers were about as effective as a leaky condom." Bannatyne peered at him with some concern. "What's with you?" he asked. "Why the look on your face?"

Gilbert watched an elderly women walk a Pomeranian by.

"I just feel sorry for Magda," he said, "that's all."

"You spoke to her again?"

Gilbert nodded. "She's going to stop by the van in fifteen minutes," he said. "She wants to talk to me first. She doesn't know you're here. You better get going or we're going to blow it."

Bannatyne's brow furrowed as he reached between the two bucket seats and grabbed his bullet-resistant vest from the back.

"Just remember," he said, "her brother's an asswipe." He double-checked the radio attached to the shoulder of his vest. "Don't go all soft on me just because she's a nice girl."

"You know me better than that, Bob."

Bannatyne gave him a doubtful look. "You live with three women," he said. Bannatyne opened the van door and stuck one foot on the sidewalk. "Now, look . . . keep in contact. Let's not fuck up. Keep an open channel. And speak loudly, for Christ's sake. I'm an old man. I'm going deaf."

"Don't worry."

"I worry," he said. "Especially with an asswipe like Barcos."

Bannatyne got out of the van, closed the door, and retreated along the sidewalk, turning right when he reached Christie Street, where he had his own car parked. God, here they were, two old guys trying to take down a Colombian cocaine cowboy. Bannatyne was right. They had lots to worry about. He felt his adrenaline building.

Ten minutes later, Magda appeared at the passenger-side window.

"Hello," she said. She glanced into the van. "So you are alone?"

"Do you see anybody else?" he asked.

"And you're not going to hurt him?"

The earnest look in her eyes was painful to behold.

"I'm not going to hurt him," he promised.

She nodded. "I have phoned his lawyer," she said. "His lawyer knows what is going on and he will be expecting our call. We will get this all sorted out."

Gilbert stared at Madga, amazed by how sweetly obtuse she could be. Shooting two men in the head at point-blank range in front of seven Club Lua witnesses wasn't something that could be sorted out easily. Barcos was going to jail for a long time.

"So you'll give me a signal?" he asked.

"I will wave to you like this." She demonstrated with ballerina-like grace. "Then you can come over and take him back to your car."

"Okay," he said. "I'll be watching. You've done the right thing, Magda. Your brother will thank you for this."

She blushed, pleased by this praise. "I hope so," she said.

She left the Windstar and walked across the park. Some teenaged boys at the picnic table flicked their chins over their shoulders and watched her—she was a Latina goddess. They stared at her longingly, eyes pining away. She walked all the way across the park and sat on the bench by the wading pool.

The light in the sky faded to black, like the end of an old-time movie. Gilbert reached for his bullet-resistant vest, slipped it on, and engaged the radio attached to its shoulder.

"Five-twenty-four, this is nine-sixty-nine, do you copy, over?"

Bannatyne's gruff voice crackled over the radio. "Ten-four on that, nine-sixty-nine, over."

"The bait's in position, repeat, the bait's in position, copy?"

"Copy that, nine-sixty-nine, over. All units standby, repeat, all units standby, over."

Gilbert waited for the man of the hour, Oscar Barcos, to show up. He lifted his Beretta Nine from the floor and gave it a quick check. Bannatyne was right about the old revolvers—they hadn't been that good, not even at close range. At least he could actually aim this new Beretta with a fair degree of accuracy, even though he hadn't fully mastered the gun's strong kick yet. He cranked a round into the chamber, stuck the safety on, and slid the weapon into his holster.

A halo of moths flew around the tennis-court lights. Two girls detached themselves from the knot of teenagers at the picnic table and drifted diagonally across the park. Gilbert heard them laugh. He thought of Nina, how her own carefree summer nights in Topham Park might forever be a thing of the past. An ambulance raced down Christie Street, lights flashing but no siren. He wanted to hold onto Nina forever, to somehow make her anxiety disappear, to give her a guarantee of a long and healthy life. But such guarantees were beyond a father's power. A raccoon lumbered out from under a cedar bush, looked around, its eyes catching stray beams from the tennis-court lights, then retreated into the shadows under some large maples. Gilbert could only hope—and even pray—that Nina's second HIV test had in fact been a false positive.

Fifteen minutes later, Barcos, a short, skinny man in his late twenties, turned the corner at Christie and Hillcrest. While of obvious Hispanic origin, he nonetheless had kinky hair, evidence of an African ancestor somewhere in his blood. He wore a white tennis jersey untucked over baggy beige cargo pants. He had a curious way of walking, sliding his feet over the grass as if the soles of his shoes were magnetically attached to the ground.

Magda stood up and waved to her brother. Barcos glanced around nervously. Gilbert knew Barcos had to have a gun. He wouldn't be wearing baggy cargo pants with so many big pockets if it weren't to conceal a weapon.

Barcos shuffled across the park, his white shirt looking blue in the harsh glare of the sodium lamps.

The cocaine merchant reached the bench by the wading pool fifteen seconds later.

He hugged his sister, kissing first one cheek, then the other. Gilbert again felt sorry for Magda. He wanted to give Magda a chance to work it her way, allow her at least a few minutes to talk to her brother before he called Bannatyne. So he stalled with the radio, knowing Bannatyne was going to give him shit later.

Brother and sister sat on the bench by the wading pool. They spoke for nearly two minutes before Barcos, jumping to his feet, looked wildly around.

Here we go, thought Gilbert.

Barcos gestured angrily at his sister. Gilbert heard his voice, raised and furious, chastising Magda in Spanish. He knew the young Colombian was going to bolt any second. Gilbert couldn't hold off any longer. He gripped the radio on his shoulder and spoke quickly.

"Five-twenty-four, this is nine-sixty-nine, do you copy?"

"Copy that, nine-sixty-nine. Do you have a ten-twenty-five on the suspect yet, over?" asked Bannatyne

"Ten-twenty-five on that, and he's a code Six-AD. Repeat, armed and dangerous, and ready to run, copy?"

"Copy that, nine-sixty-nine, and will alert all units."

"Copy that, and over," said Gilbert.

Barcos, after a last few harsh words to Magda, walked quickly toward Hillcrest Avenue, trying to remain calm, acting as unsuspiciously as possible, under the sad impression that this tactic might work. Gilbert watched with mounting apprehension. Madga leapt to her feet, ran after her brother, grabbed his wrist, pleaded with him, but he shook her away.

Gilbert drew his weapon, got out of the van, and ran into the park. He aimed his gun at Barcos with both hands.

"Police!" he yelled. "Get down on the ground! Get down on the ground right now!"

Barcos, validating Al Valdez's characterization instantly, pulled a gun from his pocket and fired twice at Gilbert, the reports rending the humid summer air like a pneumatic drill pounding concrete. Both shots missed Gilbert. Gilbert dove to the ground. He shot his own gun, aimed to the left of Barcos, making sure the bullet skidded safely into the ground, a warning shot, enough to get Barcos headed the other way. Barcos turned and bolted toward the hill, heedless of the obstacles that might lay ahead. Magda screamed. The teenagers at the picnic table took cover. The kids on the swings jumped off and sped out of the park.

Gilbert spoke into his shoulder radio again. "Five-twenty-four, we have a ten-fifty-seven on that, repeat, we have a ten-fifty-seven times two, over."

"Copy that," said Bannatyne.

"Suspect is headed south down the hill." Gilbert sprang to his feet. "Am in pursuit."

Magda ran up to him. "Don't shoot him!" she cried. "Please don't shoot him!"

Gilbert raised his hand. "Stay here!" He gripped her by the arm and forced her back. "Just stay here and get down on the ground!"

He left her there and ran toward the hill, fifty years old but feeling like a young man again. Barcos was a white streak in the shadows ahead of him.

Gilbert heard sirens in the distance—Mike Strutton coming with backup. Neighborhood dogs howled in response to the sirens. Everything was sharp. Everything was clear. His knees were good. The big aspirins were working for a change. He felt flexible and strong. Maybe it was because of Regina. Maybe it felt so easy because he knew he had to do this for his wife, throw Barcos at Marie Barton as a way to stop her from looking at Regina.

Barcos disappeared down the hill.

Gilbert reached the crest of the hill and saw the cocaine merchant struggling through the knee-deep weeds. Barcos disengaged himself from a particularly nasty thatch of pink thistle and dodged around two black locust trees. The weeds got smaller, and he headed toward the exit at Christie and Davenport. Gilbert was afraid he might get away.

But then Gilbert saw Bannatyne huffing out of the shadows

down there, ready to stop Barcos, his great belly under his flak jacket as impressive as Buddha's.

Barcos saw Bannatyne and turned around and ran the other way.

Gilbert sped down the west side of the hill to cut him off.

A few seconds later, two radio cars roared into position at either exit.

Barcos, now realizing both exits were blocked, retreated up the hill. It didn't matter that Gilbert was coming down the hill after him. Barcos simply raised his weapon and fired at him again, intent on shooting his way out.

Barcos missed Gilbert yet a third time.

Gilbert gained speed and dove straight for the little man. He crashed right into the Colombian. Barcos raised his hands to protect himself and accidentally smashed Gilbert's right cheek with the grip of his pistol.

They tumbled into the pungent weeds. Gilbert made a grab for the man's gun. He stuck his finger in through the trigger guard and lodged it behind the trigger. A few seconds later he yanked it free.

"I've got his gun!" he shouted to Bannatyne. "I've got his gun! Don't shoot!" He turned. He saw uniformed officers running up the hill from Turner and Davenport. "Don't shoot!"

Uniformed officers swarmed around Gilbert and the Colombian a few seconds later.

They ripped Barcos away from Gilbert and forced the suspect to lay facedown on the ground.

Barcos, the fight gone out of him, simply allowed himself to be handcuffed.

Who should be one of the arresting officers but Constable Virginia Virelli? Her blond hair was tied back tightly under her police officer's cap, and her face was flushed by the night's warm, humid air.

She knelt beside Gilbert as two officers yanked Barcos to his feet.

"Are you all right?" she asked. She pointed to his cheek. "You're bleeding. Do you want EMS?"

"*Oscar?*" a shrill voice called from up the hill. "*Oscar, estas tu bien?*"

Barcos swung round and looked up the hill.

"*Magda, vete al casa,*" he cried in a tired, irritated voice. "*Vete al casa ahora mismo.*"

Gilbert glanced up the hill, struggling to catch his breath.

"That's his sister," he told Virginia.

"That's really starting to bleed," said Virginia.

He touched his cheek, pulled his fingers away, and saw blood. "It's not *too* bad," he said. "More of a scrape, I think. I don't think I'll need EMS." He swallowed a few times as sweat beaded his forehead. "I'll have my wife put some iodine on it when I get home."

Virginia helped Gilbert to his feet. "That was good," she said. "You really did a good job. I can tell you've been doing this a long time. Especially the way you disarmed him." She looked around. "Where's Joe?" she asked. "Isn't Joe with you?"

"This is Bob Bannatyne's case," he said. "Barcos is his guy." He glanced up the hill again. Magda worked her way down through the tall weeds. "Could you do me a favor?" he asked. "Could you take his sister down to your car? Her name's Magda.

Try to be nice to her. We need to keep her somewhere out of the way while we question her brother."

"Sure," she said. She started up the hill.

"And by the way," said Gilbert, "how are you and Joe doing?"

She stopped, a shy grin coming to her face. "Good," she said. But then she frowned. "Only he . . . he's got this thing with his hair right now."

"Yeah?" said Gilbert, acting innocent.

"He got it cut really short." Her frown deepened. "Too short."

"Yeah, I noticed."

"No, I mean really short. He looks like . . . like he's been sheared. I tell him I like it. I mean, what else am I supposed to say? But it's . . . you know . . . *hideous*. I wish he would let it grow long again."

"Do you want me to tell him?"

She shook her head, bewildered. "Don't bother," she said. "He says he never listens to you. Especially when it comes to style."

GILBERT AND BANNATYNE ESCORTED BARCOS to Bannatyne's unmarked car on the corner of Christie and Davenport. Constable Virelli took Magda to her own car.

Once they had the suspect at Bannatyne's car, Gilbert told him the deal.

"If you come clean on Glen Boyd's murder," he said, "we'll give you a break on the Club Lua killings. We've got solid evidence that puts you at Boyd's apartment the night he was murdered."

"I want my lawyer," said Barcos.

"Give me his wallet," said Bannatyne. "I want to see if I can find any receipts from Club Lua. Fuck his lawyer."

Gilbert dug in Barcos's pocket and handed Bannatyne the man's wallet.

"I didn't kill no Glen Boyd," said Barcos.

"We know you were down there at nine-thirty," said Gilbert. "That's exactly when he was killed."

"I was on the subway going home at nine-thirty," said Barcos.

This didn't jibe with Gilbert.

"On the subway?" he said. "Your sister told us you drive a Porsche."

"These cuffs are too tight," said Barcos. "I'm going to charge you with police brutality."

"The cuffs are fine," said Gilbert.

Barcos squirmed, bending his wrists to illustrate his point.

"My car is in the shop," he said. "And leave Magda out of this. I don't want you guys talkin' to her. She's *my* sister, and she don't need no fuckin' cops harassing her."

"We've got you down at Boyd's at nine-thirty," insisted Gilbert.

"I was on the subway going home," countered Barcos. "And I never killed no Glen Boyd." Barcos looked frantic as he fumbled for a legitimate-sounding story. "Fucker . . . fucker tried to rape my sister." His eyes widened, as if he were pleased with this story. "I rough him up a bit, teach him a lesson for that, but I didn't no fuckin' kill him."

Gilbert stared at the little Colombian man. Boyd tried to rape Magda? He glanced at Bannatyne, not believing it for a minute.

"He tried to rape your sister?"

"Yeah."

"So you broke his arm?" said Gilbert.

"I don't know about no broken arm," said Barcos. "I rough him up a bit, teach him a lesson, that's all. I get on the subway and I go home. I didn't no fuckin' kill him."

"And he tried to rape Magda?"

"He don't fuck with my sister. No one fuck with my sister."

It sounded lame. But then Bannatyne took something from Barcos's wallet.

"Barry," he said. Bannatyne held up a subway transfer. "You better check this out."

Meanwhile, Barcos was going all macho on them.

"He lucky I didn't break his leg," he said. "Magda don't want no ugly dago shitbag grabbin' her ass. Teach him a lesson."

Gilbert took the transfer. He glanced over it. The transfer, printed at Osgoode Hall station on the evening of June first at 9:34 P.M., shifted the timing in the Colombian's favor. A drop of blood fell from Gilbert's cheek onto the transfer. Shit. His case against Barcos, because of this transfer, was slipping away from him.

Bannatyne gazed at Gilbert's cheek with some concern. "That's bleeding," he said.

Gilbert dug into his pocket, pulled out a napkin, and pressed it to his cheek.

Any defense attorney would use this transfer to demonstrate an airtight alibi for Barcos. If Barcos and Deranga had been in Jay's Smoke and Gift at 9:17, then in the subway at 9:34, they wouldn't have had the time to kill Boyd at 9:30.

The Colombian looked at the transfer. He caught on in an instant.

"You see?" he said. "That's my transfer. I was on the subway, like I told you. Got the time right there."

Gilbert felt frustrated. What was he going to do now? How was he going to stop Marie Barton from indicting his wife? He shouldn't have been so damn confident about Barcos. He recalled Tim Nowak's concern about the timing, remembered the staff inspector's exact words. *Nine-seventeen is not nine-thirty. And we can't be absolutely certain Barcos and Deranga went to GBIA after they left the smoke shop.* Gilbert grasped desperately for other logical explanations because he didn't want this arrest to slip away from him. Barcos could have found the transfer in the subway station. People were always throwing transfers away on the subway station platform. Maybe Barcos saw one, recognized it as a chance to build an alibi, and pocketed it for future use. Gilbert had to pick holes in the Colombian's story any way he could.

"Tell us where you got this transfer from, Barcos," he said. "Did you find it in the subway station? If you cooperate with us on the Boyd murder, we'll go easy when it comes to Deranga and Munoz."

Barcos's eyes blazed. "I want my lawyer."

Gilbert tried a different tack. "So Boyd tried to rape your sister," he said, as if he thought it were the most far-fetched thing he had ever heard. "C'mon, Barcos. The only reason you went down to Boyd's on the night of the murder was to kill him. You thought he was rolling up your network here, cooperating with police to bust your guys, so you strangled him. Don't give me no rape-story bullshit."

"No way," said Barcos. "The only reason I went down there was to teach the fucker a lesson. I want my lawyer."

The rape story still felt thin to Gilbert, a typically ill-conceived cop-out a gang member might use. Yet because Barcos didn't deny his own actual presence at GBIA on the night of the murder, offering this rape story instead, Gilbert couldn't discount it entirely. He looked at the subway transfer again, now with its spot of blood. He wanted to go home tonight and tell Regina that it was all over, that the asswipe was in jail, and that they didn't have to worry about Boyd anymore. But how could he do that when he had this transfer in his hand, and when Barcos's rape story sounded like it might have at least a smidgeon of substance?

He handed the transfer to Bannatyne. "Bag it," he said. "I'm going to check his story with Magda."

Magda leaned against Virginia Virelli's radio car at the corner of Davenport and Turner. She was crying. Officer Virelli tried to calm her but it didn't do any good. Magda looked at Gilbert as he approached. Her eyes grew apprehensive. Her tears stopped.

"Is he all right?" she asked.

"He's fine," said Gilbert. "He's in custody." He softened his tone, realized that if he was going to get anywhere with his verification, he would have to play good-cop with Magda. "He's not going to hurt himself or anybody else. And that's just what we want. You did the right thing, Magda."

"I didn't think he would run away," she said. "I was sure he would see sense." A knit came to her brow. "I thought you were coming alone," she said. She gestured at the police officers. "Where did all these people come from?"

Gilbert looked away. "He fired at me three times," he said, justifying the police presence.

She grew subdued. Her disillusion was profound.

"I'm glad you had help," she admitted, her voice tremulous. She glanced around. "What's going to happen to him now? Where are you taking him? I guess I should call his lawyer."

Gilbert hesitated. He wanted verification on the rape story, but didn't feel it appropriate to talk about it in front of Virginia. An issue like this had to be handled sensitively.

"Constable Virelli, could you assist the other officers, please?" he said. "We're trying to recover the cartridge shells from the shots fired."

"Yes, sir," said Virginia.

Virginia climbed the hill to help the others. Gilbert faced Magda. They stood under the boughs of a maple tree. The light from the streetlamp, shining through the leaves, freckled the area with dappled shadow.

"He's in big trouble, isn't he?" said Magda.

Gilbert wished he could tell Magda something reassuring. But he couldn't. He pulled the napkin away from his cheek, saw that the bleeding had nearly stopped, turned the napkin over, and wiped the sweat from his brow.

"I think Detective Bannatyne outlined what Oscar faces when he spoke to you at your home a couple of weeks ago." He paused, looked at her steadily, and decided to get it over with. "My own case is different."

Her eyes narrowed. "You have a case against him, too?"

"Oscar says you know Glen Boyd."

The color climbed to her face. "Yes," she said.

"He was murdered recently," he said.

Her face changed again, as if deep inside a quiet calamity unfolded, one she struggled bravely to hide.

"I am aware of this," she said, her voice now fearful.

"And we thought your brother might be involved, but now we have some evidence to the contrary."

Her eyes brightened. "Really?" she said.

Her optimism irked Gilbert.

"This evidence we have," he said, plowing grimly on, "is evidence you might help us verify." He forced a grin to his face. "And by helping us, you might help your brother." As if all he wanted was to set Oscar free, just like she did. "He says the only reason he went to Glen Boyd's on the night of the murder was to . . . you know . . . to teach Boyd a lesson . . . because he said that Boyd . . . well . . . he made a move on you."

She looked at him curiously, nodded, then wiped the tears from her eyes with the back of her wrist. "I will do anything to help my brother," she said.

Gilbert felt something fading inside. His own certainty about himself, and about how he was handling this case was going fast. "So what your brother says is true, then?" he asked.

Her eyes widened in distress. "Yes," she said. Gilbert felt like raising his fist to the heavens and shaking it at the Gods of Homicide. "I went to Mr. Boyd's office to collect a certified check for Oscar."

So. *Pay up or die.* Boyd had come up with the cash after all.

"And this was when?" asked Gilbert.

"The end of May," she said.

This then explained the fresh packet of cocaine. Boyd had restored his credit with the boys from Barranquilla.

"So what happened?" he asked, his tone now gone sour.

Magda looked at the emerald ring on her finger.

"Mr. Boyd was nice . . . at first. He asked me in. He offered me a drink, rum swizzle, genuine stuff from Bermuda, what we sometimes drank in Barranquilla. While he was fixing our drinks in the kitchen, I noticed all the photographs. He has so many photographs. And he knows so many famous people. He had ones of Carlos Santana. I love Carlos Santana. I asked him how he knew Santana. He told me he's known Carlos Santana for thirty years. He told me stories about Santana. They were good stories, and I laughed a lot. The time went by. I thought nothing of it until I started feeling strange.

"I thought I was getting drunk. I thought the rum swizzle must be strong. But then I grew scared. The way I was feeling . . . it was so . . . strange . . . and I told him I felt sick, and he smiled at me and said I should lie down on his bed for a while. But then I remembered something my brother had once told me. He says sometimes a man will put drugs into a woman's drink . . . and I felt so strange . . . so strange . . . I knew that this is what he must have done. I sniffed at my drink. It didn't smell right. I took another small sip but spit it out. It didn't taste right. I don't know why I didn't notice it when I first drank it. I looked at his kitchen windowsill and I saw all sorts of pill bottles there." Gilbert remembered the pill bottles they'd found on Boyd's kitchen windowsill, three different kinds of tranquillizers among them. "Then I looked into his eyes and I knew what he was going to do. My brother has always warned me about this. He says there are drugs. He says men will try this from time to time."

A cat leapt onto the fence post at the bottom of the hill, looked at them, then jumped into the tall weeds. This revelation—about Magda's drugged drink—disturbed Gilbert. And yet, knowing what he knew of Boyd, it didn't surprise him. Boyd always got what he wanted, no matter what he had to do to get it. Moths circled around the streetlight on the corner. He felt sorry for Magda, that she should have to become another of Boyd's victims. In that way, they were part of the same club. But drugs! The old date-rape scenario. What a heinous and revolting crime. Gilbert's takedown adrenaline eased.

"So did he . . . did he actually rape you?"

"I don't think so," she said. "He got me to the bed somehow, I don't remember how, and I passed out for a minute or two." Her eyes misted over. "Then I woke up. I tried to get up, but I was really wobbly."

"I can't believe he put drugs into your drink," he said. "What a creep."

"He was lying next to me," she said. "He tried to kiss me but I pushed him off. I felt stronger. Maybe it was because I was so scared. I got to my feet, hurried down to the street, and got a taxi home."

"You didn't call the police?" he said.

"No," she said. "We are new to this country. I was afraid to. And when I got home, Oscar told me he didn't want me to call the police, that he would handle it himself." She glanced at Bannatyne's unmarked car. "Oscar was furious when I told him about it. That drug Mr. Boyd put in my drink made me feel sick for two days afterward. Sick to my stomach, and clammy. Pale and clammy. I'd never seen Oscar so mad."

Gilbert glanced at Bannatyne's car, too. He could see Bannatyne smoking a cigarette now. Oscar defending Magda's honor. No one was all bad, even if they were bad enough to shoot two best buds at close range. Gilbert felt horribly sorry for Magda. What an ordeal. But he was also disappointed by how his strongest suspect was now off his list. Barcos's subway transfer alibi was airtight, and his sister had verified the rape story. Gilbert had rushed his own sense of logic. He was beginning to think there was no possible way he could remain objective on this case, not when he had a personal stake in its outcome. Yet it was because he had such a personal stake in its outcome that he had to work on it so hard. With Barcos, his bias had gotten the better of him. But he vowed to control his bias from here on in. Though nothing would have made him happier than to book Barcos on the Boyd murder, he knew he had to be careful, and that he couldn't be fettered by his own tunnel vision again.

Gilbert and Bannatyne went to a bar after the Barcos takedown. Gilbert usually limited himself to one beer, but tonight he ordered a boilermaker: beer, with a shot of Canadian Club straight up on the side.

"You shouldn't be so hard on yourself," said Bannatyne. "You're allowed to be wrong once in a while."

"I'm going after Judy," he said. "If it isn't Barcos, it's got to be Judy. She has a history a violence. She throws food at waiters. She smashed Boyd over the head with a guitar. She lied to us about Scaramouche. Now we have a parking receipt that places her at the scene of the crime in and around the time of the murder. She's got a tenser bandage around her wrist. I'm convinced she injured herself when she strangled Boyd. I'm certain the skin scrapings under the fingernails of Boyd's left hand will end up belonging to her. Tomorrow, I'm going to phone the DNA guys to see how the comparison test on her is going. Joe found a hair in her rented car."

Bannatyne looked at him skeptically. "Tim's watching you, Barry. I'd be careful. He doesn't want you touching it. You could really fuck things up for yourself if you stepped out of bounds."

"Then I'll get Joe to phone them."

Bannatyne sighed. "I'd leave Joe alone," he said. He took a sip of beer and placed his glass on the coaster. "You got to work behind the scenes, Barry. If you stumble on anything useful, and can firm it up so that it really adds something, that's when you show it to Joe. But if Tim so much as gets a whiff of you poking your nose into it, he's going to come down hard. He told me so. So just tiptoe around a bit and find some new angles."

"What new angles?" said Gilbert, exasperated by the whole thing. "There aren't any new angles. Judy's the only angle I have, now that Barcos is out."

Bannatyne frowned. "Play it smart, Barry. Let Joe worry about Judy." Bannatyne sat back on his bar stool and took another sip of his beer. "Now . . . Nigel Gower was working on some finger-prints for you. That's a possible angle you might look at."

"The plate and the coin jar," said Gilbert.

"Right," said Bannatyne. "The plate and the coin jar. Has he made any headway on that?"

"He's found Boyd's prints on both. Plus a half-dozen mis-cellaneous ones on the plate."

"And has he had any luck identifying the miscellaneous ones on the plate yet?"

Gilbert knocked back his shot of Canadian Club. "He's going through the system," he said. "He hasn't had any hits yet. But I'm sure some of them must belong to Judy. She's always tossing things around. She tossed the phone at Boyd. I'm sure she threw the plate at him as well."

"What about Phil?" suggested Bannatyne. "Phil what's-his-name."

Gilbert shook his head as he felt the first anesthetizing effects of the Canadian Club numb his body.

"So far we have no physical proof that links him to the scene of the crime," he said. "He had to be in New York the next day for the release party of his new record, and he says he was at home packing. We can't verify that, but the guy's so fixated on his career, I'm sure he wasn't even thinking about Boyd."

"Yes, but what about this Palo Alto business?" asked Bannatyne. "And what about when he tried to launch his solo career and Boyd lost all his money?"

"All that was a long time ago. I'm sure he's had time to cool down."

"Yes, but what about the threats?"

"Look, Bob, I'm not going to close the book on Phil as a suspect, but from what I've seen of him so far, he prefers to get his revenge in court. There's nothing physically linking him to the scene of the crime the way there is with Barcos and Judy."

"Okay, okay," said Bannatyne. "But didn't this Phil guy tell you that Boyd had a lot of enemies?"

Gilbert looked at his old partner. "Yes," he said.

"Well . . . maybe you have to widen things. Boyd gypped a

lot of people. A *lot* of people, from what you were telling me. Any of who might have done the goods on him the night he was murdered. Maybe you guys aren't even in the right ballpark yet."

"Our strongest evidence points to Judy and Barcos. And now that Barcos is out of the picture, that leaves Judy."

"Yes, but maybe you should look at Boyd's books more carefully. Maybe you have to make a list of all the lawsuits he's been involved in over the years. Maybe it's not only Phil who's made threats. It could be any of the bands or other groups Boyd's gypped over the years. And maybe it's not even a question of the people he gypped."

Gilbert lifted a brow. "What do you mean?"

"Look what happened tonight," said Bannatyne. Bannatyne tapped his wide, gristled chin a few times. "We found out Barcos broke the guy's arm because he tried to rape Magda. And I know you don't like to remember all that shit from way back when, him taking Regina to France and all, but you remember what you said to me the morning after she took off? You said you wanted to kill the guy. Maybe there's some other guy out there right now who feels the same way. Maybe you and Barcos aren't the only ones."

"Please, Bob," he said. "I don't like being compared to Barcos."

"I'm serious, Barry," said Bannatyne, brainstorming now. "Maybe there's another victim out there like Magda who has an angry boyfriend or brother. Or several other victims, with several other boyfriends or brothers. Maybe it's just a case of menfolk getting even for wrongs perpetrated against their womenfolk."

"It's possible," said Gilbert.

"Of course it's possible," said Bannatyne. "The man's a notorious womanizer. He put drugs in Magda's drink."

Gilbert felt his anger flare. "The sick fuck," he said.

"This sex angle theory is something you definitely should be checking out. Or, like I said before, it could be the gypping."

"I'll check out his previous lawsuits," said Gilbert.

"And don't forget Phil," said Bannatyne. "Just because he's not physically linked to the crime scene doesn't mean he wasn't involved. It could be the Hell's Angels after all."

Bannatyne was right. These three angles—the gypping, sex, and Phil angles—had to be looked at more carefully. The gypping theory wouldn't take too much work. The sex angle theory would take more, but he would have to do it for Regina's sake. And he would have to review everything he had done on Phil, and maybe dig around for more background information. He grinned at Bannatyne. He was still learning lessons from the man after all these years.

"Thanks, Bob," he said. "Thanks for giving me some perspective." He took a sip of his beer. "I really need it on this one."

Regina was waiting up for him at the kitchen table when he got home shortly after one that morning. She immediately rose from her chair and looked at the gash on his cheek.

"What happened?" she asked.

He fudged a bit. He didn't want to distress her. He didn't want to tell her that Barcos had hit him in the face with his gun. "I tripped against a fence," he said.

"Did you get him?" she asked.

Her voice sounded hopeful, and he hated to disappoint her. "Yeah, we got him . . ."

She gave him a inquiring look. "But . . ."

He frowned. "But he's not the guy," he said. "He proved his alibi." Gilbert explained to her about the subway transfer. "So Bob and I went out for a drink and thrashed through some other possibilities. Other angles we might look at."

"But I thought you were off the case," she said. He looked away. He couldn't hide anything from Regina. "Barry . . . if Tim wants you to stay away from it . . . especially because I'm a suspect . . . it's not going to wash well with him if he finds out you're poking your nose into it."

"I'm going to work quietly," he stipulated. "Bob came up with some great ideas and I'm going to look at them, that's all. If I find anything, I'll show it to Joe. I'm not going to let them near you, Regina. I'm not. You don't need this right now. Not with Nina the way she is. Neither do I. I'm going to pursue it."

She took a deep breath, walked back to the table, and sat down. She finally nodded.

"You're right," she said. "I don't need it. I'm trying to look after my child. I don't want anything to interfere with that. That's priority-one as far as I'm concerned."

"You see?" he said. "You agree with me. I have to do something."

She shrugged. "Why do we have to be locked in this stupid box?" she asked.

"Who knows?" he said. "But I plan on clawing my way out of it as fast as I can."

She shook her head. "Nina had a bad crying fit tonight."

His face sank. "Shit," he said. Then Regina's eyes filled with tears. "Regina . . . no . . . don't." He walked up to her, put a chair next to hers, and sat beside her. "Don't do this to yourself."

"I can't help it," she said, and wept.

His own eyes misted over. "Don't worry," he said. "These new angles. They're good. I can work with them. And I don't care what Tim says. He's just going to have to understand. We need our energy for Nina, not all this other bullshit."

CHAPTER
SEVENTEEN

AT WORK THE NEXT DAY he was restless and desperate to break the Glen Boyd case any way he could. But he had to be careful. He knew Bannatyne was right. Nowak would come down hard.

He glanced over his shoulder and saw Nowak talking to Carol by his office. For some reason this made him feel like an outsider. He was torn. In a paramilitary organization like the police force, chain of command was important. An officer was expected to obey his superior, no matter what. Yet he couldn't just sit here and do nothing while the net closed around his wife. So he started working on Bannatyne's angles.

He logged onto the Internet and accessed the Ontario Courts web page. From there, he clicked onto the CACTIS link. Using his password, the Computer Assisted Case Tracking and Information System took him to the search screen, and gave him the option to search cases by docket number, defendant, plaintiff, Crown Prosecutor, and defending attorney.

He found five lawsuits against Boyd, over and above the seven Phil Thompson had filed. Some of the names looked familiar—disgruntled old rockers and punkers from the past. In all cases, Daniel Lynn was the defending attorney. He phoned Daniel Lynn, Boyd's lawyer, to ask him about these cases.

"We're digging around for other possible suspects in the Glen Boyd case," he told Lynn. "I've just gone into the CACTIS search screen, and see that you're defending him in five different lawsuits besides Phil's. I know you said Phil might be a possibility, and we're still investigating that angle, but what about these other plaintiffs? Any possibility they might have had something to do with Boyd's murder?"

"I don't think so," said Lynn. "The five plaintiffs don't live in Toronto, and I don't believe they really have the temperament. I wouldn't want you to waste a lot of time looking too carefully at them because I don't think your effort will yield any useful results."

Gilbert glanced at the CACTIS screen one more time. "Okay," he said. "By the way, thank your uncle for that pound of Blue Mountain coffee he sent me. My wife and I are really enjoying it a lot."

"I'm sure the pleasure was all his," said Lynn. "Like I said, he's always looking for Blue Mountain converts."

As Gilbert hung up, he felt as if he had at least eliminated one angle, the lawsuit angle.

He spent the next half hour checking websites that had

information about Phil. He read about the Houston and Denver arrests, the one for playing naked on stage and the one for throwing his lighted guitar into the audience. There was a lot about the new CD as well. Over and above that, nothing established Phil as a likely suspect. Nor did Gilbert come up with anything useful when he reviewed the existing evidence on Phil.

So he turned his attention to the sex angle. The thing to do was to draw up a list of all the women Boyd had dated in, say, the past three years. Find his black book, or consult with Stacy, Todd, whatever he had to do, then draw up a supplementary list of male relatives, friends, or boyfriends of these women. The task seemed huge. Yet from past experience he knew many other investigations started out just this way. It would take time. Marie Barton would probably indict Regina before he could finish. So be it. If he couldn't preempt an indictment against Regina, he could at least work hard toward her ultimate acquittal. He lifted a pencil and tapped his paperweight a few times. To determine if this angle in fact had some validity, he would first find out if Boyd had a history of sexual assault. Bannatyne's theory would hold a lot more weight if multiple offenses had occurred in the past.

Carol Reid walked down the aisle of desks. Nowak had disappeared into his office.

When she got to Gilbert's desk, she spoke in a low voice.

"I just thought I'd better warn you," she said. "Tim's drafting an arrest warrant for your wife." Gilbert's face sank at the news. "I don't know when he's going to serve it, or if he's going to serve it at all, but he's having me get it ready. That's what we were talking about just now."

Gilbert glanced over Carol's shoulder at Nowak's office.

"Does Joe know?" he asked.

"Tim says yes," she said. "I'm sure Joe and Gord are doing everything they can to work on other suspects. They're in your corner, Barry. So am I. But Tim's sticking to procedure. He's letting the Crown Prosecutor run the show."

"Thanks, Carol."

Once the squad secretary had gone back to her office, Gilbert felt even more desperate. Nowak never sat on warrants. If he was drafting one, he would use it. Gilbert figured he had until Friday. Then the uniforms would come to his house. He went back to Bannatyne's sex angle theory with renewed diligence.

He checked Glen Boyd's prior criminal history a second time, hoping to find something that might demonstrate a history of sexual assault. He checked municipal records, widened his search to include the entire Province of Ontario, then all of Canada.

He failed to find anything besides the few minor drug busts he'd uncovered already, the bad-check charge, and the public drunkenness arrest. Tellingly, the public drunkenness arrest had happened at the Zanzibar, a strip club, after Boyd had harassed some of the girls.

Gilbert turned his pencil end on end. Nothing in Canada. But Boyd had lived in the United States, most recently his ten years with Judy Pelaez in San Francisco. Boyd might have a criminal record in San Francisco. But a request to San Francisco would necessitate Nowak's involvement, and of course Gilbert's hands were tied in that regard. So he thought of his brother, Howard Gilbert, a homicide detective with the Miami-Dade Police

Department in Florida. He knew Howard would be only all too happy to help him.

He phoned his brother.

After a few minutes of fraternal small talk, Gilbert told Howard about the Boyd case, and how he was working this new sex-assault angle.

"If Marie Barton indicts Regina, that'll be it for Jennifer's tuition," he told Howard. "The lawyer's fees will kill us. I'm wondering if you could check whether Boyd has any sex-related priors anywhere in the States. He lived in San Francisco with Judy Pelaez for ten years. You could probably get the info faster than I could. I'm trying to shake something loose here."

"I'll try to get back to you by the end of the day," Howard told him. "Did Boyd go under any aliases?"

"Not that I know of," said Gilbert.

"Give me a chance to dig around," said Howard.

Gilbert hung up.

While he waited, he took the elevator to the seventh-floor evidence repository. Maybe if he had another look at all the physical evidence, he might think of something else.

As the clerk let him through, he felt guilty, wondered if the clerk knew he was off the Boyd case or not. He thought the clerk might say something, but the clerk gathered all the vouchered items and brought them to his table without comment.

Gilbert started first with the blond hair, now in a plastic bag. He held it up to the light. He recognized it as matching Regina's hair, knew that as evidence against his wife it couldn't be refuted. What the hell was one of her hairs doing in the victim's bed? Marie Barton would use this blond hair to win her case.

He put the hair away and lifted the scarf. The scarf was in a bigger plastic bag. This, too, would be used by Marie Barton. The suspect bought the scarf at Hazelton Lanes, she would argue. And then she would show the jury the charge-card slip Joe had turned up at Neck and Neck. Was this not a reasonable linkage, she would ask the jury?

And what about Regina's perfume? He opened the bag and took a whiff. Regina's perfume all right. Marie Barton would no doubt use that, too.

He looked next at the broken plate, the one with men on donkeys crossing mountains. He could see where Nigel Gower had dusted for fingerprints. Looking at the broken plate, its two ends attached by the hanging wire, got him thinking of Judy again. Had Judy been the one to throw the plate? She was always throwing things at Boyd. The broken plate convinced Gilbert more than ever that Judy had to be Boyd's killer.

He tried to step back from it, take an objective look at it, become that perfect cipher of criminal evidence, the homicide detective.

Was he missing something here? No. The more he looked at it, the more he really became convinced of Judy's culpability. She was high-strung. She was the kind of woman who got caught up in her own emotions, and who couldn't control her anger. He lifted the bag and had a close look at the rim of the plate. Certainly that rounded edge would explain the crescent-shaped welt on Boyd's forehead. And if Judy threw the plate, or otherwise used it as a weapon, the latents would be good, deeply etched. If only Nigel could find a damn hit on them. But it was unlikely he would find any hits in Canada. He knew Judy had prints on file in the U.S. When she'd smashed Boyd over the head with her guitar, she'd gone to jail. That meant prints. Those prints would be on the FBI's AFIS database. But to put in a request to the FBI's Automated Fingerprint Identification System would require Nowak's signature. And how was he going to get Nowak's signature when he was off the case? The whole thing left him rattled.

He went back downstairs. He phoned Nigel Gower in the fingerprint section, forgetting for the time being about the sexual-assault angle.

"Nigel, I'm just wondering how the fingerprint identifications are coming along on the Glen Boyd case?" he asked, trying to sound innocent. "Have you found any matches on the miscellaneous latents yet?"

A pause ensued. "I thought you were off the Boyd case, Barry," said Nigel.

Shit. Nigel knew.

"I'm still helping out," he said.

"No," said Nigel. "That's not what we've been told." Gilbert heard some rustling of paper on the other end of the line. "I've got the memo right here, Barry. The memo's specific about you. I'll get in trouble if I help you."

"Just tell me if you've found anything yet."

He heard Nigel sigh. "I'm sorry, Barry, but I . . . you

know . . . this came right from the staff inspector's office. I wish I could help you but I can't."

"You're not going to find anything on any of the Canadian systems," he told Nigel. "You're going to have to put in a request to AFIS."

"That would need the staff inspector's signature."

Gilbert felt his frustration mounting. "Can't you just do this for me, Nigel?" he asked. He thought of Regina. "It's really important."

"Barry, I can't talk to you about this. My boss is motioning to me right now. Something about a public relations risk. He's shaking his head. I wish I could help you, but I can't."

The two men ended their conversation.

Gilbert rested the receiver gently in the cradle, took a few deep breaths, and tried to control his anger. One thing was certain: Nowak was serious about keeping him off the case. Memos? Good God!

"Barry?"

He turned around. It was Carol again. "Hi," he said.

"Your brother called," she said. "He wants you to call him."

"So soon?" he said.

"Yes," she said.

So he dialed Howard.

"It didn't take as long as I thought it would," said Howard. "You're right. Boyd's got a bit of a history. Three counts of sexual assault, but none of them resulting in convictions. The first was in Lake Tahoe in 1991. He was organizing and promoting a bikini contest there and had sex with one of the contestants. She says she was forced against her will, but witnesses say she was flirting, and that was enough to get an acquittal. The second was in Albuquerque in 1995. Boyd was at a Christmas party and forced himself on a young lady. She didn't come forward until a month later. The fact she delayed things sank her case right from the start. So . . . you know . . . a couple of cases like that, and statistically speaking, it means Boyd might be a serialist, which would bolster Bob's theory."

"What about the third case?" asked Gilbert.

His brother sighed. "The third case." Howard seemed reluctant to go on. "It's ugly. But it's all too typical. It happened in San Francisco. It's dated just eight months ago. When he was down there visiting his family. I spoke to the detective in the Sexual Assault Squad responsible for the case, a guy named Victor Tran. He remembers the case clearly because the assault was perpetrated against Boyd's own daughter."

Gilbert's reaction was one of utter revulsion. "He assaulted Morningstar?"

"She was sixteen at the time," said Howard. "Not a nice thing for your father to do. A common victim profile, though. A girl under the age of eighteen raped by someone in her own household. Just like the Mariana Relós case I worked on."

"Boyd makes me sick," said Gilbert.

"All these guys make me sick," said Howard.

"So why isn't Boyd in jail?" asked Gilbert. "Why is he up here in Canada? He should be rotting in a U.S. prison somewhere."

"Judy got him off the hook," said Howard. "She phoned Tran after the arrest and told him Morningstar had been making the whole thing up. She protected Boyd. When Tran questioned

Morningstar, she backed her mother's story, said she'd made the whole story up because her father wouldn't give her the car to use for a night out. Tran didn't buy it for a minute. But he still had to let Boyd go because Morningstar refused to testify."

Once Gilbert had finished talking to his brother, he sat at his desk thinking for several minutes. While Howard's information lent credibility to Bannatyne's sex theory, it more obviously reinforced his own idea that Judy might be the guilty party after all. Was he having tunnel vision again? He didn't think so. He ran it through his mind one more time. Judy comes up here for the ultimate reconciliation dinner. Boyd doesn't even show up. On top of that, he tells her he's seeing another woman. But even before all this, he rapes Morningstar, and that in itself is motive enough to strangle the guy. Judy loses her temper and in a fit of rage kills Boyd. Boyd can't defend himself because his arm is broken, maybe by the Colombians. He pinches her arm with his left hand and gets her skin caught under his fingernails. She's not a strong woman, and there's minimal trauma to Boyd's hyoid bone and thyroid cartilage, but she manages to kill him just the same, even though she sprains her wrist in the attempt and now has to wear a tenser bandage.

He grinned, feeling excited about all this. It fit nicely together. As a bonus, it covered Bannatyne's sex theory, too. He didn't see a downside. He could detect no bias.

He pushed away from his desk, stood up, and walked to the window. He had to talk to Judy again. At the hotel. Away from Nowak's prying eyes. If he could squeeze a confession out of her, he might wrap this case up before Nowak moved against his wife.

*   *   *

Judy Pelaez had neither hope nor expectation in her eyes when she opened the door for Gilbert.

"So what?" she said, when he told her they knew about Morningstar.

"So it's true, then?"

"You can believe whatever you want."

"Okay," he said. "In that case, it's another piece of compelling evidence. It must have been horrible for you. And I understand that . . . you know . . . it might have driven you to extremes. But now it's time to . . . to fix it all."

Her eyes narrowed incredulously.

"What are you talking about?" she said. "You think I killed Glen?" Her lips stiffened. "You've gone crazy. Either that or you're desperate. As for Morningstar, she loves her father as much as I do. Glen didn't know what he was doing when he did that. And I made Morningstar understand that. It might seem monstrous to you, but let's not forget, Glen was sick at the time, really sick, with all the drugs and alcohol. He's a difficult man, I'm the first to admit that. Even so, he knew he had done something terribly wrong once he had sobered up."

She turned away, walked to the couch, and sat down. This was going to be harder than he thought. She crossed her legs and gazed at him through her tinted prescription glasses as if she thought he were the most annoying man in the world. He walked to the back of the chair and rested his hands on top of it.

"Judy," he said, "why are you making this hard on yourself? And on your kids? Like I say, what Glen did to Morningstar is just one more piece of compelling evidence, especially in the way of motive." He took his hands away from the back of the chair and squared his shoulders. "Not that you didn't have a huge motive to begin with. He stood you up, had you come all the way from San Francisco for what was to be your big reconciliation dinner, and never bothered showing up. Then he told you he was seeing another woman. If that's not enough, he raped your daughter. And it's not only motive. It's the physical evidence."

"What physical evidence?" she asked.

"Judy, we've already gone through the evidence with you," he said. "The parking receipt that places you at GBIA at the time of the murder. The restaurant personnel at Scaramouche not being able to tell us that you were actually there. Your history of violence. Why don't you just give up? It would be so much easier."

Her lip curled. "Are you always so preposterous?" she asked. She took off her glasses, and the muscles around her eyes tightened. "I would never kill Glen," she said. "Look . . ." She cast around for words. "I don't know you . . . and you don't know me . . . but I'm a . . . a widow now, so why don't you just leave me alone? I hate what Glen did to Morningstar. And I should have done something about it. But I didn't. I just wanted to . . . to bring my family together. So why don't you leave me in peace? I want to bury Glen, that's all. I want to be a good widow." A frantic smile came to her face. "Because I sure as hell wasn't a good wife." Her smile disappeared. "He . . . he hasn't got anyone else besides me. I'm the only one who cares about him. Everything you're saying is ridiculous. So if you don't mind . . ." She pointed to the door. "I'm really tired. I want to drink a sherry, take a couple of aspirin, and go to bed for the afternoon."

"C'mon, Judy," he said, refusing to be put off. "Let's not kid ourselves. Let me spell it out for you one more time. You have a history of violence. The salad plate you threw at that waiter in Barcelona. The room you trashed in Dallas. Your previous assault on Glen with that guitar during the 'Lost in Love' tour. Then Glen stood you up. You came all this way. And what did he do? He threw it in your face. He told you he had another woman. And let's not forget Morningstar. As for the hard evidence, I have the parking receipt. I have Scaramouche. I even have that tenser bandage around your wrist. You hurt your wrist when you strangled him. Why don't you just come clean about it, and we can end all this right now?"

She stared him straight in the eye. "Got you," she said. She took a cigarette from the pack on the table, stuck it in her mouth, and lit it. "My wrist." She lifted her wrist. The smoke swirled around her head. "Good point." She sat back on the sofa. She drew her left foot up under her right thigh. She smiled, as if she thought he were more ridiculous than ever. "I've had my bad wrist since 1985. Chronic tendonitis. I hardly have the strength to brush my own hair." She leaned forward. Her voice hardened. "Which means I wouldn't have the strength to strangle someone, would I? If you need proof, I'll have Dr. Lukow in San Francisco send you the medical notes. Think of him as my expert witness. He runs a special clinic for musicians. The tendonitis is from all the guitar playing. I'm lucky if I can play fifteen minutes a day. I'll have him fax the notes. Or should he mail them?"

Gilbert didn't know what to say. She was right. She was absolutely right. And he didn't know how he could have missed it. His bias was still so strong, and he was still so determined to clear the case any way he could for the sake of his wife, that he couldn't see even the simplest things. He hardly had the presence of mind to respond to Judy. His confidence in himself was badly shaken. He couldn't trust himself anymore.

"The fax machine is . . . we're having a problem with the fax machine right now," he said, because under no circumstances did he want Nowak to pick up the fax and see what he was doing. "If you could have him courier the notes to me in the morning, that would be fine."

"Okay," she said. "I've got your card. You'll have them tomorrow. Now . . . if you don't mind . . . I'm tired. There aren't any little bottles of sherry left in the cabinet. I'll have to call room service."

So he left, broadsided by Judy's tenser bandage the same way he'd been broadsided by Barcos's subway transfer.

As he walked with distracted steps along Jarvis Street to his car, he felt like a ship blown out of the water. This was what bias did to you, he thought. It made you misread things. The tenser bandage. Meant to prove Judy's guilt, it now in fact proved her innocence. Dr. Lukow would be sending notes in the morning, and that would be the end of it. Judy had an expert witness with documented proof. Strangling a man for Judy was a physical impossibility. Her left wrist couldn't take it.

He shook his head. How could he have been such a fool? He kicked a discarded Coke can into the gutter. Maybe he would have to draw up Bannatyne's proposed list of sex-angle suspects after all, just to keep himself busy, and to make the case stop nagging at him so much.

DR. ANTON LUKOW'S NOTES ON Judy's tendonitis arrived in a FedEx envelope just after lunch the next day. Gilbert read the notes with increasing consternation. Judy had indeed developed the condition in 1985, and had suffered from it ever since. Dr. Lukow, in a separately dictated letter, made it clear that the pain and weakness in Judy's left wrist would make it physically impossible for her to strangle someone. Gilbert gathered up the notes, and, taking a surreptitious glance over his shoulder, left the Homicide Office, went downstairs, crossed Grosvenor Street, and walked to the Coroner's Building to get a second opinion.

He found Dr. Blackstein in his office.

"I wonder if you'd take a look at these notes and tell me what you think," he asked the coroner. "If her wrist is this bad, could she strangle someone?"

Dr. Blackstein checked over all the reports and the various

dated entries Dr. Lukow had made regarding Judy's wrist since 1985. He read Dr. Lukow's dictated letter. When he was done, he sat back and pressed his hands against his desk.

"Given the extent and severity of her tendonitis," said Blackstein, "I have to agree with Dr. Lukow's assessment. She wouldn't have had the strength or tolerance in her wrist to strangle Boyd." The coroner shook his head. "I'm afraid she hardly has the tolerance to pick up a bag of groceries."

As Gilbert returned to headquarters, his mood plummeted. The heat was oppressive. He took out a handkerchief and wiped his forehead. He felt frustrated by his own pig-headedness. He entered the cool, air-conditioned headquarters with a sigh. He felt like he didn't know how to be a cop anymore.

Back in the squad room, he found Nowak waiting for him.

"Barry," said the staff inspector, "could I have a word with you?"

"Sure."

"In my office?"

He followed the staff inspector into the office. Gilbert had the FedEx envelope under his arm, and felt conspicuous with it. Nowak walked to his chair but remained standing. Gilbert waited. He sensed he was in trouble.

"Barry," said Nowak, "it seems we have a problem. I've been told by Philip Mayhew in Auxiliary Services that you contacted Nigel Gower and requested information regarding fingerprint identification in the Glen Boyd case." Nowak paused, his face hardening. "Is this true?"

Gilbert stared straight ahead. "Yes, Tim," he said. "It's true."

"I've also checked the evidence log," said Nowak. "You're

on file as having requested the hair, the jar, the plate, and the scarf. You did this after you were pulled from the case. Is this true as well?"

"Yes, Tim," said Gilbert. "That's true as well."

Nowak sighed and scratched the back of his neck. "Did I not make myself clear?" he asked.

"Tim, this is my wife we're talking about. I can't stand by and watch it all happen without trying to do something about it."

Nowak sighed again, as if he were disappointed in Gilbert.

"Barry, that's a separate issue," he said. "Right now I'm concerned with your insubordination. Philip Mayhew called Deputy Chief Ling about the whole matter. Ling in turn called me. And he was extremely angry." Gilbert kept his eyes straight ahead. "I'm going to have to insist, Barry. No further interference. You disobeyed a direct order. And that's serious." Nowak shook his head. "I wish I could offer you more flexibility on the case, but I can't. Ling made it clear to me that you're to stay away from it. The risk of a public relations fiasco is too big. I don't believe Regina did it any more than you do. And if it goes to trial I'm sure she'll be acquitted. But in the meantime, we have to make Ling happy. He emphasized that he *would* punish you if he discovers any further breach. Suspension without pay, or possibly even a transfer from the Homicide squad. You're on an extremely short rope here, Barry. So don't pull it too hard."

"I'm so glad Judy's innocent," said Regina. "I always liked her. Glen should have had the good sense to stick with her."

Gilbert and Regina were finishing up the supper dishes together later that day.

"Glen was never strong on good sense," he said. He was still feeling rankled by everything. "And I'm glad she's innocent, too. But it means I still have zip. Nothing I can take to Joe. Meanwhile, Marie Barton is polishing her case against you, and Carol's drafted your arrest warrant."

"You should tell Tim about Judy's tendonitis," she said.

"I can't do that," he said. "One more breach, and I'll be punished. I might be transferred out of the squad. And then I'll never get a chance to work on the case, not even behind Tim's back. Tim's going to have to find out for himself. I can't believe I've been so stupid. First the subway transfer, then the tenser bandage. I'm a better cop than that. I know I am."

After finishing the dishes, he went up to the spare bedroom— a room he had turned into his own personal den—and brooded.

He sat on the hide-a-bed, an old piece of furniture he and Regina had owned since the 1970s, brown and ratty, starting to fall apart, but comfortable. A swath of green broadloom covered the floor, a refugee from the bungalow on Merritt. He felt flummoxed by the case. His old stereo—a Technics turntable, a Marantz amplifier, and a couple of Koss speakers—sat on a shelf on the wall. His old LPs were packed in milk crates. He really felt he had been straightjacketed on the case once and for all. He didn't know what to do. He felt tense. He got up and flipped through his old albums. Maybe if he listened to some music he might relax.

He came to Mother Courage's 1977 release, *Give You My World*. Naturally, as he was involved in the Glen Boyd case, he decided to give it a listen. He pulled it out and looked at the cover photo. The band members were all so young. Phil stood off to one side, isolated from the rest, an exceedingly tall, thin man wearing jean cutoffs, a denim shirt opened to reveal a tanned chest, and what looked like a Yankees baseball cap over his long flowing hair. Michelle Morrison, as radiant as an angel in white satin bell-bottoms, gave Phil a sly but coy look. Ted Aver, clutching drumsticks in one hand and a Heineken in the other, looked bored out of his skull.

Gilbert switched on his turntable, put the record on, scooted back to the sofa, and let the changer do the rest.

As he listened to the first side, he continued to brood. Barcos was off the list. So was Judy. Nothing physically linked Phil Thompson to the crime scene. All this necessarily strengthened Marie Barton's case against his wife. It removed any doubt a jury might need to acquit her. He considered the concept. Doubt. He had a sudden notion that his wife might be guilty after all. Compelling evidence linked her to the scene. She was strong enough to physically perpetrate the attack, what with her muscle-training classes. And she was eminently capable of keeping a secret, as Marseilles had so amply demonstrated. If he were a complete outsider, would this be the way he would be thinking? Would this be his unbiased assessment of the case?

His brooding quickly ended as the last cut on the first side of *Give You My World* started.

The tune, called "Stacy," was sung by Phil Thompson. Just as Roger Daltry sometimes let Pete Townsend sing, so Paul Harding had given Phil a chance.

As Gilbert listened to the lyrics, he felt he had stumbled across a lucky break, one that might exonerate his wife.

Stacy, you're so spacey,
And you rock like AC/DC.
You're my Sunshine and my K.C.,
You're everything to me.

Stacy, this is crazy,
'Cause in love I'm kinda lazy,
And I never thought I'd need you
Like I do.

The first two verses rolled along with a honky-tonk feel, lots of piano, and slide guitar.

Then came the chorus. It was the chorus everybody remembered, three simple words, but never a greater hook.

Yes, I do,
Yes, I do,
Yes, yes, I do.

He remembered how in the dozen or so weddings he'd attended in the 1980s, "Stacy" had always been the wedding-band song of choice. The words "I do" made it real wedding material.

As he continued to listen, he pondered Phil's relationship to Stacy Todd.

Stacy, you're my Beatles,
Don't need no grass or needles,
Don't have to boogie all night long,
Just have to sing this song.

Stacy, you're the only one,
I think that we can have some fun,
And I never thought I'd want you
But I do.

When Phil sang the chorus again, his voice soared with passion. *Yes, I do. Yes, I do. Yes, yes, I do.* Gilbert remembered the photographs of Phil and Stacy on Phil's vanity wall, the one in the French Alps and the other one in the Caribbean. He was certain the Stacy in the song had to be Stacy Todd. Did Phil have a thing for Stacy, then? Because that might work. Especially because Regina had told him Boyd had a thing for Stacy as well. He recalled Regina's exact words about Boyd and Stacy. *He's half in love with Stacy Todd.* Might that be the triangle he was looking for, a love triangle, that sometimes quintessential shape of murder?

As he pondered the possibility, he remembered his first visit to Stacy's apartment two days after the murder. He tried to recall whether he'd seen any evidence of Phil: photographs, clothes, or other possessions. He remembered the GUITAR SUMMIT '99 coffee mug Stacy had been drinking from. That might indicate Phil's presence to a certain extent. Was it possible, then? Should he trust this? Or was this just another gut feeling gone awry?

He needed corroboration, he decided. Gut feelings were fine in certain situations, but when it came down to it—and especially in light of his proven bias in this case—he needed hard, solid evidence. He needed someone who could verify Phil's relationship to Stacy, someone outside the case, someone who wasn't liable to mention it to Nowak, and someone who would have the right information.

That meant Ted Aver.

Ted Aver lived on Maple Street in south Rosedale in an old renovated mansion two blocks away from the Rosedale Ravine. As Gilbert crossed the footbridge over the ravine, he stopped to admire the view. Lofty maples soared from the depths below him. A cardinal flitted from branch to branch in the nearest maple. Cars, looking as small as Tonka Toys, meandered along the winding Rosedale Ravine Road.

Ted's teenaged children were out. His wife was at work. Ted was alone in his wheelchair, sitting at his computer, tracking some of his many investments when Gilbert knocked on his door.

"I read about Oscar Barcos," said Ted. "Thank God you got that maniac off the street."

They went into Ted's living room, an open-concept affair with the walls painted white and the second-floor staircase exposed at the back. A drum set, rigged with all Ted's handicap contrivances, stood in the corner. A fresh pot of dahlias sat on the large oaken table in the bay window's recess.

Ted brought Gilbert a glass of ginger ale from the kitchen. Gilbert took a sip, and was refreshed by how cold it was.

"I'm just curious," he said. "For the record . . . are Phil Thompson and Stacy Todd . . . you know . . . a couple?"

Ted stared at the Persian rug for several seconds before he answered.

"Periodically," he finally said. "When they're not driving each other nuts." Ted drew back and squinted. "They're like Mount Vesuvius," he said. "They're pretty from a distance, but every so often they erupt. And then they have to give themselves time to cool off. Phil's a workaholic. He lets the domestic side of things slide whenever he's working on a project. He'll forget about bathing for days at a time. He's gone through a lot of maids because he doesn't pick up after himself. He's a real pain that way. The roadies used to hate him because he never took responsibility for his own stuff, especially when he was writing songs. Stacy, on the other hand, is a neat freak. God forbid if you walk on her floor with dirty shoes. Which Phil has done on many occasions. You get two people like that together, and there's no flexibility . . . and . . . well . . . what do you expect? They love each other passionately . . . but they've never learned to cohabit successfully."

Gilbert watched a monarch butterfly land on an ivy leaf outside the bay window.

"That song . . . 'Stacy' . . . the one off *Give You My World* . . . it's definitely about Stacy Todd, then?" asked Gilbert.

"Oh, yes," said Ted. "That was a bit of a surprise hit for us. No one thought it would take off the way it did. But then all the wedding bands started covering it . . . and I guess . . . you know . . . it got some longevity that way."

"And what about Glen Boyd's relationship to Stacy Todd?" he asked. "Do you know anything about that?"

Ted gave him a sly grin. "I think you're getting at something here, Mr. Custom's Man."

"I'm just trying to establish . . . the kind of dynamic . . . I want to get a feel for Boyd, his friends, and his associates during the last weeks of his life."

Ted's face settled.

"No, I think you're trying to bust Phil."

"I just want to investigate the possibility that he and Stacy—"

Ted raised his hands, stopping Gilbert. Gilbert saw callouses from drumsticks.

"If you think Phil had anything to do with Glen's murder," said Ted, "you're wrong." Ted looked away, as if the idea pained him. "Phil's the original peacenik. He would never hurt a flea. Do you realize how out of character that would be?"

Gilbert tried to backtrack as unobtrusively as he could. "So as far as you know, the relationship between Stacy and Boyd was strictly a professional one," he said. "Stacy was his secretary and he was her boss."

Ted frowned. "I didn't say that," he said. "Glenny was an asshole around women. Stace knows that. Stace knows how to handle herself. I won't say it's been easy for her. She's always been independent. Phil has money. He could easily look after her. But she doesn't want that, insists on having her own job. So she sticks with GBIA. Working at GBIA is all she's ever done. She was twenty-two when she started. If Glenny gets a little touchy-feely, she just puts up with it because she likes her job a lot and doesn't want to lose it. She knows how to handle Glenny. She's always been good that way."

"So . . . Phil knows about this? The way Boyd has this touchy-feely thing with her?"

"Yes. And occasionally he gets pissed off about it, but come on, Glenny's harmless. The world's full of harmless old stoners, and we just have to learn to tolerate them. Phil trusts Stacy to handle herself, and she always has, so if you think you might have an angle there, you don't. Besides, I thought Barcos was your man."

"No," said Gilbert. "His alibi holds up."

Ted shook his head doubtfully. "Well . . . I wouldn't be looking at Phil. He's not the type. He's gentle. Like I say, he's the original peacenik. He would never kill anybody."

CHAPTER

NINETEEN

WITH A CAREFUL GLANCE OVER his shoulder, and a look around the squad office, Gilbert, getting sick of the cloak-and-dagger routine, called up the Boyd case file on his computer the next morning. He clicked on the autopsy report. Luckily, the case-file software had no audit tracking system. He could take a look at the Boyd investigation with impunity.

His ideas about his new angle were now starting to gel. Here was Dr. Blackstein's diagram of the body, the ligature marks sketched in darkly around Boyd's throat. He double-checked the toxicology addendum, which listed all the drugs and medications found in Boyd's apartment. Any number of the various tranquillizers discovered in Boyd's medicine cabinet or on his kitchen windowsill could have been used as "date-rape" drugs. Looking at this list of hammer-blow medications simply confirmed Gilbert's growing suspicions.

He skimmed through the entire document. He wanted to find out if Blackstein had taken any combings from Boyd's pubic area. As expected, Blackstein hadn't bothered with combings. Combings were invariably taken from female murder victims when rape was suspected. This case didn't fit that profile at all.

He called Dr. Blackstein's office. When Blackstein came on, his voice was rough, hoarse, and sore sounding.

"You've got a cold?" asked Gilbert.

"God, yeah."

"There's nothing worse than a summer cold."

"God, yeah," repeated Blackstein.

Gilbert told Blackstein what he wanted. Blackstein sighed.

"I was just about to go home to sit by my pool for the rest of the day. I'm sick, you know."

"As I was saying, there's nothing worse than a summer cold."

"If you knew what was good for you," said Blackstein, "you'd come over here and catch a dose of it yourself. We could sit by the pool together and drink Bloody Caesars all day."

"If you could just do this one last thing for me before you go to your miserable fate." Gilbert had to employ a strategy to keep this latest request from getting back to Nowak. "And I'll make it easy for you, Mel. Don't bother dictating an addendum to the preliminary report. Just give me a verbal on it. Add your findings about the combings when you dictate the final report, along with whatever you get back from Toxicology on the possible overdose. That way, you'll be able to get to your Bloody Caesars sooner."

While Gilbert waited, he went to the front of the Homicide

office. He grabbed one of the complimentary newspapers, the *Toronto Star*, took it back to his desk, and searched for any follow-up stories by Ronald Roffey on the Boyd case. He discovered one on page four: NO FIRM SUSPECTS FOUND YET IN GLEN BOYD MURDER. He frowned. He considered the story so much journalistic baiting, and profoundly desired to put Roffey in his place.

Blackstein called back a half hour later. "You're right," he said. "I found three blond pubic hairs tangled up in his."

Gilbert felt both elated and relieved. At last he was getting somewhere with this, and Roffey be damned. But he still had to be careful. He was treading dangerous ground.

"Don't bother sending the samples through the usual channels, Mel," he said. "I'll come over and pick them up personally. We've been asked to move quickly on this by the deputy chief."

"The old greased-lightning routine," said Dr. Blackstein. "What else is new?"

But in fact, Gilbert felt like Harry Houdini, forced to solve the case with his arms and legs shackled.

He drove to Stacy Todd's apartment later on, taking a consent-to-search form with him. He parked across the street and filled in some of the blanks—his name, his badge number, Stacy's address, and a blanket statement about what he may need to voucher.

He got out of the car, dodged afternoon traffic, knocked on her door, and waited, but after a few minutes, concluded she wasn't there.

So he got back in his car.

He knew he was taking a risk. If this search proved fruitful, he would have to tell Nowak he was working the case without authorization. Who knew what Nowak might do? It was a chance he was willing to take.

He waited. He would wait all day if he had to. He had to do what he could to prove his new theory. He remembered Stacy's condition the day he had taken her to GBIA, how she had looked so ill. He remembered how she'd gone to the hospital on the night of the murder, Mount Joseph, according the wristband in her bathroom wastepaper basket, supposedly for diabetes. He remembered how she had been so pale and clammy, like Magda. All this was tantalizing, but he was determined to be a cop from here on in, so he wanted a definitive lock on some hard evidence before he concluded his theory was true.

Stacy Todd pulled up in a taxi an hour later.

Gilbert gave her a chance to get inside, then walked across the street and knocked.

"Oh," she said, when she answered the door. "It's you. Hi."

"Hi," he said. "Do you have a few minutes?"

She hesitated. Her shoulders rose. Was she scrambling, he wondered?

"I have to go out," she said.

"This won't take long," he said.

She paused, but finally said, "Sure. Come on up."

He followed her upstairs to her apartment.

When they reached the landing, he presented her with a consent-to-search form.

"I have to look around," he said. "I hope you don't mind."

She looked at the form through her big-framed glasses. Pink blotches appeared on either cheek. "I *have* to let you look?" she said.

"No," he said. "This is not a search warrant. This is a consent form."

"Why do you want to look?" she asked.

"Because we have to rule you out," he said. "We may need some materials from your apartment to do that."

"Oh," she said, sounding relieved. "If that's the case . . ." She took the form and signed it.

He went into the living room and snipped a few strands from her rug with a pair of scissors, just for show. Stacy watched him. Then, continuing the charade, he went to the dining room where he bagged a thread from the curtain. He felt awkward. During a search, he usually steamrollered right ahead, regardless of who was watching. But if his suspicions were correct, and Boyd had indeed raped Stacy, then, despite any involvement she might have had in his murder, he necessarily felt sorry for her.

She retreated to the kitchen, so ill at ease she looked as if she was going to be sick.

That's when he went where he really wanted to go, the bathroom.

He wasn't hoping for much. In fact, he wasn't hoping for anything at all. If she was such a neat freak, the bathroom was bound to be antiseptically clean. But he knew he had to try. He lifted the toilet seat. The toilet was spotless, and smelled of Comet cleanser. There wasn't so much as a coil of pubic hair anywhere. Same thing with the floor.

He continued his sordid little search. He felt he was really invading her privacy. He looked and looked, but he couldn't find anything, not even behind the old water radiator.

He then pulled away the shower curtain and saw a drain-trap placed over the drain. He pulled the drain-trap away and found, stuck in its mesh, the squalid bit of evidence he was looking for, a single hair, of the coarse curly pubic type, blond, perhaps a match to the ones combed from Boyd.

Here was an interesting twist, he thought, one he would have to tell Sexual Assault Staff Inspector Vivian Gannett about after it was all over: combings taken from the rapist, not the rape victim.

He bagged the hair, then started looking around for any of the medical equipment associated with a diabetic. He opened the medicine cabinet and looked for insulin, hypodermic paraphernalia, a glucose meter, test strips. Nothing. He went to the bedroom and looked for the same things. Still nothing. He went to the kitchen and searched all over. Stacy stared at his every move. He didn't find anything like a glucose meter or other such equipment anywhere in the kitchen either.

"What are you looking for?" she asked.

He turned to her. She looked tired. And jumpy.

"Nothing," he said. "I'm finished."

"And you found what you were after?" she asked.

"That'll be for the lab to decide," he said.

He left. He felt miserable. If his theory was true, what Stacy was feeling now was what his wife must have felt after she had come home from France. Used, abused, and humiliated. He descended the two flights of stairs to the street. Not that he thought Stacy had killed Boyd. Phil had likely avenged her. But that was beside the point. What he had here was a woman who had been put into an impossible situation against her will. He hated to think that once he finished his investigation he would end up making her suffer even more.

Gilbert took the combings from Boyd and the sample extracted from the drain-trap in Stacy's apartment to the Centre of Forensic Science. While fingerprint identification was an official part of the Police Auxiliary Service, hair and fiber comparisons were carried out by the Centre. Gilbert shook his head as he climbed the steps to the front door. He hated to sneak around like this. But at least he could be reasonably certain that there was no memo from Nowak's office circulating around the Centre. He could get the comparison done quickly and quietly.

If the wait was quiet, it certainly wasn't quick. He had to wait three hours. The wait would have been days had he not decided on the easiest method of comparison. The technician finally handed the report to him around five-thirty.

He could have gone the DNA route. He glanced at the report as he strolled back to his car. Or he could have gone for neutron activation analysis. But both these methods would have taken far too long, and with his wife's arrest imminent, time was of the essence. So he'd gone for a straight microscopic comparison.

As he read the report, he saw that all hairs were definitely identified as human pubic hairs, blond, all with a similar distribution of pigment granules, all structurally the same. The report concluded that the hairs most probably came from the same individual, but warned, based on criteria from the Royal Canadian Mounted Police forensic lab, that there was a one in eight hundred chance the two samples might not be a match.

Gilbert stopped on the sidewalk and considered this. Given the Horsemen's odds, it was a fair certainty both samples came from Stacy. He was now convinced, given all the evidence, that Boyd had indeed drugged and raped Stacy on the night of June first. He tapped the report a few times. Yet he still didn't feel safe enough to take it to Nowak. Or to even mention it to Joe. Not when Nowak had been so firm about his suspension and possible dismissal. There was so much at stake. He might lose his job. And he loved his job. Before he revealed any of this to anybody, he needed to definitively place Phil and Stacy at the scene of the crime in and around the time of the murder. That meant obtaining Stacy's hospital record. He had to establish her movements that night, and that meant starting with Mount Joseph Hospital.

But how was he going to get her hospital record? A hot wind raked some dust in the street. He would need a court order. He would have to go to Justice Dave Lembeck. But he couldn't go to Justice Dave Lembeck. Lembeck was sure to have the memo from Nowak's office. He put the comparison report in his briefcase. Damn. Another roadblock. And he wasn't sure how he was going to get around it.

When Gilbert got home that night, he found Regina and Nina waiting for him with apprehensive faces in the front hall. He immediately thought Nina's test result had come back positive.

But such wasn't the case. The test result hadn't come back at all.

"Mike Topalovich called you," said Regina. "He said it was urgent."

"Daddy, why would Mike call you?" asked Nina, her eyes full of trepidation. "Have you been talking to him?"

Gilbert didn't answer. He put his briefcase on the floor, lifted the telephone, and dialed Mike's number immediately.

Regina and Nina stood by, watching with wide, mystified eyes.

Mike picked up after the third ring.

"Hi, Mike, it's Barry Gilbert."

"Oh . . . hi, sir."

"What's up?"

Mike paused. "Well, sir, I've got some news. And I think you're going to like it. Carolyn finally got in touch with me. My third pre-Nina sex partner? They were on holiday. They have relatives in the United States. That's where they were."

"Great," said Gilbert. "And did she give you her test results?"

"Yes, sir," said Mike. "She doesn't have it. She's clean. Vashti's the one I caught it from."

Gilbert sagged in relief. Vashti came after Nina. Which meant Nina was now free. She could leave that awful place, the land of the terminally ill. He glanced at Nina, and already she looked different. Like the aura of death had left her. Mike would have to stay behind and face all the frightening demons himself. He felt sorry for Mike and Mike's family. Mike had turned out to be such a nice guy.

"Thanks, Mike. I really appreciate everything you've done. You're a good guy."

"It's the *least* I could have done, sir. I'm just glad it worked out for Nina. I'm *really* glad."

Gilbert hung up. He turned to his wife and daughter. He didn't know how to begin.

"Yes . . ." he finally admitted. "Yes . . . I've been speaking to Mike. I had to . . . to find out for myself. I had to *do* something. I couldn't stand by and wait. I had to get the timing of the thing." He explained about Carolyn, the two other girls, and Vashti. "And because Carolyn's negative, it means Mike caught the infection from Vashti. He met Vashti after Pascale's party. Which means he was infection-free at Pascale's party. Which means you're not HIV-positive, Nina."

The color climbed into Nina's face. She sat quickly on the hall chair—as if her legs were about to give out. She lifted her hand with a tremor to her forehead and her eyes clouded with tears. Regina gave him a questioning look. He could see she wanted to make sure he had his facts right. He gave her a covert nod while Nina struggled to come to grips with her unexpected release from HIV purgatory.

Then Nina sprang to her feet and threw her arms around Gilbert, knocking him off balance. Regina grabbed him and steadied him.

"Thank you, Daddy," she said. "Thank you, thank you, thank you."

He was immensely relieved. It put things in perspective. His urge to protect Nina, to rescue her from that bad place, had been extreme. That same urge compelled him to protect Regina. And that's what he would do. He would protect Regina. First as a husband, then as a cop. And he would do it without bias this time.

In bed later on, Gilbert told Regina about the new Stacy angle.

"He was friendly with her whenever I was down there back in the spring," said Regina. "Too friendly, in my opinion. Too free with his hands."

"That's what Ted Aver told me," said Gilbert.

"I could tell she didn't like it," said Regina. "But I can't believe he would . . . then come to think of it . . ."

She trailed off.

"He doesn't treat women nicely, does he?" he said.

"No," she said. "He doesn't. In France, it finally felt all wrong. It was a power trip to him, nothing more."

"You see?" he said. "That's what I'm talking about. I think I have a real shot at this. I'm finally starting to feel like a cop again. I'll go down to the hospital and start asking questions. I'm sure I'll find something."

"You know what?" She looked out the window, where a summer gust billowed the sheer curtains. "Marie Barton's case against me, and Tim's arrest warrant? They both seem so . . . so ridiculous . . . so far away from me right now. As far as I'm concerned, your biggest case of the year is Mike Topalovich. And you've solved that one, Barry. I don't care about Marie Barton's case. Or Tim's arrest warrant. I'm just glad we got our little girl back. Don't let anybody ever tell you you're a rotten cop. Because you're the best cop in the world. And you're also the best husband and father."

CHAPTER
TWENTY

AT WORK THE NEXT MORNING, as a blistering sun rose over the east end of the city, Gilbert came into the squad room and saw Lombardo and Nowak talking in Nowak's office. He gave them a quick glance, then beelined for his desk, feeling guilty about all his covert work on the Boyd case.

He was just getting settled when Nowak called him in.

"Barry?" he said. "Can I see you?"

Had he gone too far, he wondered? He got up, and, like an errant student who's been called to the principal's office, trudged to the front. Had Nowak been talking to Blackstein? Or to the Centre of Forensic Science about the hair samples?

Gilbert was sure he was going to be disciplined, that he might even lose his job, but when he got to Nowak's office, both Nowak and Joe smiled at him.

"Good news, Barry," said Nowak. "You don't have to worry about your wife as a suspect in the Glen Boyd case anymore. We've received firm evidence that's changed the Crown's mind. Joe and Gord arrested Judy Pelaez early this morning in her hotel room."

Gilbert was caught so off guard by this, he at first didn't know what to say. He glanced at Joe. His partner had a great smile on his face, his eyes bright with good news.

"Nearly seven weeks on this damn thing," said Lombardo, "and me and Gord finally get a break." Lombardo gave Gilbert a pat on the back. "We got the final DNA testing back on the other skin sample. It's a match to Judy Pelaez. It was enough to convince Marie Barton to go ahead with Judy instead of your wife. You and Regina can rest easy. You don't have to worry about sabotaging Jennifer's education money to pay for legal fees."

Gilbert, put on the spot, just stared at them. He wondered if Judy had said anything to Joe or Gord about her tendonitis during the arrest this morning. Scarier still, had she said anything about his own meeting with her four days ago?

"So you took her into custody," said Gilbert. "And did she say anything?"

"No," said Joe. "She kept her mouth shut." He frowned. "She had this smug smile on her face. We asked her a few questions but she told us she wasn't saying anything, and that we would have to talk to her lawyer."

Gilbert was relieved. "And who's her lawyer?" he asked.

"She's going with what's-his-name," said Joe. "Boyd's lawyer. Daniel Lynn."

Gilbert thought of the pound of Blue Mountain coffee. "Lynn's a nice guy," he said. "I like him."

Lombardo tapped his chin a few times. "There's something different about you," he said. "Wait a minute. I know what it is. You just called a lawyer a nice guy. I thought the terms were mutually exclusive."

Nowak and Lombardo had a good laugh about that. But Gilbert thought: *God, what a jam*. He had to work fast. He was happy Regina was off the hook, but now that Judy was facing prosecution, and the department a major embarrassment, the pressure was still on.

"When's her arraignment?" asked Gilbert.

"In a few days," said Nowak. Nowak's smiled faded, as if he sensed an ulterior motive in Gilbert's question. "I know you usually go to arraignments, Barry, but I'd appreciate it if you stay away from this one. Ling called me again. He was checking up on you."

Shit. He looked helplessly at Joe. Now he felt he couldn't even go to Joe.

Gilbert went back to his desk and tried to work while Joe went out to buy celebratory cappuccinos for all. He couldn't concentrate. He kept wondering how he was going to get a court order to obtain Stacy's records from Mount Joseph Hospital.

As he brooded over the problem, he tried to fit the events of June first into a loose chronology. Judy Pelaez arrives at the apartment a little after eight. Whether she went to Scaramouche was now beside the point. She goes upstairs to GBIA and she and Boyd have a fight. Their fight, as usual, gets physical, and in all the pushing and shoving, trace amounts of Judy's skin get stuck under Boyd's fingernails. Then she leaves. A little before nine, Oscar Barcos and Francesco Deranga arrive. Boyd grabs Deranga, and trace amounts of Deranga's skin, et cetera, et cetera. The two sell Boyd coke and break his arm. They get to Jay's Smoke and Gift by 9:17 and board the northbound train at Osgoode Station by 9:34. Boyd takes drugs to kill the pain. He's so whacked out on painkillers he hasn't the sense to go to the hospital. But what happened *before* Judy? Had Boyd indeed raped Stacy? And what happened *after* Barcos and Deranga? Did Phil and Stacy indeed go to GBIA to avenge that rape? If he could answer those two questions, he might have his killer.

But first he had to prove Stacy's visit to Mount Joseph Hospital. Who could he get to help him?

Then it dawned on him. Daniel Lynn. He might have an ally in the lawyer.

He called Daniel Lynn after lunch. He asked for the lawyer's opinion on the Pelaez arrest.

"It's utterly preposterous," said Lynn. "I've known Judy for the last thirty years, and I'm convinced she would never kill anyone, least of all a man whom she so desperately loved. Tell your staff inspector he's made a big mistake. I've got medical notes from her doctor. Judy suffers from chronic tendonitis in her left wrist. It dates back to 1985. From all the guitar playing. I spoke to her doctor over the telephone. A Dr. Lukow. I filled him in on the situation and he tells me it would be impossible—absolutely impossible—for Judy to exert the necessary force to strangle the man, given the state of her wrist."

"I have the same information," said Gilbert.

"You do?" said Lynn. "Then why in God's name did you arrest her?"

"It wasn't me," he said.

Gilbert explained his own situation, how and why he had been yanked from the case.

"But I'm still going to break the case come hell or high water," he said. "Which means I'm looking at Phil again."

He told Lynn about Phil and Stacy's relationship, about the hair comparison report and how it indicated Boyd might have raped Stacy, and finally about Stacy's admission to Mount Joseph Hospital.

"But if I'm going to prove her admission, I have to get her hospital record," he said. "I need a court order to get her record. I can't get one through the usual channels. Like I told you, I'm not even supposed to be working this case."

"You needn't worry about that," said the lawyer. "Let me phone Justice Wayne Oulds. He's an old friend of mine. He has his office in Osgoode Hall. He can be trusted. I'll give him a ring. You should have your court order in no time. Pop down in a hour. I'll make sure his secretary has it for you by then."

Once Gilbert had his court order from Justice Oulds, it took him a while to find the Health Records Department at Mount Joseph Hospital—the department had recently moved from the basement to the third floor.

"The department looks a lot smaller," he commented to the receptionist, glancing around.

She grimaced. "We can hardly move in here," she said. "I don't know why they put us here."

He presented his court order from Justice Oulds. "We believe this woman may have come to your Emergency Department on the evening of June first. If so, we'll need a copy of her records."

The receptionist glanced the order over. "I'll take this back to the release-of-information desk," she said. "If you wouldn't mind taking a seat."

He took a seat. He felt an inkling of satisfaction. He was on the hunt, and he was getting close. This was a quest. A quest to save Judy from prosecution, one to spare the department a huge embarrassment, and also one where he would at last confront Boyd and ultimately bury the old stoner for good.

The receptionist came back five minutes later with a copy of Stacy Todd's chart.

Gilbert glanced through the latest reports. All of them were dated June first. He was getting a good feeling about this. The registration form indicated that the triage nurse had admitted Stacy Todd for urgent care on Friday the first of June at 6:33 in the evening. Preliminary diagnosis had been marked as possible overmedication. The registration clerk had typed Stacy's address, telephone number, and health card number on the registration sheet. The nurse had printed her vital signs—pulse, blood pressure, and temperature—in the appropriate spots. He flipped through some previous notes from other admissions—an ear infection two years ago, a bad cough three years ago, and a fractured collarbone five years ago—but saw absolutely nothing about diabetes.

"She's not a diabetic?" he asked.

The receptionist nodded toward the chart. "That's all we have," she said.

He flipped back to the June first admission. He looked at the doctor's note. The doctor's note was illegible. While he was encouraged that Stacy Todd had in fact been here on the night of June first, this doctor's note, because of its illegibility, was virtually useless as a piece of legal evidence.

He showed it to the receptionist.

"Can you read any of this?" he asked.

She looked at the sheet. "No," she said. "But I know it's Dr. Charbonneau. He's one of the worst."

Gilbert took a deep breath and considered his next move.

"Is he in the hospital today?" he asked.

She lifted her phone and dialed. "Julie, is Dr. Charbonneau here today?"

Dr. Martin Charbonneau was in fact on duty in the Emergency Room.

Gilbert made his way to the south end of the building and took the elevator to the first floor.

He asked the triage nurse in Emergency where he might find Dr. Charbonneau.

"Check the fast-track nursing station," she suggested.

He went through the big double doors, passed a man with a bleeding arm, a leukemic boy with no hair, and an old woman with the yellowed skin of a jaundice sufferer.

After asking again at the fast-track station, he was directed to a diminutive middle-aged doctor who stood at the X-ray viewing panel examining the X-ray films of someone's broken hand.

"I remember her well," said Dr. Charbonneau, once Gilbert showed him the note. Dr. Charbonneau had a calm, clean, professional look, and smelled faintly of rubbing alcohol. "She came in here, and she said someone had given her drugs. She wasn't sure what kind. They were slipped into her drink." Dr. Charbonneau raised his eyebrows, as if to convey both surprise and cynical resignation. "She exhibited some mild symptoms of overdose." He pointed to a deeply etched squiggle in his note, and Gilbert, looking at it a second time, deciphered the word "overdose" in and among the doctor's Picassoesque scrawl. "We observed her," said Dr. Charbonneau. "I asked her if she thought it might be a police matter." His voice grew firmer. "She said no. One of her friends picked her up. And that's why I remember the case so well. It was none other than Phil Thompson, of Mother Courage." He shook his head. "You never know who's going to walk in here. Do you know Mother Courage at all? From way back when?"

"Yes," said Gilbert. "Do you remember what time Phil Thompson came in?"

Dr. Charbonneau scratched his beard. "It must have been around nine o'clock," he said. Dr. Charbonneau shook his head as a nostalgic grin came to his face. "Mother Courage was big in Trois-Rivières, where I come from. All of Quebec loved them. It's too bad they broke up. I always thought they were one of the best bands going."

Gilbert approached a Middle Eastern taxi driver. The driver was in his mid-twenties. He sat in an aging Crown Victoria taxicab smoking a cigarette while he waited to move up the taxi-stand queue outside Mount Joseph Hospital.

"How are you today?" asked Gilbert.

The driver looked at him suspiciously. "Not bad," he said.

Gilbert showed him his badge and identification. "I'm wondering if you can help me," he said. Gilbert gave him a bit of background on what he was trying to do. "So what I want to know is, were you working here on the first of June?"

The driver nodded. "I work here every day," he said.

Gilbert withdrew a color scan of Phil Thompson's face, one taken from the new *Phil Thompson Unplugged* CD, and handed it to the taxi driver. Having made a side trip to buy the CD after his visit to Dr. Charbonneau, he now had copies of Phil's picture.

"Do you remember picking up this fare at all?" he asked the taxi driver.

The driver looked at the scan. It showed a rakish portrait of Phil, hair masking half his face, finger cymbals held to his eye.

Gilbert knew asking this particular driver, a man of Arabic extraction, was a long shot—Phil Thompson's star status, even in the western world, had been waning for years. But he was running out of drivers to ask.

The driver looked at the scan and handed it back to Gilbert.

"No, I have not seen this man," he said.

Gilbert curbed his disappointment. He looked up and down the taxi stand. All the drivers had his card. They would all ask around. And they would call him if anything turned up. Gilbert believed this was his only approach. With Phil's driver's license suspended, Gilbert was convinced the aging rock star took cabs everywhere, and had in fact taken one down to GBIA after Stacy's discharge.

"Thanks," he said. "Keep the picture. Maybe you'll remember differently tomorrow. Here's my card. Call me if you do."

He gave the driver his card and strolled back to the shade of a grubby little maple in a concrete planter. Was it useless, then? He could spend the next two months asking cab drivers about Phil Thompson, and not get anywhere with it. Memories grew dim. Seven weeks was a long time. Calling cab companies hadn't worked either. They had nothing suspicious on their run sheets.

By four-thirty, he still hadn't had any luck. Thirty-nine cabbies now had Phil's picture, and thirty-nine had Gilbert's card. He was tired. He took a sip of his third Gatorade. The constant heavy traffic on University Avenue was getting to him. He longed for the quiet of Regina's garden.

He decided to go back to headquarters. He would have to hope that one of the cabbies called him.

On the way back, he swung by the Coffee Nook, a hole-in-the-wall joint with no tables or chairs, just a take-out counter.

While he waited for the counter-help to bring him his coffee and bagel, the radio played Phil Thompson's new hit, "Old Dance Partner."

"Steadily climbing the charts, Phil Thompson's comeback song from *Phil Thompson Unplugged*," said the deejay. "Everybody grab your old dance partner, and put on your dancing shoes. We're gonna dance the night away."

As the counter-help came with his coffee and bagel, Gilbert nodded toward the radio. "Are they playing that a lot?" he asked.

"Every couple of hours," she said. "A lot of people like that song."

To prove her point, she moved her head to the music while she took his money.

When he got back to headquarters, he found Joe Lombardo there. Gilbert decided it was time to tell Lombardo the truth. As much as he didn't want to get Joe in trouble, Gilbert finally felt he needed help. Besides, he longed to be working with Joe again. Things hadn't been the same without Lombardo.

"Joe," he said, "I haven't been entirely honest with you. I've been working some angles on the Boyd case all this time."

He started first with Judy's medical chart from Dr. Lukow's office in San Francisco. He took the FedEx envelope out of his briefcase and handed it to Joe. He watched Lombardo's face sink as Joe read Judy's medical notes and the special letter dictated by Dr. Lukow.

"But we've already arrested her," complained Joe. "We've booked her."

Gilbert shook his head. "She's got tendonitis in her left wrist," said Gilbert. "She's had it since 1985. I showed these notes to Dr. Blackstein. He thinks she wouldn't have had the strength or tolerance in her wrist to strangle Boyd."

Joe read the medical notes again, his brow darkening as his lips tightened.

"No wonder she had such a smug smile on her face when we arrested her. When Marie Barton sees this, she's going to freak. She's going to bite Tim's head off. She's going to bite *my* head off."

Next, Gilbert handed Joe the pubic hair comparison report.

"All hairs belong to Stacy," he said. Gilbert gave him the background on the Stacy angle. "I'm sorry I went behind your back like that, Joe, but I had to do something. I would have told you . . . only Tim called me into his office, and he read me the riot act, and I didn't want to get you in trouble. Now . . ." He leaned forward and looked at the documents on his desk. "I've got Stacy's medical chart, and that proves she went down to Mount Joseph Hospital on the night of the murder. And I've got this doctor who tells me Phil picked Stacy up after she was discharged. Phil picked her up in and around the time of the murder."

"So now you're trying to place the pair at GBIA after they left the hospital," said Lombardo, catching on quickly.

"Yes."

Lombardo frowned. "Jesus," he said. "You really should have come to me sooner. I could have helped you with all this."

"I didn't want to put you on the spot. I didn't want to get you in trouble with Tim."

Lombardo's eyes narrowed. "Tim never should have yanked you from this case in the first place," he said.

"Tim's concerns were legitimate," said Gilbert. "I don't blame him at all."

Lombardo nodded. "So what are you going to do now?"

Gilbert sat back in his chair. "I think Phil and Stacy must have taken a taxi down to GBIA after they left the hospital," he said. "So I've been down there all day canvassing cabbies."

"Wouldn't Phil drive his own car?" asked Lombardo.

"He can't drive right now," said Gilbert. "His license has been suspended for driving under the influence."

"That's right, too," said Lombardo.

"I haven't had any luck canvassing cabbies," said Gilbert.

Lombardo considered the problem. "Did you call the cab companies?" he asked. "They keep records, you know."

"Yes," said Gilbert. "They have no fares originating from Phil's address on that night. Stacy must have called him on his cell. He must have hailed a cab from somewhere else when he came to the hospital."

"And you spoke to all the evening-shift cabbies at Mount Joseph?"

Gilbert felt his face sinking. He felt like an idiot. "Jesus," he said. "I spoke to only the day-shift."

Lombardo grinned. "That's why you should have come to me sooner," he said. "I'm younger. I have more brain cells than you do."

After a pizza slice and a Dr Pepper at Domino's, the detectives got in Gilbert's Lumina and drove down to Mount Joseph Hospital to canvass the evening-shift cabbies.

Gilbert sat on the edge of the big concrete planter with the grubby little maple. Joe did the canvassing. Joe insisted.

Gilbert was tired, enervated by working all day in the heat. Also, he was sixteen years older than Joe—and the sixteen years between thirty-four and fifty took their toll, something Joe would find out soon enough as his birthdays rolled by one by one.

Lombardo walked from cabby to cabby, working the line with a persistence and high-octane attitude that Gilbert had to admire. He was glad he was working with Lombardo again, even though the young man's vigor seemed to underscore his own waning vitality. Anything seemed possible when he was working with Joe, and any case solvable, even one as personally difficult as this one.

Around ten-thirty, Joe waved him over to a cabby at the end of the line.

"Barry," he called. "Come over here. I found a guy."

Gilbert got up and walked over. His knees gave him a pinch.

Lombardo stood beside a cabby. The cabby was a tall man, around fifty years old. He had long hair flowing thinly from a bald pate, a beard, and a big, pitted, alcoholic's nose. He wore a blue Stevie Ray Vaughan T-shirt, a denim vest, and, oddly, pink-tinted sunglasses. His arms were thick, muscular, and the right one had the name BARBARA tattooed in big green capital letters on it. The cabby held a clipboard of sheets. Joe put his hand on the man's shoulder.

"This guy says he took Phil Thompson and a woman named Stacy to a Queen Street address on the evening of June first," he said.

The driver held up all his sheets.

"I got it right here," he said, "on one of these fare sheets. If only I could find the damn thing." The man had a thick Newfoundland accent. "I should be pruning these someday, but housekeeping's never been my strong point." He flipped through the sheets with a hopeless look in his eyes. "Nope. I can't find it. But I remember Phil Thompson. One of my old girlfriends loved Mother Courage way back when. I know he lives in Toronto, and

I've seen him in and around Queen Street a time or two before. I can't say I was a big fan, but I listened to them, just to keep my girlfriend happy."

Gilbert glanced at Lombardo, then turned back to the driver. "Do you remember the actual address you took them to?"

The cabby scratched his head, his eyes narrowing as he searched his memory.

"I could point it out to you if we drove downtown," he said.

"Then why don't we do that?" said Gilbert.

The cabby grinned, as if he thought Gilbert were trying to fleece him.

"As long as you don't mind payin' the fare," he said.

"Don't worry," said Gilbert. "We'll pay the fare. You're sure you can take us to the right place?"

"I know the exact place," said the cabby.

They got in the taxi and headed south to Queen Street. At this time of night, the young fashion freaks and bar-goers strolled the trendy strip. Gilbert saw a couple police cars cruise by. The lights were bright, the shops were as diverse as condom shacks and head joints, and in front of the City TV building, boogie freaks danced on the sidewalk as music from an open-air broadcast of the station's weekly dance show boomed across the pavement. The driver, whose name Gilbert saw from the identification panel on the backseat was Brian Kelsey, got conversational.

"So you use those German shepherds for your K-9 unit?" asked Kelsey.

"Yes," said Gilbert.

Kelsey nodded. He reached for the dash, lifted a photo, and handed it to Gilbert.

"That's my baby," he said. The photo showed an aging Doberman. "Dobermans get a bad rap," continued Kelsey. "Everybody thinks they're vicious because of all that Hollywood crap they see about them. But really, all my Ginger wants to do is sniff your hand and be friends. It's them German shepherds you have to worry about."

"I always liked German shepherds," said Gilbert, remembering Queenie.

Kelsey nodded, prepared to be polite about it.

"If you get a good one," stipulated Kelsey, "they're fine. And if you give it some proper sense in the first two years of its life, you should have no trouble. But you got to remember, the Nazis used German shepherds as guard dogs, and at heart, they're really vicious. Not so with Dobermans. You know what the Nazis used Dobermans for?" Kelsey glanced in the rearview mirror and smiled at them with nicotine-stained teeth. "They used them to deliver messages. What's that tell you? It tells you the Doberman is a hell of a lot smarter than the German shepherd." He nodded. "A Doberman knows a hundred-and-thirty English words, and a German shepherd knows only three. I bet my Ginger knows at least two hundred English words by now."

Kelsey repeated this theme one way or the other, elevating his own Ginger into a kind of super-dog, until he pointed out a building on the south side of the street: none other than the offices of Glen Boyd International Artists.

"That's the place," said Kelsey. "Phil went upstairs by himself. I took his chick to another address further west of here, over by Ossington."

Gilbert stared at the edifice, an old shopfront building from the early 1900s, painted over with a bright op-art design that fit right in with the rest of the trendy commercial neighborhood. At least Stacy hadn't gone up with Phil. That would get her off the hook as an accomplice.

"Do you have a rough idea what time you dropped Phil off?" asked Gilbert.

Kelsey scratched his head, thinking. "Had to be between nine and ten," he said. "The bars were just filling up."

"And you'd be willing to sign a statement to that effect?" asked Lombardo.

Kelsey glanced over the backseat and grinned again. "It depends on how big a tip you give me," he said. "I'm always willin' to do extras if the tip's big enough."

GILBERT AND LOMBARDO PULLED UP to Stacy Todd's grimy brownstone at seven o'clock the next morning. A street sweeper rumbled past, soaking the street with its sprayer, the water immediately turning to steam on the warm asphalt. An inmate from the Centre for Addiction and Mental Health wandered through the dewy grounds across the street; a Filipino hospital attendant watched the patient closely. A breeze blew from the south, carrying the funky smell of the summertime lake. A streetcar clanged across the intersection at Ossington and Queen.

Gilbert parked half up on the sidewalk.

He and Lombardo got out and crossed the street to Stacy's place.

"I've been meaning to ask you," said Gilbert. "How's Virginia?"

Lombardo frowned. "I'm not sure she likes my hair the way it is. She says she does, but I'm getting a different vibe."

"Really?" he said, acting innocent.

"What do you think of it?" Lombardo asked him. "I want your honest opinion."

Gilbert gave Joe's chopped hair a forbearing glance.

"I think you should have left it alone."

Lombardo's eyes glimmered with regret. "I wanted to hide the bald spot," he said.

"You don't have a bald spot, Joe," said Gilbert. "And if you do, it's so small you can't notice it. Mike Strutton always has to say something. That's what you got to realize about Mike. He's a jerk that way."

"So you don't think I have a bald spot?"

"No."

"I knew it," said Lombardo. "Strutton's an asshole."

"If he's an asshole, why did you listen to him?" asked Gilbert.

"You know what I think?" said Lombardo. "I think my hair's going to grow back thicker, now that I got it shaved. That's what my barber says."

"Joe, it'll probably grow back the same."

"I don't think so," said Lombardo. "My scalp's had a chance to breathe."

"You should stop having so many theories about your hair," said Gilbert. "It's unhealthy. Your hair's your hair. Leave it alone."

"My mother says my hair's my best feature," said Joe.

"Then why did you cut it off?"

"I panicked," said Joe.

"The next time you panic, I'll make sure there aren't any scissors around. In the meantime, just grow it back."

"I'm going to," said Lombardo.

Gilbert knocked on Stacy's door.

It took nearly five minutes, but Stacy finally answered.

She stood at the bottom of the stairs in a blue terry-cloth dressing gown. Her glasses were on, but they were askew. A lock of blond hair hung over her forehead in a fetching way. She looked caught off guard, alarmed to find them standing at her door so early.

"Next time, could you call before you come?" she said.

"We wanted to catch you before you went out," explained Gilbert.

"You still should have called," she said. Her friendly attitude from previous visits was gone. "What do you want?"

Out on the street, morning rush-hour traffic was building quickly.

"Do you mind if we come in?" asked Lombardo.

She flicked her eyes coldly at Lombardo.

"Could we make it some other time?" she said. "I have someone here right now."

It occurred to Gilbert that Phil Thompson might be upstairs.

"Okay, so we'll get right to the point," said Gilbert, not at all pleased by the reception they were getting. "We have reason to believe you have knowledge of Glen Boyd's murder."

She didn't miss a beat.

"How?" she asked.

He outlined his evidence: the matching hairs, her trip to

the hospital, her taxi ride to GBIA with Phil. "We know that Phil went upstairs alone," he said, "and that the taxi driver took you home by yourself. But we also know that you and Phil are a couple. We believe he must have told you."

In this way, he hoped to shake something loose, dump it on her all at once the way Bob Bannatyne might. Her face remained impassive. He realized what Ted Aver had said about the woman was true: despite the seed cakes, mint tea, and gift baskets, she knew how to handle herself.

"Isn't that nice?" she said. "So what are you going to do now?"

Gilbert stared at her. It wasn't working. Taking it to the next step by getting her to implicate Phil, was, at least for the time being, an unattainable objective. Still, he made one last try.

"We might have to book you as an accomplice if you don't cooperate," he said, though he had no intention of doing any such thing, knowing how much she had suffered already.

"Then go ahead and book me," she said.

He really wanted to cut the investigation short by getting her to cooperate, but it was obvious she wasn't going for it.

"So you admit to some involvement then?" said Lombardo, going out on a limb.

Stacy stepped adroitly around this snare. "If you're going to arrest me, do it now, and let's get it over with. I'd like to post bond. I've got things to do today."

"Let's go, Joe," said Gilbert.

Joe made his own last try.

"Were you, or were you *not* involved in the murder of Glen Boyd?" asked Lombardo.

Stacy gave him a saccharin smile.

"When and if you arrest me," she said, "you can speak to my lawyer about it. Right now I've got someone here with me. I'm sorry you've come all this way. Can I go back inside now? Or should I really get my pants on?"

Despite her legal gamesmanship, Stacy looked worried, as if she sensed the end was near.

"Go back inside," said Gilbert. "But stay in Toronto. Things would really go from bad to worse if you tried to leave."

"I have no reason to leave," she said, and shut the door.

As Gilbert and Lombardo headed back to the car, he felt sorry for Stacy. She didn't deserve this. Boyd had forced her into this situation. And yet Gilbert had no choice but to press forward with the investigation, and to bring the case to a satisfactory close. That made him mad. Especially at Boyd. Boyd, he thought, was a one-man Armageddon, bringing destruction wherever he went.

Gilbert drove to the Metro West Detention Center later that day to visit Judy Pelaez. Judy sat across from him in an orange prisoner's uniform. The uniform, a coverall, looked too big for her.

"I'm sorry about this," he said. "I didn't want it to happen this way. I'm not on the case anymore. But I'm trying to rectify things for you as quickly as I can."

She grinned placidly, distantly. "He's a never-ending story, isn't he?" she said, her voice tender, in its soprano range.

"Who is?" he asked.

"Glen."

He didn't know what to say to this. He reached across the table and put his hand over hers. "I think you'll be okay. I'll make every effort to finish up quickly."

She looked at his hand. "You sometimes don't act like a cop."

"Think of me as your friend," he said. "I'm not sure you've had too many of those in the last little while."

She lifted her gaze. Her grin melted like a snowflake on a child's tongue. She looked so blue—the bluest bird in the world.

"It's not that I don't want friends," she said. "But somehow Judy always gets in the way. No one likes me."

He smiled.

"I like you just fine," he said. He sat back. "By this time next week, you'll bury your husband. Then you can go back home. This place is bad for you. Morningstar and Delta want you back. And that's where you should be."

Faced with Stacy Todd's intransigence, Gilbert had no choice but to get Tim Nowak on his side before he could proceed any further. Only through Nowak could he get the full backing he needed to go ahead with his next step.

Gilbert and Lombardo, partners again, approached the staff inspector shortly after ten the next morning.

Gilbert outlined to Nowak his chain of evidence.

While Nowak agreed it was a fairly solid piece of work, his lips puckered when Gilbert told him it meant the squad would have to release Judy Pelaez. A puckering of the lips on the usually unflappable staff inspector meant Nowak was truly rankled.

Against those puckered lips, Gilbert felt he had to push his case to the limit. So he set out his documents.

"This is Judy Pelaez's medical chart from San Francisco," he said. "Both Dr. Lukow and Dr. Blackstein agree she wouldn't have had the strength in her wrist to strangle Boyd. And this here," he said, lifting a few stapled sheets, "is the report on the hairs. You can see for yourself. The hairs combed from Boyd match the one I vouchered from Stacy's bathtub drain. And right here we have Stacy Todd's medical chart from Mount Joseph, along with a statement signed from Dr. Charbonneau about Phil coming to pick her up. And this final sheet is a statement signed by Brian Kelsey, the taxi driver who drove Stacy and Phil down to GBIA on the night of the murder. As for background, Ted Aver's agreed to come forward. He'll sign whatever we need him to sign. And if it's not enough, Victor Tran's agreed to send Boyd's arrest record from San Francisco. Likewise, Madga Barcos is willing to testify."

The staff inspector tapped his fingers slowly, meditatively, against his desk. Then he stopped. This sudden cessation of finger movement unnerved Gilbert. Nowak's head turned smoothly, as if on greased ball bearings. His face was as calm as the Dalai Lama's. He raised two fingers.

"Two things, Barry," he said. "Number one: insubordination."

He gave the word a chance to settle. He turned to the window and tapped his fingers a few more times. He actually looked hurt, as if he couldn't believe one of his own would go behind his back this way.

"I don't know what I'm going to do about that," said Nowak. "I gave you a warning and you deliberately disobeyed me." Nowak let a second or two tick by, his silence emphasizing the gravity with which he viewed the situation. "I'll have to talk to John Ling about it. I may even have to talk to Chief Fantino." He turned to Gilbert. "But before I do, I'm required to write a Letter-of-Incident to Human Resources. Then Human Resources will send recommendations." A vein now stood out on Nowak's temple. "I'm not sure what they'll say. They might recommend suspension. They might even want me to transfer you out of the squad. At the very least, they'll recommend I cancel your next merit raise." The staff inspector's voice hardened. "Then I'll have to talk to John Ling. Ling may opt for your immediate termination. That's his prerogative. Because we can't be doing this, Barry. This is bad news. I can't have a lot of loose cannons running around behind my back. We have to act as a unit. Especially on a high-profile investigation like the Boyd case."

Nowak folded one of his fingers, indicating he was about to get to his second point. But before he could, Lombardo jumped him.

"Tim," said Lombardo, "Barry just saved your ass." His brow was one dark line. "Does it even matter to you if we get the right perp or not?" Lombardo shook his head, up on a moral soapbox. "Or is it just a matter of numbers to you, clearing the board as fast as you can so you can make us look as good as possible?" Lombardo sighed theatrically. "Barry hands you the real perp on a platter, and all you talk about is his next damn merit raise."

Nowak let his remaining raised finger sink slowly to his desk.

"Joe," he said. "Barry handing me the perp on a platter, as you call it, and the insubordinate way in which he went behind my back aren't linked as far as I'm concerned. They're two separate issues. They come under two different policies."

These words straightjacketed Lombardo. Joe sat there wanting to fight, but Gilbert gave him a cautioning glance. The boss was the boss. You had to listen to the boss when the boss talked about insubordination. And while Gilbert found Nowak's tenacious adherence to policy at times inflexible, at least the staff inspector could always be counted on to be consistent.

Nowak's head swiveled smoothly toward Gilbert again. Beneath the surface of his pale gray eyes, Gilbert saw a flicker of emotion.

"My second point, Barry," he said. He gestured at the reports. His shoulders eased, as if now that they were talking shop again, they could put personal discord behind them. "You have a good circumstantial case against Phil Thompson here. I'm the first to admit that. You've got motive. You've linked him to the crime scene in a convincing way. But if we're going to pull an about-face on Judy Pelaez, it's got to be airtight or else Roffey's going to have a field day, and that will just make Ling madder. I need something that will place Phil in the actual apartment at the time of the murder. More than just this taxi driver's statement. Especially because some of the other evidence points to other suspects."

"Yes, I know," said Gilbert. "I came to the exact same conclusion. And that's one of the reasons I've come to you at this point. Without your input, we can't go any further."

Nowak tapped his finger twice more against the table. "How so?" he asked.

"Evidence indicates there was a struggle before the murder," said Gilbert. "A jar of coins was thrown. So was a decorative plate."

Nowak nodded. "I've seen both pieces of evidence," he said.

"Nigel Gower has Boyd's fingerprints on the coin jar, and a strong set of miscellaneous latents on the plate that he hasn't identified yet. The impressions are deep, which makes sense if the plate was thrown. Joe told me yesterday that Nigel's now searched all the Canadian fingerprint databases, including the RCMP's, and has come up with nothing. But Nigel hasn't yet put in a request to AFIS down in the States, the FBI's Automated Fingerprint Identification System. I believe the miscellaneous latents on the plate belong to Phil Thompson. He's never been fingerprinted in Canada. But while on tour in Denver in 1979, he lit his guitar on fire and threw it into the audience. He was subsequently charged with reckless endangerment and battery. Which means he was fingerprinted down there. Which means his prints are on file with AFIS."

"I see where this is going," said Nowak.

"In order to authorize an AFIS search, I need the staff inspector's signature. If we send our request down today, we could have our hits as early as tomorrow, especially if we limit our search request to the parameters of Phil's Denver arrest."

When Gilbert got home later that evening, he found Regina and the girls wearing bathing suits in the garden, waging war against the fescue and the crabgrass again.

Nina spotted him on the back deck, dropped her little metal

gardening claw, and beelined straight for him. She threw her arms around him.

"Dr. MacPherson phoned," she said. "My latest test came back negative. You were right. We don't have to worry, Daddy. I'm not going to die. And I've learned my lesson. I'm never going to practice unsafe sex again."

He winced. "Why don't you practice no sex at all?" he suggested. "There's something to be said for abstinence."

Though at the moment, as he looked at Regina in her bathing suit, he couldn't think of what it was.

Still, he was relieved about the whole thing. His wife and girls went back to their weed pulling. He watched them. Sometimes the world did what it did, and there was nothing you could do to stop it. He felt lucky that things had turned out this way. He couldn't always protect his wife and daughters, but he could always love and cherish them, no matter what the world threw at them.

Nowak slid the AFIS fingerprint report onto his desk and nodded serenely.

"It looks good," he said. "The prints lifted from the plate match Phil's AFIS set. On nine points of similarity, too, one above our guideline. I guess that means you and Joe can work on Phil's arrest warrant. I'll draft Judy's release papers."

Gilbert sighed. "You know what?" he said. "I'd sooner hold off on Phil's arrest warrant just now. He's not going anywhere. He's too busy rehearsing for his tour. Let's just wait."

"Wait for what?" asked Nowak. "We've got everything we need." He tapped the AFIS report. "What more should we wait for?"

"We should wait for Dr. Blackstein to give us his final ruling on the manner of death," said Gilbert. "All we have is his preliminary one. Let's take another few days. Let's wait for the final report. I called Mel earlier today, and he says he's expecting the toxicology results back any time now. I don't doubt that Boyd died as a result of strangulation, but if it turns out to be respiratory failure due to a drug overdose, and we go ahead and arrest Phil, we're going to look bad. Judging by the way you feel about the Pelaez arrest, Tim, you don't want that."

Nowak stared at Gilbert for nearly five seconds.

"Thanks, Barry," he finally said. He lifted a document from his desk. "Carol typed this up for me this morning. It's your Letter-of-Incident. I was going to file it with Human Resources this morning. And I was going to phone John Ling this afternoon." The staff inspector ripped the letter in four pieces and dropped it into the wastepaper basket. "But I think we'll let things quietly slip by. Once I tell John Ling what you've done for the case, I'm sure he'll feel the same way."

CHAPTER
TWENTY TWO

ON THE WAY TO WORK the following Monday, Gilbert saw Phil Thompson's picture on the front cover of *NOW* magazine. *NOW* magazine, free, distributed in newspaper format from vending boxes all over the city, was *the* entertainment bible to Toronto's Generation X: a smorgasbord of personal ads, club and concert listings, and movie, theater, and restaurant reviews. Every issue showcased a local talent. This week, *NOW* showcased Phil Thompson.

Gilbert pulled over to the curb and grabbed a copy from the corner vending box. In the picture—a poster-sized one—Phil wore a suit, an earring, and a string tie. His Jesus-length hair flowed over his shoulders, and he gazed at the camera with calm importance.

Gilbert flipped to the feature article.

After a long hiatus, Phil Thompson is finally back. Phil Thompson Unplugged *is now platinum, and the former Mother Courage guitarist will embark on a twelve-city North American concert tour next month. His hit single, "Old Dance Partner," is number seven on the Billboard Chart, and it looks like it's going to climb even higher.*

Gilbert shook his head. Just when things were looking up for Phil, things were looking down. Gilbert wasn't sure Phil deserved it. Phil had been terribly wronged by Glen Boyd. He tossed the paper on the passenger seat. He pulled out into traffic. Phil, after twenty years of trying, was finally back on the charts. But that wasn't going to make one bit of difference when Gilbert went to arrest him.

At work, Gilbert found the results of the toxicology test waiting for him on his desk. He hesitated before looking at them. He hoped for a twist. He felt sorry for Phil Thompson because of all the things Glen Boyd had done to the man. He felt he had a lot in common with Phil Thompson. They both had old scores to settle with the concert mogul, and they both knew what it was like to suffer because of Glen Boyd. He wanted to pull out findings in the toxicology report indicative of an accidental overdose. He wanted the results to exonerate Phil so that the guitarist's born-again musical career might stand a chance. He hoped this opening of old wounds might turn out to be nothing more than a big pointless kafuffle, a last bitter joke played by a dead man. But these wishes, he knew, were just another example of his bias creeping into the case, and he quickly suppressed them. He mustered a stiff professionalism. He opened the toxicology report and read.

His shoulders sagged.

While a high concentration of cocaine, Prozac, and morphine had been found in Boyd's bloodstream, the amounts, even when combined, weren't fatal, and therefore, the ruling on the manner of death was homicide, namely, strangulation.

Gilbert's lips stiffened and his eyes narrowed. He gripped his mouse and clicked the arrest warrant template to his screen. He filled in the blanks. Boyd, throughout his life, had victimized countless people: all the dreamer rock musicians he had bilked; all the women he had left broken-hearted or otherwise sexually duped; even his landlord, if the credit agent coming to the door on the night of the murder had been any indication. Gilbert typed in his own name in the spot marked ARRESTING OFFICER. But Phil Thompson was perhaps Boyd's biggest victim: Palo Alto, the solo album fiasco, and now Stacy. In regard to Boyd's own culpability, and in a purely vigilante sense, justice had been served. Gilbert typed in Phil's name, then sketched in the details of the crime. Yet in the strictest legal sense, Gilbert had no choice but to serve this warrant.

He extinguished his last bit of bias.

People simply couldn't go around killing people, no matter how much they had been victimized.

Gilbert drove with Lombardo later that day to Phil Thompson's residence, the renovated church.

They found Phil and Stacy in the backyard drinking iced

tea. The sky was sunny and the flowers bright. A small fountain, made of tan-colored stone, splashed playfully in the back. A starling, as dark as gun metal, high-stepped through the grass back there, stopping every now and again to peck the ground.

"Philip Thompson," said Gilbert, "you're under arrest for the murder of Glen Anthony Boyd. Could you please put your hands behind your back."

The former Mother Courage guitarist gazed at Gilbert and Lombardo serenely from under the cool shade of the gazebo, at peace with himself, as if he had just spent the last week at a meditation retreat. He stood up, leaned over, and kissed Stacy.

"Give Clifton, Simhi, and Lynn a call," he said. "I might as well get Danny to represent me, now that I've dropped everything against GBIA. Look after the place. Don't let anybody touch those tapes."

"They're safe with me," she assured him, and gave his hand a squeeze.

Phil turned to Gilbert. "How long does the bail process take?" he asked. "It's been a long time since I've been arrested."

"A few days," said Gilbert. He thought of Justice Wayne Oulds. "If Daniel Lynn's your lawyer, maybe sooner."

"He is. Thanks. Are you going to arrest Stacy, too?"

"We've decided against that," said Gilbert.

Phil gave him a glance; in another life they might have been friends. "Thanks," he said again.

Phil put his hands behind his back. Lombardo cuffed him.

"Lead the way," said the guitarist.

Gilbert led him away from the gazebo—away from the

woman who rocked like AC/DC, his Sunshine and his K.C., his Beatles, the woman, who, in the end, had become as much a victim as Judy, Regina, Magda, and Morningstar.

A few days later, Gilbert and Regina caught coverage of Glen Boyd's funeral on the evening news.

Over a thousand people attended.

The camera panned and zoomed, selecting this musician or that musician, rockers from times gone by, yesteryear's flower children, headbangers, and punks. At the center of it all was a tiny woman, the bluest bird in the world, dressed entirely in black, legendary folk goddess Judy Pelaez. Delta and Morningstar flanked her—giant children compared to their mother. The veil did little to hide the peculiar grin on Judy's face.

"Why's she grinning like that?" asked Regina.

Gilbert stared at the grin. What did that grin mean? Was Judy finally happy? Did she grin because she at last had an unassailable right to Boyd? Out of all the hundreds of women who had slipped between Boyd's sheets, did Judy Pelaez finally feel she had beaten them all? Or was it just plain relief? Maybe now that Boyd was dead she wouldn't be the bluest bird in the world anymore.

"I don't know," he said.

A quick-edit switched to eight pallbearers—former Diodes bassist Ian Mackay was among them. They maneuvered Boyd's walnut casket through the throng on the church steps to the waiting white hearse. Gilbert glanced at Regina. She seemed upset by the funeral.

"Are you all right?" he asked.

Her lips pursed in mild distress. "I'll never forgive myself for what I did to that baby in Marseilles," she said. "Or for what I did to you. As for Glen . . . I don't know . . . he should have had the good sense to stick with Judy."

Gilbert rested his hand on her knee. "He wasn't a one-woman man," he said. Read *sexual predator,* he thought, but didn't mention this to Regina. "That's just the way he was."

In a related story, Gabriel Pavey, the courthouse correspondent, reported the latest on Phil Thompson's legal status.

"CFTO News has learned that former Mother Courage guitarist Phil Thompson will enter a plea of voluntary manslaughter in the strangling death of concert mogul Glen Boyd. Thompson's defense attorney, Daniel Lynn, has been meeting with Crown Prosecutor Marie Barton most of the afternoon, and they expect to have the deal finalized before they go home tonight. This comes on the heels of the widely publicized arrest of folksinger Judy Pelaez."

A segment with Staff Inspector Tim Nowak came on. A bouquet of microphones rose toward Nowak's chin. Tall, serene, and unruffled, he spoke calmly to the gathered reporters.

"The Metropolitan Toronto Police Force sincerely apologizes to Judy Pelaez, to her family, and to her many fans for her arrest. When we arrested her, we acted in good faith, with the evidence we had in hand, and on the advice of the Crown Prosecutor. We booked Ms. Pelaez on what we thought was a compelling and prosecutable case. We did so solely in the interests of public safety. Chief Fantino will send Ms. Pelaez a personal letter of apology. Our lawyers are working on an out-of-court settlement which we believe will generously address any perceived damages. We regret this unfortunate incident, but don't see how we could have acted any differently, given the circumstances and the information we had at the time of Ms. Pelaez's arrest."

Gilbert grinned. This was Nowak's specialty: say you're sorry but never take the blame. It would frustrate the hell out of Ronald Roffey.

Curious about the details of Phil Thompson's plea bargain agreement, Gilbert phoned Daniel Lynn the next day.

"The plea was in exchange for a lighter sentence," explained Lynn.

"Did you take him to Justice Oulds?" asked Gilbert.

"Yes."

"And Marie Barton was okay with that?"

"Justice Oulds was one of Marie's professors at law school," said Lynn. "She had no objection."

"So what's the deal?"

"Six years, which means he may get out in as little as thirty months."

"Good," said Gilbert. But he still wanted more detail. "Did he actually tell you what happened that night? How it ended up with Boyd dead like that?"

"The story goes that Phil and Stacy went to GBIA after Stacy was discharged from the hospital," said Lynn. "Stacy went home while Phil went upstairs. Phil was naturally furious when he found out what Boyd had done to her. He doesn't get angry often, but when he does, he's a mad dog. He got there, and Boyd was using the scarf as a sling for his broken arm. They argued. They pushed. Glen threw a big jar of coins at Phil. Phil lost his temper. He threw the plate at Glen, then went at him with the scarf. He says he wasn't intending to kill Glen. He just wanted to scare him. He says he was hardly pulling on the scarf at all." This, then, explained the slight trauma, thought Gilbert. "But obviously he was pulling hard enough and long enough to murder the poor man."

Gilbert thought about it. "The whole thing's so sad," he said.

"I know," said Lynn. "That's why I advised a plea. I didn't want to make it any sadder by trying to fight it. It was by far the wisest course for Phil."

"Too bad Phil was making a comeback," said Gilbert.

"Yes."

"And of course his tour's been cancelled?"

"Yes," said Lynn.

"And record sales are going to drop off, aren't they?" said Gilbert.

Lynn sighed. "Phil's a great musician," he said, "but he's now also a murderer. That's not the best thing for record sales, long-term, is it?"

It was Friday, and the evening was a muggy one, with a big red sun setting beyond the Don Valley. Gilbert was driving home from headquarters. He was glad he didn't have to work this weekend. He wanted a chance to unwind from the Boyd case.

As he drove, he kept thinking of Phil, Judy, and Boyd, icons of their time, fading into the past. They belonged to the 1970s. And now the 1970s were over. Was it hard, he wondered, when you were famous, to watch yourself go out of style? It certainly seemed to have tortured Phil for the last twenty years. When he thought of Phil, Judy, and Boyd, he thought of lava lamps, mood rings, and pet rocks. He thought of platform shoes, three-piece white suits, and yellow ribbons around old oak trees. The decade, the 1970s, now lay across his heart heavily. It had been real, so real, but now it was gone.

He remembered the polyester leisure suits he used to wear as a detective in Fraud, his long hair and sideburns, and how, when he and Regina went to parties, he'd sport a signs-of-the-zodiac medallion around his neck. In the seventies, there had been muggy summer nights like this one. There had been the smell of traffic, such as he was getting through his open window, and the promise of a July weekend, such as he had before him. There had been love, hate, and murder. But there had also been something else, a feeling that the times were different, that they had finally changed, and that the world was never going to be the same again. He mourned. As much for the decade as for the lost chance it represented.

In his driveway, he opened his glove compartment and took out Phil's new CD. He got out of the Windstar and walked to the front door. As he opened the front door, Regina came out of the dining room and greeted him in the front hall.

"I thought we'd have a barbecue," she said. She looked at him more closely. "What's wrong? You look a little down."

"I'm fine," he said.

She hesitated. "No," she said. "You're not."

He grinned a sad grin. "I'm just a little blue about this Phil thing," he said, "that's all." He held up the CD. "I bought his new CD. I thought we'd have a listen before supper. Or do you want me to get the barbecue started first?"

Sympathy glimmered in her eyes. "We can order out," she said.

He raised his eyebrows. "Swiss Chalet?" he suggested.

"Swiss Chalet," she said.

While Regina went to order the food, Gilbert put his brief-case down and went into the living room. He opened the new CD, put it into the machine, and cued Phil Thompson's current hit, "Old Dance Partner."

It turned out to be a song about farewells. As Gilbert listened to the lyrics, his sadness deepened.

Say good-bye,
To that plane in Casablanca,
Say good-bye,
When Bogart walks away,
Say good-bye,
To an old dance partner . . .
And to our dance-floor yesterdays.

Phil sang in a mellow, easy voice, his backup singers joining him on the words "Say good-bye." The song was lilting and nostalgic, had bongos and a washboard as its percussion instruments, used an easy shuffling rhythm. Some bridging material followed the opening chorus.

> *A fragment of what we felt,*
> *A glimmer of what we knew,*
> *And of that song we danced together,*
> *It's gone like morning dew.*

Phil's voice now took on an urgent quality, as if he were trying to capture something, perhaps those fleeting years when he'd been a young man.

Regina came into the living room and sat next to him.

"This is pretty good," he said.

"It sounds good," she said.

They both listened. Another "Say good-bye" chorus went by with slightly different words. Then more of the bridging material.

> *All the songs we used to sing,*
> *And the things we used to do,*
> *And that night we danced forever,*
> *Is gone for me and you.*

Gilbert frowned.

"There you go again," said Regina. "What's wrong?"

Phil Thompson played a solo on acoustic guitar. "I don't know," said Gilbert. "Maybe it's the nature of my job. I brood on mortality too much."

They listened to the final chorus.

Say good-bye,
To the ghost who lives in Graceland.
Say good-bye,
To Gene Kelly in the rain.
Say good-bye,
To an old dance partner . . .
My step will never be the same.

"He's right on target," said Gilbert. "This guy can write songs. And it's too damn bad he's gone and ruined his career forever. I hear a song like this, and I can't help thinking of our old Ford Pinto, or how I was so freaking nuts about Jefferson Airplane, or how you used to wear your hair long and parted in the middle. Us boomers . . . we're all growing old."

She leaned her cheek against his shoulder. "It's not so bad," she said. She kissed him and smiled softly. "Growing old is fine if you have someone to do it with."

She had a point. He'd made his pivotal life decision in the 1970s—his decision to grow old with her. And so the 1970s were always there in the background, informing his current situation. He stroked her hair. The song shuffled toward its close. She came back from France, and he stuck with her. That was his decision. The best decision he'd ever made. He felt lucky. Luckier than any rock star on the planet. He had preserved this . . . this magical thing he had with Regina. *A fragment of what they knew. A glimmer of what they felt.* It was all still here. In her soft smile, and in the tender conviction of her voice. Having nearly lost it, he knew how precious it was. The seventies were over. But he knew what he had with Regina would last forever.